THE WITCH DOCTOR'S OPAL

BUNYIP BOOK 1

TRISTAN A. SMITH

LARGE PRINT EDITION

To my parents, Ross and Pauline, with all my love and gratitude.

THE OPAL

TRISTRAM JONES WAS a child who wanted to be good. Unfortunately, his idea of what was good was limited by the Jehovah's Witness religion.

Tristram's parents were not Jehovah's Witnesses. His father was agnostic, and his mother was eccentric.

Holly, his mother, was a strong, intelligent woman with her own peculiar ideas on spirituality. One of her peculiar ideas was that Tristram was blessed by Jehovah whilst she was pregnant with him. Hence, she was quite proud when at ten years old, Tristram organised his own bible study with a young elder for the small country town of Bairnsdale.

Russell, Tristram's father, approved of the moral fibre that his son was developing under the influence of the Witnesses. However, he hoped along with

Holly that Tristram would eventually lighten up. Fear of God makes a serious child.

Today, everybody was serious.

Tristram sat in the front row of a Presbyterian Church and listened sceptically to the eulogy. He noted every contradiction to Witness dogma with zealous scorn.

His little sister Saffi, two years younger than he, sat beside him and nursed their little brother Jase. Jase was four years old. Both Tristram's siblings were blonde, attractive children, and he felt ugly in contrast with them. Saffi had large, gorgeous blue eyes, and little Jase had curly blonde hair and dark hazel eyes that shone like a sparrow's. Tristram, on the other hand, was a skinny asthmatic child with brown hair, freckles, and a big nose. He did like the colour of his eyes, which were hazel like his mother's. Other than that, he had decided from an early age that he was ugly, and that the only advantages that he could hope to nurture were his intelligence and imagination.

Toby Jones, their grandfather, lay hidden in a beautiful casket behind the old priest. It was the middle of April when Granddad Toby died. He was only fifty-eight.

"Do you know why they call it the Dead Sea?" The old priest suddenly asked Tristram.

"Yes." Tristram replied with a cynical glare.

The priest returned a kindly, paternal smile.

"Yes? Very well then, young fellow. Why it is called the Dead Sea?"

Tristram shrugged. "Because they throw dead things in it."

Startled laughter rippled across the audience.

"It is called the Dead Sea because nothing lives in it." The priest corrected, turning his attention to the audience. "Many sweet waters run into it, but none leave it. A greedy entity, it keeps all that comes to it. Yet, despite all the sweet water that pours into this accursed sea, it remains utterly salty and undrinkable. No beautiful birds float on its surface. No coloured fish swim in it. It tries so hard to fill itself with *life*, but it remains *dead*."

After a calculated pause for the audience to reflect, the priest smiled down at Tristram.

"Do you think there is a lesson in that?"

"Probably." Came the petulant response.

The priest chuckled.

"Ladies and gentlemen, like a body of water, we have in each of us a body of *spirit*. And just like a body of water, the spirit in our bodies is constantly being replenished by outside sources. The *love* of our heavenly father, and the love of our *fellow human beings*, trickles and flows between us. But unlike the Dead Sea that takes all and gives nothing, we can pass on the love that dwells within us. I see today, a lot of love and respect for this man, Toby Jones.

Clearly, he gave more than he kept, or there wouldn't be so many of you here today..."

Later, when the sermon had concluded, it was time for everybody to walk past the open coffin and pay their last respects.

Tristram stood at a distance and watched his mother approach the coffin.

Holly was more charismatic than beautiful. She had a lean and curvaceous figure, but her face was rather masculine, with a prominent nose that she had inherited from her father.

Holly beckoned to her children. "Come and look at his face, Tris. You too, Saffi – bring Jase with you."

Holly was adamant that her three children would understand and accept death. The fashionable psychology of the time was to let children see and perhaps even touch the dead, so that they did not form any unhealthy misconceptions.

Tristram stood his ground. "No."

Holly smiled patiently.

"I won't force you, but it will help you to look at him." Her voice was low and mellow.

Tristram shook his head.

"Alright." Holly nodded. "Saffi?"

Saffi looked up at her brother.

"I will if Tristram will."

Tristram crossed his arms. "I will not."

Tristram's father came and stood beside Holly. Tristram marvelled at how handsome his dad looked.

Russell Jones often described himself as a 'short, fat, hairy guy with glasses' – which was true but misleading. The description hints at ugliness but Russell was not ugly. He had simply settled for being comfortable rather than handsome. In a suit, however, with his raven hair brushed and his beard trimmed, the glasses folded neatly in his breast pocket, he looked almost regal. His steel, dark blue eyes and broad shoulders became more apparent than his pot belly, short legs and long torso.

His father's appearance affected Tristram. It was one of the first occasions that he saw him as a role model.

Tristram marvelled at how the family looked to his dad. He noticed his uncle, Russell's younger brother by eight years, a man in his own right – yet now looking up to his older brother in the day of darkness. Tristram saw a similar look in the eyes of Saffi and Jase, whenever they looked at him. He understood that one day, he would stand where his father was, and Russell would be a cold, grey corpse in an ornate wooden box...

"Come and see him, Tris. You won't get another chance to see him." Russell asked with quiet composure. His voice was light and muted, with an accent that was English. In times of high emotion, Russell abandoned his Australian accent in favour of the more cultured one that he had used in Nottingham, England, when he was a boy.

Grandma Joan tried to lead Tristram to the coffin, but he politely and firmly refused yet again.

"I do not need to see him, Grandma. He is not there. He has gone. That is just a corpse now."

Joan did not press the issue. She was not that sort of grandmother.

"I think you're quite right, darling-heart." She said. "He is somewhere much better. I am absolutely sure of it."

Joan's voice was strong and clear, with a jovial Australian ring to it. Though a grandmother and five years older than her late husband, she seemed youthful. Her hair was dyed and in auburn curls. There was a roguish yet motherly air about Joan, and a substantial intellect behind her grey-blue eyes.

Today, Joan was beside herself with grief. Tristram sensed in her a panic and disbelief that were contained only with superhuman force of will.

He took her hand and placed in her palm a large opal.

Joan gasped as she recognised it. "*Tristram...*"

"He gave it to me so that I would remember him." Tristram answered. "It has pieces of his soul in it."

Eight days earlier Tristram Jones was utterly inconsolable. Anxious hope and realistic despair fought a raging duel inside him. Morbid curiosity waited to see if Granddad Toby would really die.

Tristram did not understand the meaning of 'bowel cancer'. It therefore became a half-formed, malevolent shadow in his mind that grew in him day by day. A gauntlet of nightmare filled nights and forlorn, prayer filled days had all but crushed him. He was rapidly losing health, and this worried his parents. Holly and Russell decided to let Toby talk to the boy from his death bed; even though they felt that the sight would repulse and sadden him. Toby had a way of reassuring people that no matter what, everything would turn out fine.

Grandma Joan ushered Tristram up the dark hallway of her and Toby's old house. It was a charming, weather-board house in East Geelong. The house had been renovated over the years with patience, love and gentle happiness. Intricate floral wallpaper reached from the thick carpeted floor up into the high ceilings. Grandma's kitchen still had a wood and coal stove and oven – things that she would not trade for the finest modern technology. It was a house that sighed with a contented love, even as Toby lay dying within it.

Before Tristram was ready, Joan led him into their bedroom. She gave Toby a cup of tea and a kiss and was rewarded with a brave smile. She left him and Tristram alone.

Tristram was afraid to approach the bed. Everything in the room was neat and comfortable. The morning light through the windows gave the scene a peaceful, ethereal glow. However, Toby provided a ghastly contrast in the romantic picture. He was a skeleton wearing pyjamas. His breathing was laboured. Tristram was about to make a quiet exit when Toby looked up and gave him a craggy, beautiful smile.

"How's my racing ferret this morning?" He asked in a light, husky voice with a pleasant English accent. He and Joan always called the children racing ferrets whenever they had recently had a bath and combed their hair.

Tristram smiled and came to his side. Granddad Toby was still with him after all. He was about to tell him how good it felt to see him, when Toby suddenly tensed his whole body and coughed a terrible, violent cough. Sweat glistened on his forehead.

"Should I get Grandma?"

Tristram was on the verge of panic, but Toby settled again with a sigh and a pained smile.

"No...it's alright, Tristram. It's not as bad as it seems."

In his health, Toby was a tall, well built man with an ever-present grin that gave way only to heart-felt smiles. Like Joan, he had a youthful energy about him. He laughed heartily and often, and his whole body quivered helplessly at the deep mirth that welled inside him. He loved music – lived it. There wasn't a song he didn't know off by heart. The children would shake their heads in wonder when he would suddenly burst into a song in the middle of their conversations, having been reminded of a tune by some key word or phrase.

Today, Toby's light was fading, but it was a most magnificent light. The yellow mask of death would have been an unbearable horror if it weren't for the radiance of Toby's soul, gently beaming out from his kind eyes.

"I heard music this morning." Toby began dead-pan. "Jazz music. Stan Kenton."

"Did you?" Tristram answered poker-faced.

Toby's light blue eyes twinkled.

"Tristram...were you *dancing* in the other room this morning?" He asked with playful suspicion.

Tristram went red and grinned. "No."

Toby narrowed his eyes and smiled. "No? I think you *were* dancing in the other room, Tristram."

Tristram giggled. "Just one dance."

"Ah-ha. Just one dance. Was it with a beautiful woman?"

"It was Grandma."

"Ah..." Toby sighed with pleasure. "Then it *was* a beautiful woman..."

A flash of life and memory washed over Toby's face. He grinned and grunted with amusement.

"What's so funny?" Tristram asked.

"I can't dance, Tristram. I have two left feet. It doesn't stop me dancing though." Toby smiled.

Tristram returned the smile, and then it vanished as he realised that his granddad would never dance again.

Toby read the change in his expression. He made eye contact with Tristram and then carefully reached out a closed hand.

"I have something for you." He said solemnly. "Something...to make you feel better about what's going to happen."

"Nothing can do that, Grandad." Whispered Tristram, tearfully.

Toby smiled and opened his hand. He was holding a large, tear shaped opal about the size and girth of a hazelnut. It was the colour of the sky on a bright blue morning. Luminescent reds, pinks, oranges, purples and greens swirled and wheeled within in it like tiny galaxies.

"Do you know what this is, Tristram?"

"It's an opal."

"That's right. A very special opal, with a long and rich history."

Toby placed the opal into Tristram's hand.

Immediately, Tristram felt a most unusual sensation from the opal. It was cool to the touch, but it made him feel warmer, as if someone were embracing him from the inside.

Toby's eyes glowed briefly with an excited joy.

"*Do you know what this is made of?*" He asked in a way that sent a thrill through Tristram.

"Glass?"

"No."

"Quartz?"

A gentle chuckle from the dying man. "*Quartz?*"

Tristram shrugged. "I don't know."

Toby took a long, deep breath, and then gave the most contented smile that Tristram had ever seen.

"Memories." He said finally with quiet triumph. "It's made of memories, Tristram. Look closely at it, can't you tell?"

Tristram gave a sad smile at the fantasy.

"You don't believe me?" Toby asked, with mock indignation. "Pick one of the tiny colours and look very, very closely at it. What is your favourite colour?"

"Green."

"Look at one of the greens."

As Tristram focused on an olive-green speck he instantly became aware of a temperate rainforest. He could smell wet, earthy smells and he could hear bird calls, and a rushing stream in a gully nearby. The sensation passed like a transient daydream, and he was back in Toby's room again. The colour seemed to flash and roll into the other colours like a speck in a kaleidoscope.

The boy was positively startled.

"A rainforest!" He shouted.

"Tasmania." Explained Toby with a vindicated expression. "A rather recent memory. The sensations are what you feel first, but with practise you can feel the emotions and the thoughts of the memory as well."

"I see a beautiful sunset." Tristram was being flooded with sensations.

"There are many of those." Smiled Toby.

"I feel sad, though."

"It must have been just after Sally died. I still miss that old dog. Do you remember how she used to say 'mama' to Joan?"

A mirth trickled into Tristram as the pink and orange colour rolled away to be replaced by a pearly hue.

"Yes, I can see her now, wagging her tail." He frowned. "She is very young."

"She wasn't always an old dog, you know."

"I see purple flowers..."

"Port wine magnolias. I admire them every year."

"There is so much blue..."

"I love the ocean on a clear morning, and I love looking up into the sky...I think everybody does."

A deep, rusty red colour suddenly arrested Tristram's attention. He tensed and then his face set in a bitter, determined scowl. He began to wheeze roughly.

Toby's face became anxious.

"What are you seeing now?"

"The red desert...It's night time. It's cold and there are so many stars..." Tristram's voice was filled with awe.

"Oh yes, that one. That memory isn't mine, Tristram. It is a strange, disturbing memory."

Tristram felt a terrible hatred. He had a headache from a troubling dream.

"*Beware of thieves...*" He hissed.

"Don't focus on that colour, Tristram." Warned Toby, but Tristram was in a trance.

"My left leg feels funny...it doesn't bend the way it should."

Suddenly Toby snatched the opal from Tristram's hand.

"I'm sorry." Tristram breathed, startled.

The concern on Toby's face lingered as he looked into Tristram.

"Opals like these, Tristram, are made from all sorts of memories and feelings. Each colour you see in it is a moment, a memory, an emotion. You need only hold the opal, and whatever passes through your mind is accepted by it, you see? And then the opal translates the experience into a fragment of colour. Unfortunately, the opal does not discriminate between pleasant and awful memories. It keeps *everything* given to it, the bad and the good. Do you understand?"

"Yes." Tristram nodded.

"Like the others before me, I have made a very

great effort to only hold the opal when I have something pleasant to give it." Toby continued, looking seriously into Tristram. "In a funny way, it is a positive mirror of my whole life. That is what the opal is, Tristram. It is a container with the best memories of my life – of lots of other lives. Do you see?"

Toby enjoyed the thought for a moment.

"I will try to give the opal only good memories." Tristram murmured.

Toby nodded. Then he frowned.

"I am worried that you might be too young for this, Tristram." He continued. "But life is unpredictable, and we have no choice in some of the hurdles set before us. The opal is... special and dangerous, like life itself. Take the journey the best way you can. This opal is yours now; make it even more beautiful with your own life. But remember not to dwell on the rusty red colours. At least, not the ones with the limping witch doctor."

"*Witch doctor!?*"

Toby sighed with a resigned smile.

"I presume that he has been dead for decades, but from my own experience and the legend told to me by the opal's previous owner, he was an aboriginal witch doctor."

"How did you know he was limping?"

"When you experience his memories, you know what it is like to be him."

"What did he look like?"

"He was an aborigine. I don't know which tribe he belonged to, but aborigines of many tribes seemed to recognise and fear him. He was very unusual, Tristram. I once saw his reflection in water and he had orange eyes. Rich orange, like the peel of the fruit."

Toby frowned as he ruminated on the strange character of the witch doctor.

"Tell me more." Tristram asked eagerly. "Is he wicked?"

Toby looked perplexed "I don't know. His memories are all bitter. But not just bitter. His feelings were cold, hateful, determined...very determined..."

Toby began to drift into his own thoughts, tackling an old puzzle that he could never quite solve.

"It doesn't matter." Toby concluded, finally. "The point is that his dark memories are a part of the opal, just as trials and tribulations are a part of a lifetime... but trust me, Tristram; it is the good that is worth holding on to, always. Remember the pleasures of life and remember also the lessons of heartache – but let the heartache go. You must learn this, Tristram."

Toby reached out and held Tristram's hand.

"I will, Granddad." Tristram solemnly promised.

"Treasure the opal; make it beautiful, like a mirror of your soul, made by wonderful memories from your life. And one day, Tristram, you will realise that you no longer need the opal, and on that day, you should pass it on to someone special, as I passed it on to you today."

A silence of some time passed between them, in which Tristram's mind swam in a whirl of thought and Toby breathed slow, painful breaths. Tristram did not know what to say, and Toby understood.

"It's time for you to go out and enjoy the sunshine and the fresh air."

"OK, Granddad." Tristram answered with some relief. He looked into Toby's faintly smiling face and knew that he should hug him tightly.

Yet he couldn't. A shame filled his stomach as he realised that he was repulsed by Granddad Toby's dying body. Toby's beautiful spirit was unreachable in that emaciated flesh.

Tristram stood forward and tenderly shook Toby's hand.

"I love you, Granddad."

"Take care, Tristram."

Just before Tristram reached the door, Toby spoke again.

"Tristram?"

"Yes?"

"Could you please take that cup of tea outside and empty it on the camellias?"

"OK."

Tristram took the cup beside the bed and Toby gently touched his arm.

"Could you tell Joan that it was lovely? I would like her to think that I was able to drink it all and that it made me feel better."

Tristram gave a teary nod, and then left his grandfather forever.

Tristram kept the opal secret from that day. He dared not to show it to anyone, until the moment that he felt Joan needed it most, as they stood beside her husband's coffin at the funeral.

"Is that an *opal*?" Russell asked in an incredulous whisper.

Tristram closed his hand over the opal with an anxious jealously.

"Yes, it is." Joan answered resolutely. "And Tristram is going to take excellent care of it. Aren't you, Darling-heart?"

"Yes." Tristram answered solemnly.

"I don't know that I would trust a child with such an expensive heirloom, Mum." Russell objected. "I mean, do we know how valuable it is?"

"It is absolutely priceless." Joan answered. "And I am certain that Tristram would not part with it for all the world."

Holly knelt down and looked Tristram in the eyes.

"We're not going to take the opal from you, Tris." She said. "But we should put it in a bank-safe until you are old enough to look after it."

"No!" Tristram shouted. "I *am* old enough to look after it. You say I am responsible, but you don't trust me!"

"It will still be yours; it will just be in a safe place."

"No! Granddad gave it to me to look after, no one else!"

"Don't shout at us, Tristram." Warned Russell. "We're your parents. We're not trying to rob you; we're trying to do what's best for you."

"You don't look after any of your other toys." Added Holly coolly. "What if you lose it? What if some other kid steals it from you? Give it to us to look after; you know it's for the best."

"No!" Tristram was on the verge of panic. "You don't understand – I have to look after it. Me only. You don't understand. Grandma!"

Joan answered his appeal.

"Toby, for reasons of his own, has given Tristram the responsibility of looking after this opal. It is a very special opal. I fully believe that it is a piece of Toby's very soul – and he gave it to Tristram, and so Tristram *must* keep it. I will not have it otherwise."

This last command was not going to be disputed by Holly and Russell at that moment, though the issue was hardly finalised in their minds.

Accepting their silence as acquiescence, Joan then turned a serious but kindly eye on Tristram.

"Now then. Tristram, you are now responsible for keeping this opal very safe – because you know better than anyone else how precious and priceless it is. But you *must promise me* to put it somewhere safe and secret and not to tell a *soul* where you keep it. Will you promise me this, Tris?"

"I promise, Grandma." Tristram answered sincerely.

"Then it is settled." Joan kissed Tristram on the forehead. "I know that a promise from my number one grandson is a promise that will be kept. Now let us say no more of the matter."

The issue was put to rest for the remainder of that sad and solemn day. It remains only to describe two other characters that witnessed that exchange: Tristram's maternal grandparents, particularly one Stewart MacDougall.

The rough old farmer was another personality in this picture whose dress was out of his usual character. Granddad Stewy had foregone his cheap shirts and casual trousers for quite a smart grey suit. The grey wisps of his fine hair were neatly combed over his forehead, rather than flying in the haphazard directions that usually attracted the silent criticism of his gentle wife. He was a short, barrel-chested figure with ropey, sinewy limbs that were forged from years of labour and perseverance in the face of adversity – his mettle was fired in the harsh kiln of the dry Wimmera country of Western Victoria. His face and forearms were permanently tanned. His eyes had a determined gleam behind cheap glasses that sat on a bulbous nose.

Stewart's hazel eyes lit up and flashed when Tristram gave the opal to Joan.

He sighed worriedly when the discussion of the opal had ended.

"Well, Jack..." Stewart began in his deep, nasal drawl. "That's a bit of a worry."

Mary Allison MacDougall was a true lady, and never liked the rough, farm nickname of Jack.

She shrugged her shoulders.

"I'm sure he'll look after it." She returned in her soft, well-spoken manner. Her gentle, musical voice was a complete contrast to the ocker boom of her husband.

"He's a good lad, Jack, but he's a child – and all children are irresponsible."

"Oh Stewart! Tris will look after it."

"Nope – he'll lose it, and it'll be a legacy lost forever."

"Holly has brought him up well, he'll be careful."

"Holly is a good mother." Stewart conceded. "So, she'll probably put us both at ease by taking it off him."

"I'm at ease as things are." Mary murmured.

"Mmm?"

Mary gave a gentle, frustrated sigh. "It doesn't matter."

"Speak up, Jack, you're forever makin' me strain me ears!"

"It doesn't matter."

"Then why did I hear something? If yer gonna say somethin' Jack, you should belt it out, so I can hear it. But no – you always just sorta mutter and mumble about."

"It was nothing, Stewart! God!"

"Well, I am going deaf, you know, Jack."

"Yes, I know." Mary mumbled. "I wish I was."

"Mmm?"

"Oh for heaven's sake, Stewart, it doesn't matter!"

"Well, you know I do worry about these things, Jack. You gotta look ahead to avoid every disaster."

"It isn't our place to meddle."

"No – we don't meddle...We don't meddle." Stewart rejoined with a mixture of great pride and reluctance.

A silence ensued whilst Stewart ruminated on the issue.

"Yeah..." He finally drawled. "We don't meddle, Jack. We'll just have to sit back in total helplessness and hope we're wrong about everything."

Mary rolled her eyes but offered no other rebuttal.

INTO THE WILD HIGH
COUNTRY

BRIGHT IS a small town near the snowfields in the high country of Eastern Victoria. It is busy in winter and beautiful in autumn. Fortunately for the Zumstein family, it was autumn now. Though they were unaccustomed to the chill, the four Queenslanders appreciated the vibrant colours of the season about them. Bright had many mature, introduced specimen trees, such as liquid amber, oak, claret ash, golden elm and birch. Hence, the place was alighted with fiery reds, warm oranges, honey goldens, and rich clarets. The foliage of the town was an invigorating contrast to the surrounding smoky evergreen of the eucalyptus forest that covered the mountains.

Hester Zumstein was never satisfied with her appearance. Her hair was short, blonde and stylish. Her blue eyes were compelling. However, Hester hated her body, because no amount of exercise would make her large behind go away. Yet, whatever lot nature had bestowed upon her, Hester was the best looking she could be. This principle dominated every aspect of her life. Her house on the Gold Coast of Queensland was large, white and polished both inside and out. The garden was wrought with fashionable palms, and granite boulders and a salt-water swimming pool. There was not a bare patch on the lawn, not a weed in the garden, not a leaf on the wide decking of the veranda. Inside, there was never a scuff on the carpet, a drop of water on the kitchen floor, or a picture crooked. At least, not for long. Order and cleanliness was Hester's special religion – but in that regard, her two children were positively sacrilegious.

Hester cast a critical eye over her boys as they sat in the car.

Pyran, a red-haired boy Tristram's age, had already lost a button on an expensive shirt. His bright green eyes squinted nervously under his mother's fierce glare. His older brother Warrick, a dark-haired lad approaching fifteen, had rolled up the sleeves on his shirt and refused to tuck it into his costly jeans. He had an angular face with narrow blue eyes that gleamed with petulant defiance.

Hester sighed sharply and gave an exasperated roll of her eyes.

"Why must you two be such messy little shits!?

God! I bought you these expensive clothes and you've already ruined them!"

"Oh, come on, Mum, I've lost *one* button." Pyran protested.

"Don't answer back! I told you not to go and get dirty, because I want you both to look nice for your grandparents. But no! As usual you have completely defied me; you bloody ungrateful pair of shits."

"Get a grip, Mum, whadya expect? Were goin' bush – were gonna get dirty anyway." Warrick smirked.

"Warrick...don't be cheeky. Tuck your shirt in and put a jumper on, it's freezing."

"No."

"Do it now."

"How about a please?"

"How about a bloody good hiding?!"

"Pfffff. Go on, then."

Hester gasped and then, eyes ablaze, reached over and slapped Warrick on the shoulder.

Pyran winced but Warrick merely scoffed.

"Weak as piss, Mum." He sneered.

Hester resorted to her back up measure.

"Karl!"

Hester's husband Karl was a tall, muscular man with thick sandy hair and a moustache. His features were a pleasing mix of his Italian and German ancestry. Karl was an easy-going man but could find no peace when his wife was agitated. It was going to be a long car trip.

"What is it, Hezz?" He asked. His green eyes showed a tired impatience.

"Warrick is being disrespectful." Hester answered vehemently.

Karl responded the only way he knew how. Warrick yelped as he received the mighty backhand, and Pyran screamed as he received a belt straight after his brother.

"Don't disrespect your mother." Karl growled.

Warrick sulked whilst Pyran tearfully protested.

"Dad! I didn't say anything! Warrick *said* it!"

"Shut up, weasel." Warrick snapped.

Hester was sorry to see her children hurt, infuriating as they were. This was supposed to be a family holiday.

"Karl, Pyran didn't really say anything worth a hiding."

"See?!" Pyran bawled, vindicated.

"You still dirtied your clothes." Muttered Karl.

"This isn't fair!"

"Pyran – stop crying, or I will give you something to cry about. Now get in the car, both of you."

Their vehicle was a brand-new topaz Farelane. The interior was stylish and comfortable, and air-conditioned – yet the four of them were restless and impatient as they zoomed along the highway.

"Can I listen to me Southern Sons tape, Mum?" Warrick asked with a trace of petulance.

"Why don't you ask properly?"

"Please?"

"No-"

"Why not?!"

"Let me finish! No, that's not asking properly."

"Jesus Christ."

"Warrick!" Bellowed Karl, "Watch your language."

"I was joking!"

"No, you weren't."

Hester resumed her lecture. "You don't say 'can I listen to *me* tape' as if you're a thick, uneducated country bumpkin."

"Alright! God! May I, darling Mum, *please* listen to *my* Southern Sons tape, *please*, Mum?" Warrick attempted with a sullen glare.

Pyran giggled and it broke the tension. Hester chuckled.

"Yes, Warrick, my polite, beloved son. You may listen to your tape."

He handed the cassette over to her and peace was obtained temporarily.

"Mum," Pyran asked, "Can me and Warrick have a drink?"

"Next service station, mate."

"Where's the next service station?"

Hester looked to Karl for the answer.

"We'll stop at Omeo." He said.

Twenty minutes later, the tiny township of Omeo finally appeared before them as they descended the surrounding high country, and it wasn't long before Karl pulled over at the general store.

As he went inside to fetch refreshments, Hester used the opportunity to talk with the boys again.

"Remember what I said. You be polite to Holly and Russ. You do whatever Granddad says *without question*. And most important boys: be really nice to Tristram and Saffi and poor, dear little Jase. They have been very upset over Toby's death."

Pyran answered first. "We will, Mum."

Hester then got out of the car to stretch her legs.

Warrick turned to Pyran and rolled his eyes.

"This is going to suck eggs."

"I know." Pyran groaned "Tristram is a bloody goody-goody, eh?"

"Yeah. And Saffi is going to cry and sook all the time. We'll have to look after Jase everywhere we go. And Mum's gonna rave on and on about how bad we are and how she wishes we were more like Holly's kids."

"It'll be good to see Aunty Holly, though, eh? She's always nice. She'll probably give us lollies."

"Whoa!" mocked Warrick, "Lollies! Whoopee-do, Pyran."

"Shut up!"

"You shut up."

"No, *you* shut up!"

"Listen," growled Warrick through gritted teeth. "You want Mum and Dad to hear us fighting? Just shut up or I'll cork ya leg."

"I'll tell dad."

"How does that help you in the immediate future?"

Pyran was persuaded by this argument.

The issue was forgotten as soon as they were on the road again, with a packet of chips each and a can of Coke.

As the Zumsteins were travelling south-east from Bright through the rugged beauty of the high country, the Joneses and the MacDougalls travelled in separate cars north through Swift's Creek towards Omeo. Tristram, Saffi and Jase had chosen to ride with their grandparents.

The occupants of all three cars were in awe of the countryside around them. The landscape was miles of rolling, steep hills which were covered in twisted gum trees. While the Joneses and MacDougall's were travelling along the valley besides the stony Tambo River, the Zumsteins were descending through winding, shadowed roads. Eventually, all three cars passed north through Benambra, (classified a town purely because it had a pub) and took a sandy gravel road that wound deep into alpine National park.

As the MacDougall's drove deeper into the forest, a sense of forboding slithered into Tristram. The sky was ebullient, the scenery dense and soaring, it was a day for adventure – yet he felt suddenly cold every now and then. He understood that this was strange, given that the windows of the car were tightly wound up and that the car heater was going. He glanced down at the opal in his palm. A tiny, rust-red speck rolled into the centre and accosted his attention...the noise of the car vanished as Tristram became engulfed by the experience of another...

He was in dry, open eucalypt forest. Bright morning light bathed the clearing and he could feel the warmth of it on his skin. A rich mixture of scents seeped into him rapidly. The smell of the gum leaves first – then the smell of dogs – and then fresh blood.

After the scents came an intense feeling of savage triumph.

The scene came sharply into focus. Tristram sneered at an old Chinese man.

The man was bald and wrinkled, with a long white beard. His black, almond eyes emanated a deep sorrow and grief. His posture was straight and strong, and he wore the dusty grey garb of a gold-miner.

The old man did not seem to fear Tristram. Nor did he seem to fear the dingos and wild dogs that circled menacingly around them.

Tristram chuckled cruelly and waved the opal in the old Chinaman's face. It was covered in blood. He closed his eyes, then ran his tongue over the opal and savoured the salty, metallic flavour of the blood. One of the dingos gave a plaintive whine – but he would not let them approach the bodies – not yet.

He then opened his eyes and held the Chinese man with a mocking look.

If only I could wither the old man with my eyes...

However, the old Chinese man had a dignity and power that unsettled him. *What further outrage would provoke him into an attack?*

Tristram knelt down beside the corpse of a young, white woman. Her hair was dark chocolate, wet from sweat. She had not screamed when he had slit her lover's throat. Nor did she beg for the life of her child. She had lunged at him like a wild animal. A mother's instincts.

The old Chinese man did not move. He stood still and watched Tristram with intense contempt.

Tristram smiled viciously, then sat the corpse of the woman up for the old man's inspection. Then he took out his knife and slit the front of her clothing. He roughly tore the blood-soaked material to expose her plump breasts. His brown calloused hands fondled them in a gruesome parody of foreplay. Her body was still warm.

Still, the old man did not move. His eyes speared into Tristram coldly.

Suddenly, Tristram heard sobbing. It was the little boy.

The sunlight gleamed in his golden curls. He was curled up beside the body of his father, who had stared at Tristram with dumb surprise and fear only a moment ago. The little boy crawled pathetically towards him and reached out his little hand to touch that of his mother's.

Tristram felt a sharp pang of pity and he stopped fondling the dead woman's breast.

He looked up at the old Chinese man, but he had disappeared. Warily Tristram scanned the surrounding gum trees.

Then he heard the pounding of hooves. Quickly he dropped the woman, jumped to his feet and grabbed the arm of the child. He yanked the boy roughly to his feet and dragged him away through the trees...

Tristram pulled his mind away from the memory, horror-stricken. He looked about the inside of the car. Saffi was looking dreamily out her window and Jase was reading a children's book on dinosaurs. His grandparents had their mind on the road and the surrounding countryside. Tristram inhaled deeply and tried to shake off what he had just experienced, as though it were nothing more than an awful daydream. However, he could not shake the astringent guilt that pooled in the pit of his stomach. Toby was right to tell him not to look at the rusty red colours.

A few large hills away, Pyran was also having unsettling sensations. Perhaps this was not unusual – he was the smallest member of a family that was constantly on the brink of outrage. Yet, even so, at the fuzzy edge of his mind, he felt as though he was heading towards some unknown and terrible climax.

When the car had stopped at their camp site, and he opened the door, Tristram Jones was born again. He ejected himself from the warm, familiar womb of the car into the cold fresh air of the bush. A wall of eucalyptus aroma engulfed him. The high-pitched call of the currawongs and the mellifluous warble of magpies thrilled him. Ivory mountain ash tree trunks soared into the bright blue morning. Sunlight danced in their emerald clouds of long leaves.

Tristram decided that this very moment should be given to the opal. He took it out of his pocket and felt its magic at work immediately. Though it felt like an ice-cube in the palm of his hand, Tristram burned inside. Then, before his eyes the opal turned a menacing sapphire. The tiny colours wriggled like a shoal of panicked fish. In an instant the colours rushed into a swirling nucleus of rusty red in the centre of the opal and disappeared.

For a second, a shadow possessed the opal, before there was a silent supernova in the centre which sent a million fragments of colour to the surface. Finally, the colours settled, and a white almond fragment floated into the centre. Tristram saw in that fragment a mirror of the forest before him, before it shrank suddenly into a tiny speck, and rolled away into the centre. The opal then showed no further signs of animation.

"Watchya got there, Tris?"

With the sun behind him, Granddad Stewy's knobby features made him look like a wooden idol. He was beaming at Tristram with proud joy, with his hands on his hips and a tobacco pipe in his mouth.

The smell of his sweet smoke had only just begun to mingle with the scent of the bush. Tristram found it pleasant.

"Granddad Toby's opal." Tristram answered, after some hesitation.

Stewart gave a thoughtful squint under the brim of his terry-towelling hat.

"Yeah?" he drawled amiably.

Before he could add anything else, a honeybee lazily buzzed between them and landed on Tristram's jumper. With quick ease, Tristram had it in his hands.

"Is that a bee, Tris?"

"Yep."

"You'd better let him go. He'll sting ya."

"No, he won't."

"Oh yeah? How's that?"

Tristram walked quietly up to his grandfather and held up the insect for his inspection. He had it pinned gently about the join between its abdomen and its thorax. Try as it might, the bee was unable to sting him.

"I've got him by the hip, see?" Tristram smiled gently.

"Well, how about that, eh?" Stewart chuckled.

Tristram let the bee fly away.

"You know, Tris..." Stewart began in a quiet, serious tone. "I was worried at first that you would lose that opal."

He waited for a response, but the boy was suddenly quiet, embarrassed and expectant.

"But," Stewart added, "I can see that you're a sensible fella. I reckon that's why ol' Toby gave it to ya."

"I won't lose it, Granddad."

"I hope not, Tris. There's more than one person's history associated with that thing."

"It is the only thing of Granddad Toby's that I have left." Tristram said with a steady, serious look. Stewart sensed a rebuke. "I will *not* lose it."

"I believe ya, Tris."

A silence passed between them before Tristram added with a trace of emotion "I miss him so much."

Stewart sighed, and smiled kindly at the lad. He puffed contemplatively at his pipe and drank in the beauty of the sunbathed bush.

"You know, Tris," he finally murmured, "Everything sorta has a way of just workin' out. No matter what sorta rough patch yer have, you always end up havin' another happy time sooner or later."

As if on cue the Zumsteins arrived, followed closely by Tristram's parents. The echo of car doors resounded about the tranquil forest and a raucous, jocular exchange erupted from the two families.

Stewart smiled broadly. "Yer see?"

THE HAUNTING POOL

"LET'S LOOK AT THEM ANYWAY." Dared Pyran in an excited whisper.

"No!" Bawled Saffi, "Granddad Toby told Tristram not to look at the red colours!"

"Saffi! Don't yell!" hissed Tristram.

The adults had not heard them. Warrick was clearly trying to impress his grandparents and his aunty by behaving entirely out of character. He was polite, cheerful and helpful. The ladies were getting merrily tipsy with white wine. Mary cackled raucously as Holly and Hester each fought to dominate the conversation. The men had fired up the gas barbeque and were standing officiously around it, exchanging yarns and jokes. They were all far too happy and loud to notice secret mischief. Even so, Tristram wished Saffi wasn't so quick to shout.

"Can I have a look, Tris?" Asked Jase eagerly in his quiet voice.

"No, Jase. You're too young."

"That's not fair!" Exclaimed Saffi. "You can't show me and not Jase, that's just mean."

"Alright! Shoosh! But not now, OK, Jase? I promise I will show you, but not now."

"Why can't he have a look now?" Saffi demanded.

"Saffi," Tristram growled, "maybe you should go and talk to Grandma-"

"No!"

Pyran joined in. "Were not going to have any fun – not anything *you'll* think is fun-"

"We want to be with you guys!"

It was time for the boys to change tactics.

"Saffi," Tristram beseeched, "I just want to show Pyran how it works. That's all. Now, I showed you how it worked after the funeral, and I trusted you not to tell anyone about it. Pyran is our cousin, so we should trust him as well."

Pyran added "Come on, Saff, it won't be so bad. I'll look at any colour you want. What's your favourite colour?"

Saffi considered the boys' proposal with suspicion before she relented.

"You can look at any colour but the red colours...I like yellow."

Tristram smiled "The colour with sweet corn?"

"Yes."

"Should've known you'd pick a food related memory."

"Shut up!"

"Alright," announced Pyran as held up the opal, "I'm gonna look at a yellow colour..."

Saffi, Tristram and Jase watched his face expectantly as he sat transfixed by the opal in his cupped hands. After about twenty seconds Pyran snapped out of his trance and smiled in sheer amazement.

"Wow! That's pretty radical, eh?" He licked his lips and wiped his bright orange fringe away from his green eyes.

Saffi asked in awe "Was it sweet corn?"

"Nah...it was fish 'n' chips!"

Tristram grinned. "Told ya you'd like it."

"Man, this is so cool. I'm hungry now though, eh?"

Pyran was turning the opal over and over in his shaking hands as he spoke. Tristram reached over and took it off him.

"That'll do for now."

"OK." Pyran murmured, disappointed.

"We will look at it again later." Tristram assured. "For now, I reckon the barbie's ready. I can smell it, eh?"

"What about me, Tris?" Jase pleaded again.

Tristram wanted to refuse but it felt awful to say

no. Jase clearly looked up to his older brother. Besides, Saffi was glaring at him.

"Alright. You guys go on to the barbie, it'll take a while for me to find the right colour. I won't be too long."

"We'll wait." Saffi returned defiantly.

"C'mon, Saff." Pyran beamed charismatically. "Let 'em be, well go get a sausage, eh? I reckon your Aunty Hester might give us all a Coke as well. Could do with one, I'm as thirsty as hell! Come on, I'll race ya!"

Saffi accepted the challenge and they raced to the others.

Tristram looked seriously into Jase's eyes.

"There's a lot of stuff in this opal, Jase. Some of it a bit too much for us kids, I reckon. That's why Granddad Toby told me not to look at certain colours. He knew I was responsible and wouldn't do the wrong thing. Can I trust you to only look at the colour I say?"

"Yes." Was the earnest response.

"OK..." Tristram turned the opal over in his hands, sampling each memory briefly. A thousand emotions floated on the surface of his mind, like the reflections of different coloured birds flying over a still lake. He breathed slowly and tried not to be swayed towards any extreme feelings. Finally, he allowed himself to chuckle at a light green memory.

"This is the one, Jase." Tristram smiled as he

pulled his mind away from the colour. "This light green speck just here."

Jase obediently looked at the chosen colour. Tristram watched his little brother's eyes light up with delight. Jase giggled happily at what he was seeing and it warmed Tristram's heart. Finally, Jase looked up at Tristram in wonder.

"Wow..." He murmured.

"What did you see, Jase?"

"I was feeding ducks, an' they were fighting an' one of them fell over."

"Oh...I see."

"It was funny." Jase beamed at Tristram. "Thanks, Tris."

"That's alright, mate. Let's go join the others, now. Don't tell anyone but Saffi and Pyran what you saw, OK?"

"OK."

With that, Tristram took Jase's hand, and led him to the mouth-watering sizzle of the barbeque.

The early afternoon rolled by, full of chat and laughter, and it wasn't long before they all found themselves on a bushwalk. They trampled along a dirt track that wound through the tall, grey and white trunks of eucalyptus. The twisted, curving boughs of the trees supported rustling clouds of long, oily emerald leaves. Dappled sunlight fell gently onto the knee-high carpet of glossy, dark green bracken fern. Before long, they descended through gullies of myrtle, lilly-pilly and towering tree ferns. As the adults jested and gossiped, the youths explored. Their minds were full of excitement and curiosity at half seen creatures in the mysterious undergrowth. The moist, earthy smell of the bush whetted their appetite for adventure, and when they finally arrived at a fast-flowing stream, they were ready to believe the fantastic.

They followed the stony stream back along its course between two gently sloping hills. Always the stream seemed to turn a corner and always the forest seemed dense and infinite either side of them. At last they came to a point where they could go no further. They were standing beside a deep pool, which was about thirty feet in diameter. Opposite them was a steep wall of earth and limestone boulders, over which the stream gently cascaded into the pool. Epiphytic ferns and mosses sprang from the rocks and the trees. Naked roots clutched boulders. There was a recess in the wall, which was barely visible behind some undergrowth.

"What a beautiful billabong!" Exclaimed Hester.

"Actually, it's not technically a billabong, Hezz, as it has a creek running through it. A billabong is always an isolated body of water." Russell explained.

"There is something a little forboding about this place." Mary murmured.

"I feel it too, Mum." Holly rejoined thoughtfully. "Perhaps this place was sacred to the aborigines."

Hester scoffed. "There's not enough tourist money in it for that."

"There's a cave over there!" Declared Tristram, before an argument broke out between the sisters. He and Pyran were soon disappointed to discover that there was no way of getting to it without getting wet.

"This region is full of caves." Russell remarked. "The caves at Buchan, the Royal and Fairy Caves, are the tip of the ice-berg. There are literally thousands of caves in these hills, most of which haven't been explored."

Tristram thought that he could almost feel the moist, empty spaces of those myriads of caves, connected to each-other via random crevices, cracks and holes. He sensed underground rivers racing through the black voids, and immense caverns with intricate networks of stalactites and stalagmites.

Suddenly a vivid image rolled across Tristram's imagination...

An immense, furry paw leaves a foot-print in the thin layer of beige clay on the floor of a cave, as water echoes in the blackness...

"I reckon we could get over there." Announced Warrick, sizing up the rocks on the left side of the pool.

"No one is going over there." Warned Hester.

"She's right, boys," Russell agreed, "it's far too

dangerous and we're miles from help if you get into trouble. Let's just sit here for a while and enjoy the scenery."

As the family sat down amongst some surrounding fallen timber and large boulders, Holly casually remarked "Not much chance of finding him here."

Tristram was the first to react. He sensed a story.

"Finding who here?"

"Big Scale." Holly replied simply.

Tristram, Saffi and Jase's eyes widened.

"Big Scale!" They breathed as they looked with sudden suspicion and excitement at the pool.

Pyran's curiosity was piqued.

"Who's Big Scale?" He asked.

"You don't know Big Scale?!" Tristram burst out. "Everyone knows Big Scale! Don't they, Mum?"

Holly smiled pleasantly at Pyran. The faintest twinkle animated her hazel eyes.

"Obviously Big Scale hasn't visited Queensland for a while."

Karl confirmed the sentiment. "It's been about ten years since he was last seen up our way, Hol".

"Who is he?!" Shouted Pyran.

Hester chuckled as Jase exploded into the conversation "He's a big, big fish, Pyran!"

"Oh, is that all?" He answered, deflated.

"No!" Scoffed Saffi. "Tell him, Mum."

"Don't you remember the story?"

"I do!" Beamed Tristram and turning to Pyran began. "Years ago, there was this bream – *Acanthropagrus butcheri-*"

The adults, particularly Hester, burst into laughter that echoed loudly about the boulders surrounding the pool.

"Acantho-what?!" Hester expostulated.

"*Acanthropagrus butcheri.*" Tristram answered. He eyed his aunty with mild surprise at her ignorance. "Otherwise known as the Black Bream."

"Oh well – God! I beg your pardon, Tris." Hester cackled.

"He knows the scientific name of all our common fish and animals, Hezz." Russell grinned. "He wants to be a zoologist one day – like Gerald Durrell. I think he'll get there too. The little bugger is forever bringing home frogs and lizards and turtles from every wet, muddy and wild place he can get to. He makes Harry Butler look like a wimp."

"Very interesting." Pyran interjected impatiently. "So, Tristram, get on with it. Big Scale is a bream..."

"Big Scale was once a small fish that got hooked by a fisherman. But he got away and kept the hook. He decided that the hook would be a trophy. Then he decided that he would fill his mouth with hooks. He would be the one fish that always got away. And so, for years he has challenged every fisherman he can, and beaten every one. His mouth is full of hooks and he has grown very, very big. Hence the name, Big Scale."

Pyran was curious but not yet enthusiastic about the story.

"Alright then...how big is he?"

"Oh..." Murmured Tristram as he tried to calculate it.

Holly interjected. "Not as big as you might think but fairly big none-the-less. He might *just* be able to fit into that pool...but then we don't really know how *deep* that pool is, do we?"

Everybody, even the adults, turned with renewed interest in the pool.

The air was still. Not a bird twittered, and not an insect hummed. There was just the sound of water...

It tinkled like tiny shards of glass as it ran over shallow stretches of the stream. It squealed as it swirled around the larger rocks and it gurgled over fallen, mossy logs. It hummed and deeply resonated as it poured into the deep basin of the pool over a limestone tongue.

The mid-afternoon sunlight was rippled back onto the underside of the large boulders on the opposing wall, lending an ethereal animation to the place.

The floor of the pool was covered in smooth, multicoloured stones that reflected the sunlight in the shallows. However, the centre of the pool was deep, dark and impenetrable.

Without being aware of it, the attention of the entire family was absorbed by the blackness at the centre of the pool. Slowly, an enchanted silence stole upon them.

Tristram was unsettled. He felt an involuntary hypnosis coming over him. As he held the opal, it grew unbearably hot and he felt as though his hand had been scolded. Yet, he was shivering with a spiritual chill, as though the jewel had sucked the warmth of life from his very being.

Holly was terrified. A sudden horrible vision flashed across her mind.

A very large animal was feeding on Jase's body at the edge of the pool, as the moon appeared above the trees...

The vision was fleeting, however, and she recovered quickly from her fright as though it were some irrational daydream.

It was Warrick who finally broke the spell. He picked up a round, smooth rock the size of a large potato, and before anybody could object, he tossed it into the centre of the pool. The ensuing splash felt sacrilegious.

"Warrick!" Hester reprimanded.

The rock plummeted into the blackness and wholly disappeared without any impression of hitting the bottom. Tristram thought that he sensed a large presence move out of the way of the rapidly descending stone.

"What?" Protested Warrick. "We've been starin'
at this pool for ten minutes! I thought it was time to
do something interesting."

"Yeah," shrugged Karl, "the day's getting on, we
should probably head back. Tris can tell us more
about Big Scale as we go, eh?"

"Yeah...alright." Tristram answered, distracted.

Ten minutes later, as they walked back to camp,
Tristram was still uneasy. It was though the stream
carried a voice from the dark heart of the beautiful
pool, that whispered within the bubbling, trickling
water...

I've seen you...

THE BATTLE WITH BIG SCALE

As THEY WALKED BACK through the bush to their camp, the children were preoccupied and serious, and Tristram had suddenly declined to regale everybody with tales of Big Scale. Hence, Russell decided to cheer the party by relating his own encounter with the legendary monster.

"We had a good day before he showed up, didn't we, Stew?"

"Yeah...had a few good ones."

"Your grandfather was there that day, and we were in a little twelve-foot tinnie on the mighty Murray river, not far from Swan Hill. Of course, I was totally out fishing Stewy-"

"Go on, McTavish!" Stewart snorted. "I was shakin' em off so yer didn't feel bad."

"You must have been shaking them off pretty hard, old man."

"There, yer hear that kids? Old Rusco is a bit of a character. I don't know how you're gonna grow up alright listening to this rot."

"Anyway," Russell continued, "we both agree that it was a good day. A lot of yellow-belly, a few redfin and a decent haul of Murray cod..."

"They were bitin' so hard I had to hide behind a tree to bait me hook!" Stewart boomed.

There was a peal of laughter from the warm-hearted audience

"Shall I continue?" Russell asked.

"By all means, McTavish! We're all in eager constipation."

More Laughter.

"Go on, Russell," drawled Hester, "tell the story and don't let this old bugger interrupt you again."

Stewart stopped in his tracks in mock indignation.

"I've just been consulted!"

"Oh God, Dad! Will you cut it out?" Hester bellowed.

"Don't you like it when I confusify me words?"

"Anyway," interrupted Russell, "all of a sudden we had a quiet patch. The fish had been off the bite for a good twenty minutes. The wind had died down completely and not a ripple broke the surface. The sky became overcast, and a spooky sort of calm came over the river. We both wound in our lines and checked our bait. It hadn't been touched. We were about to pack up and head for camp... *when we saw him.*"

Russell had his audience now, even the adults.

"About two hundred yards down the river in front of us his back broke the surface, with his dorsal fin flat against his spine. He was heading straight for us. Slowly, very slowly, he approached. Stewy and I were breathless.

Then, when he was about fifty yards from the boat, he stopped dead and raised the spikes of his dorsal fin. They stood up about six feet. We knew we were in for it then, didn't we, Stew?"

There was a thoughtful silence from Stewart as his eyes filled with awe at the memory.

"Oh yeah..." he breathed, "that was the trade-mark signal – that was Big Scale's war cry..."

"His dorsal fin stood up for about a minute, and then suddenly he dived. He did this without a sound. For a few minutes we were frantically scanning the river. Back in those days, before the mighty Murray was ruined by agriculture, you could see eight feet into the water. I know it is muddy and turgid now, and the banks are high, the water low and the old river red gums dying – but back then the river was wider, deeper, and clearer. The trees were tall and proud, a real contrast with the flat, dry wheat country with its stunted iron barks and mallees.

Anyway, after a few minutes, Stewy and I sensed that he was near our boat. We stared with our hearts pounding into the water and suddenly, he was there. Just at the very edge of the clear water, we could make out his big golden eyes watching us. They were the size of dustbin lids...and they made us cold all over. Just then, the sun came out from behind the clouds, and the light made his eyes glow under water like large reflectors. Suddenly we could also see the outline of his body. He was about the size of a circus elephant.

The other thing we could now see was his gaping mouth. It was big enough to swallow a man whole without any trouble – but that wasn't what scared us. What scared me and Stewy was the thousands and *thousands* of hooks that we could see in his mouth. There were all different colours and sizes, and many of them were rusty. Small, tiny hooks you might use for garfish were there, as well as great big shark hooks – and every other size in between.

It was our turn to face Big Scale. We knew it as we looked at him and he looked at us.

Stewy whispered "You first, Rusco. We'll use the anchor for a hook, and a couple o' big cod for bait."

I pulled up the anchor slowly and Big Scale watched but didn't move. We began to drift but he kept pace with us. It was the most eerie thing in the world, watching the sticks and the gum leaves float slowly down river as usual, with Big Scale's giant face mere feet underneath, patiently watching my every move..."

Here Russell paused, as though to recover from an exciting, terrifying memory. For a moment the only sounds they heard were the hurried tramping of their feet on the dirt track, and the crunch and snap of twigs and leaves as they walked. The bush was growing darker around them as the sun began to sink behind the mountains.

Russell continued just before Pyran could ask him to.

"Slowly I lowered the anchor down again with our two best cod pinned on each side of the pick. His eyes rolled from side to side, checking the bait from all angles. He approached the bait...but then moved away. He did this three times. Looking back, I know that he was toying with us. We were tense, so tense! He rolled over slowly. He circled our boat...and then...*he opened his mouth...*"

Russell turned to look into the faces of the children. Tristram and Saffi were smiling; they had heard the story before. Tristram thought that the story had improved markedly since the first telling. Pyran was in eager anticipation, his eyes on stalks.

"Well?" He asked.

"Well..." Russell resumed, poker-faced, "he opened his mouth – then snapped it shut again without so much as touching the bait. Then he slowly dived down into the deep until he was totally out of sight."

Russell then looked at Pyran and shrugged.

"Oh, WHAT?!" Bawled Pyran incredulously. "Is that it?! Is that the story? Man, that *sucks eggs!*"

"Pyran!" Hester warned, but she was amused.

"But it does, Mum! Why did you even bother telling that story? Gee that's rotten, Uncle Russell..."

"Actually Pyran," Russell answered in a stern, cool voice, "that isn't the end of the story. If you regain your equanimity, I may continue."

"Regain me what?"

"He means shut up, Pyran." Warrick barked. Even the cynical teenager was eager for the tale.

"Stewy and I waited for him to resurface. We waited a minute. Then two minutes. Then ten. Twenty...we started to doubt his return, but we couldn't move. Twenty-five minutes. Thirty. We relaxed into our disappointment. We didn't say a word for a whole hour. I lit up a cigarette and Stewy lit up his pipe, and we sat there in silence watching the water. The sun was beginning to set and huge flocks of white corellas were squawking in the trees, getting ready to settle in for the night.

Well, just before the sun had set completely, Stewy sighed, emptied his pipe and said "Come on, Rusco. The show's over and the monkey's gone."

No sooner had the words left his mouth, then a great uprising of water rocked the boat. In an instant,

Big Scale had rushed up to the surface from the bottom of the river, grabbed the bait and breached like a whale clear out of the water. It almost capsized the tinnie. Stewy and I hung on to the sides for grim death. We were drenched to the bone by the landing splash – and then...we were off!

Big Scale hurtled down river dragging us behind him. We thumped and bumped behind hm as if we were a speed boat on a choppy sea.

After a while we actually got used to it and even started to enjoy the ride...until – WHACK!

Big Scale rushed around a river bend and smacked us into a half submerged red gum. Luckily, we recovered, but the boat was heavily dinted – still held water though. Anyway, we both grabbed an oar and whenever something like that was about to happen again, we paddled like buggery! It was an exhausting business and really hard when the sun went down. All we had to see with was stars and shadows and Big Scales white wake in front of us – that was all.

Finally, after hours and hours it ended. He broke the line, taking our anchor and our cod, just as we were going under a bridge."

After an expectant silence, Pyran asked "Is that it?"

"I'm afraid so."

"Wasn't a bad story, but the ending could be better, eh?"

"I agree," Hester said, "it was a bit of an anticlimax."

"But you didn't even ask which bridge it was." Russell replied. With that he had their attention again.

"I said that the chase started in Swan Hill. Well... it ended...in *Mildura*."

"So?" Pyran shrugged.

"Do you know how far Mildura is from Swan Hill?"

"No...well? How far is it, Uncle Russell?"

"It's about a hundred and seventy-three kilometres."

"Whoa!"

They had arrived at their campsite. The sun had set only moments ago and the first stars had begun to appear. Raucous kookaburra calls boomed from all sides of the clearing, announcing the onset of night.

As they stepped into the clearing, Tristram noticed that they were not alone.

OLD FRED MORRIS

"Mum?"

"Yes, Tris?"

They were washing the dishes with bottled water heated from the billy.

"I saw an aboriginal man hiding in the forest."

"Did you? You sure it wasn't your imagination?"

Tristram considered this. He often imagined things that were embarrassingly easy for his parents to disprove.

"No..." He decided, as he watched the others happily gathered about the fire.

Holly eyed him shrewdly.

"What did he look like?"

"He was old. And he was wearing an old, dark blue woollen jumper."

"Anything else?"

"A green floppy hat."

"Ah...did he have a limp?"

Tristram looked into his mother's half smiling face.

"I couldn't tell." Tristram answered.

"You think he is the witch doctor from the opal."

"No, I don't...do *you* think he is?"

Holly could see that he was anxious. She was tempted to play with his highly active imagination. However, she did not want him to have nightmares. He had only just stopped having them about his grandfather Toby.

Granddad Toby. A tear came into her eyes at the thought of him. She had not grieved properly yet. Russell hadn't either. She looked at him telling jokes around the fire, every now and then falling silent as the chatter swirled around him. Russell stared into the flames, then up at the cold stars. Saffi sat sleepily in his arms and he kissed her tenderly. He saw his father in her smile.

"Mum?"

"Hmm? No, I don't think so, Tris. That old witch doctor would have died years ago. If you did see a man, he was just that – a man."

Tristram began to mull this over when another thought struck him suddenly.

"How did you know about the witch doctor?" Tristram cried. "Have you been looking at my opal?!"

"Toby told us the story, Tristram, before you were

even born. And we know that the opal is made of memories."

Tristram was positively startled. In a flash he felt foolish. He had thought that the opal's special properties were a secret between him and Toby.

"What's the matter?" Holly asked.

"Nothing."

"We haven't looked at the opal since he gave it to you."

There was a sullen silence from Tristram, but curiosity soon got the better of him.

"What did you see when you looked at it, Mum?"

"Lots of pretty colours, just like you see."

"Pretty colours? What about memories?"

"Oh yes, I saw lots of those. When I looked at a blue colour, I could imagine Toby sitting by the ocean."

*Hang on...*thought Tristram.

"You could *imagine*?"

"I saw him sitting there."

Wrong, thought Tristram. *That's not how it works. She is bluffing! But how did she know about the memories?*

"When I looked at a yellow colour," Holly continued, "I saw him enjoying some sweet corn."

Saffi!

Tristram was furious.

"What else did Saffi tell you?"

Holly knew from the look in Tristram's eyes that the game was up. She changed tactics.

"Do you *really* see Granddad's memories in that opal?"

Tristram knew that she was asking a confession from him.

If I tell her yes, she'll want to know more. If I tell her no, I would be lying, and lying is wrong.

Tristram was going red with guilt at the thought of telling a lie. This did not escape Holly's mild yet penetrating gaze.

"Tell me the truth, Tristram. Look me in the eye and tell me...remember that Jehovah can see the truth, even if you hide it from me – and He will remember forever if you tell me a lie."

Tristram looked her in the eyes, braced himself and said with a calculated shrug "I *think* I do. I *think* I see granddad's memories in the opal – but I don't know if others can."

Holly considered him.

"I think I heard Toby say once that only children can see into the opal. Maybe that's why you kids see what I don't."

"Yeah, maybe."

"You're a good boy, Tristram. We're very proud of you. And thank you for letting Saffi and Jase look at the opal. They need a good older brother."

Tristram had no answer besides a downcast glance and an embarrassed mumble.

"I've nearly finished here, why don't you join the others?"

"OK...Mum?"

"Yes?"

"What about the aboriginal?"

"*Aborigine.*" She corrected. "Don't worry about him. I'll tell Daddy and the others, but he is probably just here to enjoy the bush just like us. It was theirs first, you know."

"I know."

Do you? Holly wondered as Tristram wandered away to the fire – but she knew that now was not the time to lecture him.

Holly had also seen the aborigine. She also recognised him. His name was Fred Morris and he was the janitor at her school. He was an elderly man and was recognised as an Elder of the Koori community around Bairnsdale and Lakes Entrance. Holly often noticed him smile at bright-eyed young aborigine children as they ran past, beaming at him in the corridors. Then, once they had turned a corner, a deep sadness would emanate from him. She noticed how he was civil to the white staff – humble yet dignified.

Holly made a special effort to reach out to Fred. She was always courteous and charming, sounding him out as was her wont with all whom she encountered. Her reward was a warm "G'day Holly" in an old, rattling, nasal voice as she walked to her classroom every morning. As the years rolled by, they spoke more often, occasionally smoking a cigarette together outside the staffroom at recess.

"I'm not gonna tell 'em what I know anymore." Fred had said one morning as they smoked. He looked into Holly's hazel eyes, bitterness radiating from his deep brown ones.

"The chil'ren," he pointed, "dey alright now – but soon – smokin', pregnant, drunk, vandalisin' – violent...but dat's not da worst."

Holly waited for him to continue, but Fred was searching her face to see if she could guess what was coming.

"What's the worst, Fred?" Holly finally asked with respectful calm.

Fred reached down and picked up an empty Coke can.

"This." He said, holding it up in disgust. "Rubbish. Just thrown all over da place – they don't care."

"White kids litter too."

"Yeah, but don't yer see? Black fellas are always sayin' dat white man stole deir land – but dey don't respect da land anymore demselves. What would a black fella do wi' da land, if he had it back, eh?"

"The black people looked after the land very well before we whites came along. White man has wrecked the land, not the black man."

"Black man has changed, Holly. Look at 'im drunk in da street, beatin' 'is woman. Look at 'is house. Dirty, overgrown, rubbish everywhere – everythin' broken. He don't respect da white fella – dat's fair enough. But he don't respect 'is own people – he don't respect 'imself. His kids don't respect deir elders, dey don't respect 'im and dey don't want knowledge of deir people. But worst, Holly, worst..." He waved the can angrily "Dey don't respect da land."

A bitter sadness overwhelmed his anger for an awkward, silent moment.

"I'm sorry, Fred." Holly murmured.

"'It's alright, Holly. Not your fault. You do your best, eh? You show respect. But not da blacks – dey don't deserve da knowledge I got. Dey're like mongrel dingos – no good ta anyone. I'll keep my knowledge. When I die – it'll die wid me."

Holly was moved. Carefully and sincerely she said "That's such a shame, Fred. I think you're knowledge is precious. I wish that you'd tell me some of what you know. I wouldn't throw it away. I would treasure it and pass it on."

Old Fred eyed her thoughtfully and puffed a final puff of his cigarette.

"Well," he said finally as he stubbed out his smoke and put the butt in the bin, "maybe I'll tell ya coupla things..." He grinned and pointed to his watch. "But not today."

With that, Fred had sauntered off, leaving Holly thoughtful and full of curiosity.

It was two weeks ago that that conversation had taken place, and she had forgotten it until she saw

Fred watching the children from amongst the trees. Holly had tried to get his attention, but he had disappeared into the bush.

He probably came here to get away from people. She had thought. *Just like we did.*

THE SMELL OF MISCHIEF

"I ʀᴇᴄᴋᴏɴ Granddad's story'll top Uncle Russell's – no offence, Tris." Pyran announced from his sleeping bag on the other side of the tent.

"Yeah, I reckon you're right." Tristram replied. "I haven't heard his story yet. Dad says he's the only man in history to actually get Big Scale out of the water."

"Yeah?"

"Yeah."

"Cool...I can't wait to hear it, eh?"

It was warm in their tent, rugged up in their sleeping bags. They could just see each other's face on account of the light from the gas lamps which hissed softly outside.

"Pyran...I saw an aborigine man earlier, just as

we were comin' back from our walk." Tristram confided.

"Yeah? Shit!" Pyran exclaimed. "You don't reckon it was that witch doctor ya told me about? The one from the opal?"

"Nah...I asked Mum, and she said it couldn't have been, as he woulda died years and years ago. Still...there's a guy out in the bush somewhere."

Pyran shrugged. "Dad or Granddad or your dad – he's a black belt, isn't he? They'll sort him out if he gives us any trouble, I reckon."

There was a pause between them as they heard another outbreak of laughter from around the fire.

"Why do they send us to bed so *early*?" Groaned Pyran. "It's only eight thirty!"

"That's half an hour past our normal bedtime." Tristram answered.

"Yeah? Bloody hell. Mum usually lets me stay up 'til nine thirty – sometimes even ten o'clock. I reckon she's sent me off early tonight to make a good impression on Aunty Holly. I don't know, Tristram – why is my mum such a bitch?"

"I don't think Aunty Hester is a bitch."

"Jesus Christ, what a surprise."

"Don't use the Lord's name in vain."

"Huh? You're a real goody-goody, aren't ya? I swear it's not normal, Tristram. But don't worry, you're still alright. Better than me, I s'pose. I'm a real little bastard."

"That's not true." Tristram smiled.

"I reckon that's what most people think." Pyran's cheeky smile gave way to a sad, thoughtful frown.

"I don't think it."

"Yeah, but you're me mate and me cousin."

"Mum and Dad like you."

Pyran raised his eyebrows.

"Yeah...They do, eh?"

"But then they don't really know you."

"Yeah." Pyran sighed.

"That was a joke."

Pyran gave him a sharp look which changed quickly into a mad smile.

"No – *this* is a joke!"

Pyran suddenly forced a fart that nearly rattled his sleeping bag. They found it hilarious. The fact that they had to suppress their laughter seemed to prolong it – one child's mirth was the catalyst for the other's.

Soon Tristram was able to add to the humour with flatulence of his own.

"Pyaw! Beef chardonnay!" Concluded Pyran after a tentative whiff.

"*What?!*"

"You know how people smell wines and tell you what it is? Well, it's the same with farts."

"Smell wines?"

"Yeah. Your mum and dad probably do it."

"They don't usually drink wine."

"Don't they? Oh...So you don't know what a chardonnay or a merlin or a pinocchio is?"

"Nope."

"Shit, you're uneducated. Look, ya take in a whiff of the wine and you say gee, that's alright, or this is lolly water or hey! This is bloody awful!"

Tristram could clearly see that Pyran was imitating Hester.

"Do you drink wine?" He asked.

"Nup, not allowed – oh, mum lets us have a taste so we know what it's like, eh? But it's rotten, I'd never drink it. Peach wine's good, had that once. Mum won't buy it though – says it's lolly water. Anyway, back to farts." He let one go and eyed Tristram quizzically as he waved it over to him with his sleeping bag. "What vintage do you reckon that is? You gotta smell it, tell me the year and the flavour."

"Hmm. I reckon that's a 1987 baked bean fluff."

They laughed a little and then Tristram made another contribution to the subject. Pyran smelled it judiciously and concluded in his most pompous voice "Yes, that's definitely been in the barrel a while. I'd say that's a 1982 curried egg special."

"It's beginning to stink in here, Pyran." Tristram complained.

"You're right. Pyaw! We'd better take it easy for a bit...Hey, Tristram! Does your mum ever fart?"

"No..." said Tristram puzzled, "I don't think I've ever heard my mum fart, now you mention it."

"Yeah? Mine either. That's weird, eh? Most women don't fart. My mum certainly doesn't – and I've been especially listenin' for it since I was born."

Pyran's eyes were wide with astonished conviction.

"My dad farts, though." Said Tristram.

"Oh hell yeah, I heard him! And the smell!"

"It makes you wanna chuck!"

"Sure does! Man, I could have chundered all night after Uncle Russell let one go after tea. But he's not as bad as my dad. Oh my god! He is an expert at the egg and bacon classic."

"*The egg and bacon classic?!*"

Suddenly the tent flaps parted to reveal a tired, grumpy Warrick.

"What are yous crapping on about?" He screwed his nose up and the lethargy vanished from his face instantly as he reacted to the smell.

"Pyaw! JESUS! That's disgusting!"

Pyran and Tristram burst into hysterics.

"It's not funny you little shits! I have to sleep in here too, ya know!"

Pyran let another one go in a blatant act of defiance. This caused an immediate hysterical rigor mortis in Tristram, who had thought that he was already laughing as hard as possible.

Warrick, quite naturally, was not going to stand for such insolence.

"Right!" He spat between clenched teeth. "You asked for this, Pyran!"

Pyran panicked as the furious teenager suddenly pulled his jeans down and crawled towards him.

"Warrick! What?! It was a joke! What are you doing?!"

"I'm givin' you a fricking bare bum blast right in your putrid little face!" Was the venomous reply.

"NO!"

Both Tristram and Pyran recoiled in horror at the white, determined apparition of Warrick's buttocks.

"What's going on over there?" Hester called from the fire.

The blast happened with horrible energy and the screaming began.

"MUUUUUUUUUUUUUUUM!!!!!!!"

Hester was at their tent in an instant. She arrived just in time to catch a very smug Warrick slide his backside back into his jeans.

"What in God's name is going on here?!"

"Warrick farted right in my face!" Pyran bawled with saucer-eyed disgust.

"He deserved it – admit it, you little weasel."

"Warrick!" Hester reacted to the smell. "Bloody hell! Warrick, you are a dirty, disgusting little creep!"

She gritted her teeth and slapped him several times on his leg.

"Hey! Cut it out, Mum! It stunk like a tip before I got here!"

Karl arrived. "What's going on here?" He bellowed.

"Warrick is trying to kill the boys with his disgusting farts!"

"Pyaw! Jesus, Warrick, when are you going to grow up?"

"Dad! *They* stunk it up first!"

Karl was furious, his eyes bulging. "I think I'm going to throw up!"

"They stunk it up first!"

"Pyran?" Hester asked, her blue eyes ablaze with suspicion.

"Oh...look, maybe I accidentally let a small one go-"

"See?!"

"Pyran! God, I should've known!"

"Warrick said the 'F' word-"

"No, I didn't!"

"Right!" Roared Karl. "This is what's going to happen. Warrick, watch your language. Pyran – no more screaming or I'll give you the hiding of your life. And all of you – no more farting, got it?"

There was a fearful consent from the three boys.

"Good. Now shut up and go to sleep."

With that Karl stormed off. Hester gave Tristram a pitying look.

"You alright, Tris?"

"Yes, Aunty Hester." He was at once terrified and delighted by his aunty. She had extremes of both temper and generosity that seemed impossible to predict.

"I'm sorry that you have to sleep with these filthy shits." Hester sighed.

"It's alright..." Tristram murmured and added with red-faced guilt. "I sort of did my share of farting too."

Hester suppressed a smile.

"No more nonsense, boys, alright?"

"Alright."

"Good night."

As she wandered away the boys heard her chuckle.

"You're a bastard, Warrick." Muttered Pyran.

"You know you deserved it, shit-head."

There was an angry silence between the brothers.

"What do think we'll be doing tomorrow?" Tristram asked.

"Same shit we did today." Answered Warrick tartly.

"Dad said we might do some fishin'." Pyran remarked eagerly.

"We didn't pack any rods."

"Yeah, but Uncle Russell and Granddad did. They said they have enough rods for us all."

"Yeah?" Warrick answered, somewhat placated. "That'd be alright. You do much fishin', Tristram?"

"A little bit..."

The boys chatted quite contentedly for an hour or so before fatigue seduced them into a warm sleep. The gas lights were turned off and the adults retired to their tents. Soon, the only sounds left about the camp were the dying fire and the call of insects...

DREAMS, WITCHCRAFT AND
CRIES IN THE NIGHT

Tristram slept lightly, in a state between dreaming and awake. He was aware of his cousins breathing near him, the insects outside and the moonlight shining through the tent. He was warm and snug...

He sits by the pool in the moonlight and listens to the babbling stream. It is a warm summer night. The humidity carries sweet pollens and eucalyptus scents, whilst gentle heat emanates from the limestone rocks about him. He runs his hand over the rough texture of the rock and the dry feathery lichens. He dangles his feet in the warm water. The elegant white trunks of the mountain ash, the tallest eucalypts in the world, are brightly reflected in the pool. There is just the faintest breeze, and the long emerald gum leaves rustle gently in the surrounding forest canopy. Tristram smiles. This is a beautiful place.

He gazes up at the full moon as billions have done before and feels at peace. Suddenly he hears the laughter of children. He looks about the pool and thinks he glimpses their shadows running on the rocks on the other side of the pool. They squeal and call to each other. They began to sing a nasal, happy song.

Where are they? He sees a shadow of a child dancing out of the corner of his eye, but when he turns his head it becomes the shadow of a wattle tree.

Not a ripple breaks the surface of the pool. He looks at the perfect reflection of the stars...and two particularly bright stars catch his eye. He looks for them in the sky above, but they are not there. When he looks back into the pool the stars are bigger, like a pair of shining silver coins. They are getting closer, rising slowly up towards him. The children continue to sing.

Tristram smiles in wonder as he realises that they were eyes – he is looking at the eye-shine of some animal. Now, they are about the size of headlights. What is this creature looking up at him from under the water? He stares into those bright white eyes amongst the reflected stars, and tries to fathom the presence behind them...

Something was shaking him in the tent.

"Tristram, you awake?" Pyran whispered.

"Yes."

"Warrick's completely out of it. Ya can hear 'im snoring."

Tristram listened.

"Yeah..."

"Well? What do you reckon? Shall we sneak out and take a look at the opal?"

"Alright."

They slithered out of their sleeping bags and through the tent flaps like snakes from a washing basket. The chill outside was an unsettling contrast with the balmy night of Tristram's dream.

"It's freezin', eh?" Pyran whispered. "Let's go over to the fire."

They put some wood on the dying embers and huddled close to the warmth.

"Pretty bright night, eh?" Pyran continued. "I reckon I can see just as much now as I can in daylight."

"Yeah..." Tristram answered, rubbing his arms.

"Well?" Pyran prodded. "Where is it?"

"It's right here."

The opal was ebullient in the moonlight. The boys stared.

"Are you looking at a red, Pyran?"

"Nup. I was gonna wait for you to pick a colour out, so we could look together, eh?"

"Alright..." Tristram hesitated and then looked at his cousin.

"What?" Asked Pyran.

"Do you reckon we should do this now? Wouldn't it be better in the daylight?" Tristram looked with some apprehension into the dark shadows of the surrounding bush.

Pyran considered it.

"Why? You scared or something?"

"No way...are you?"

"Of course, not...but then... we don't really know what we'll see, eh?"

"Right."

They stood staring at each other. To face either fear or ridicule – the greatest dilemma for young boys.

Suddenly Pyran smiled.

"Tell ya what. I dare ya."

"You dare me?"

"Yeah. I dare you, and you dare me."

"OK...I dare you."

"Righto then, you're on. Let's do it."

Shaking with excitement they sat down together with the opal on the dust between them.

"Which colour?" Pyran asked.

"Let me just look..."

To their surprise, a large, rusty red fragment seemed to roll into view from the centre of the opal.

The azure colour phased into sapphire. They exchanged a fearful look.

"I reckon that's our colour, Tristram."

"Yeah...spooky how it just appeared like that."

"Want to give it a miss?"

Tristram thought hard about it, but in the end, curiosity had the better of him. Besides, Pyran was with him and he felt safe by the fire.

"No." He said finally. "Let's look at it. It's only a memory. We'll count to three and then look, OK?"

Pyran took a deep breath. "OK."

"One...two...three..."

For an instant Tristram thought that a sudden breeze had blown hot ash into his face from the fire, but then he realised that it was only sand. Red sand. He was in a desert, looking at a dawn sky with the richest rose and cerulean hues. There was not a cloud in sight. A still chill lay upon the desert, but he knew that soon a great heat would engulf the landscape.

He was anxious, and he had a headache.

His left leg bent at an unnatural angle, but he was well accustomed to it as he hobbled along in his loin cloth, with his koala skin dilly bag over his shoulder.

Finally, as he descended a sand dune, he found what he was searching for. A fresh dingo kill. It was a large female kangaroo, with short woolly fur that had a pleasant blue tinge. An elegant creature in a ghastly state – throat torn, belly ripped open, blood upon the sand. He had a hard time seeing the dingoes off her.

He put his hand into the bloody mass of kangaroo and felt eagerly through the unctuous viscera.

Good, the heart is intact.

Gently he pulled it free from the animal, tearing it out with its major blood vessels attached. He severed the arterial vessels and veins from the heart with his teeth and spat them contemptuously on the sand. He then reached into his dilly bag, and pulled out some ti-tree, five yellowed wombat incisors, a moist snakeskin and...*the opal*. With a nasal spell he tossed all but the heart and opal over the kangaroo corpse. In his left hand he held the heart, in his right, the opal. He turned his face to the heavens with his arms reaching high above him. His aspect was defiant, not supplicating.

The heart was still warm, but it was not beating.

He held the heart gently and concentrated. The opal was deeply chilled – as it always was in his hand. He let the chill run down his arm into his chest. There it mingled with the heat of his own heart, and it pained him. He breathed sharply. He had a fight on his hands...

He must get rid of the cold...

The sun began to rise and he knew this would help him. The heat in his chest overcame the chill of the opal, and he concentrated on sending that heat up his left arm and into the heart...

It was working. The heart began to beat.

It was a giddy thrill as it pulsed in his hand.

Suddenly the kangaroo twitched violently. It let out a terrified screech, and its eyes opened wide in panic.

"Tell me what the dream meant." It was not English that Tristram was speaking, but a nasal, rounded language. His voice was guttural and metallic.

The animal writhed in agony and squealed. The sunlight glistened in a rancid vapour that rose from the fur and the exposed bowels. Tristram understood that the kangaroo was pleading for the unnatural torture to stop. Blood spurted afresh from the reanimated corpse and nervous reflexes caused the animal to kick red sand violently into the air. Yellow and green intestines fell loosely out and collected the sand. A terrible life force struggled anew in matter that had accepted death. The heart in his hand pounded at an alarming rate.

"TELL ME WHAT THE DREAM MEANT!"

The kangaroo continued its awful wailing...and then suddenly Tristram heard a voice cry out. It was the very voice of life, as it cries at birth and sighs at the instant of death.

The kangaroo suddenly ceased all movement. Its eyes closed. Tristram moved in for a closer look. He prodded the animal gently, but it did not react. The heart was beating slower and slower...

He whispered, *"Tell me what the dream meant."*

Tense seconds rolled by whilst the animal did not stir. Then suddenly the head twitched horribly and faced Tristram. The eyes were wide, showing the whites. It screamed in mortal rage.

"BEWARE OF THIEVES!"

Pyran and Tristram yelped in fright. They were sitting beside the fire again, breathing rapidly and staring at each other in horror.

"What the hell was that?!" Wailed Pyran.

"Shhh! I don't know!" Tristram whispered.

"Oh God, that was awful! I think I'm gonna be sick. I can't believe what I just did!"

"It wasn't you. It was the witch doctor. Calm down or you'll wake our parents."

"Tristram...Tristram, I never want to look at that opal again..."

They sat in a nauseated anxiety for a few minutes, before Tristram's horror at the memory was replaced by a desire to comfort his cousin.

"Pyran...it was terrible, but it was just a memory. A very *old* memory. My other granddad said that he has been dead for years. So, relax...it can't hurt you."

"Yeah...you're right. I reckon I'm startin' to settle down...God..."

They sat in nervous silence for a while, as each boy's mind raced to calm the fear that hurtled through him. Tristram made a silent prayer to Jehovah. Gradually their panic diminished.

Finally, Tristram said "You know what I think we should do?"

"What?"

Tristram looked deep into Pyran's green eyes, which were wet with fear and reflected the coals.

"We should look at another colour. A happy colour."

Pyran considered this.

"What if the opal tricks us?"

"It doesn't do that."

Pyran hesitated before giving a tentative nod.

"Alright..."

"On the count of three, let's look at this purplish colour right here."

"OK."

They braced themselves and took a deep breath.

"One...two...three..."

It was a warm starry evening and she wore a rich purple dress of a material that was a delight to touch. It was soft and just a little loose on her body. Her dark, chocolate hair was fine with a gentle wave, and it fell gracefully about her shoulders and slender neck. Tristram noticed her perfume next...a faint trace of frangipani that permeated the humidity, barely detectable over the fragrance of the gardenias nearby. The garden was simple, yet elegant – a temperate approximation of an English cottage garden...a thunderstorm rumbled in the distance, and Tristram was invigorated by the moisture and electricity in the air...

She was curvaceous and a little taller than average, with a build that suggested an active life. White, ample cleavage rose and fell rapidly. The rest of her skin was tanned and almost flawless – she had a light freckling on her forearms and nose. Her face was strong yet feminine. Large, intelligent hazel eyes sparkled vividly. Sensual lips softened a determined chin. There was a rosy glow of distress about her brown face which contrasted with her usual cool. She was a woman with a formidable balance of fire and intellect. Tristram was absolutely attracted to her.

He was tall and strong himself, and a powerful heart pounded in his chest.

She moved closer, her pupils dilated in the dark. Tristram watched her transform her anxiety into righteous anger.

"You're a terrible man."

Her voice had a mellow femininity that softened her rebuke. She spoke with a mellifluous accent that was English, tempered with Scottish undertones.

Tristram could not take his eyes from hers – they were a wide window into a soul that ignited his temper, challenged his intellect and gave vivid colours to his dreams.

"I know I am late, and I am dreadfully sorry. Please don't stay angry with me. I have a wonderful excuse."

Tristram's voice was a light, pleasant tenor.

"Oh?"

"Do you believe in magic, Valeria?"

She gave an incredulous laugh. "No, Michael."

"No? Just like that, you say no?" Tristram chided.

"No. I don't believe in magic." Valeria affirmed, hands on hips.

"How can a good Christian woman like you, who believes in the miraculous powers of God, not believe in something lesser like magic?"

Valeria sighed, and her anger melted into a warm smile that sent him soaring.

"I have something for you." Tristram whispered.

"Yes?"

Tristram reached into the breast pocket of his satin vest and pulled out the opal. Valeria gasped.

"This is a very special jewel, Valeria MacAllister. If it is lost, it will find its way back to you. If it is taken from me, and I die, it will come back to my family line. That is what the old Chinese man told me tonight."

"Who is this old Chinese man?"

"He has never told me his name. He says that a

name is like a strong rope about the soul, and that he will have none of it."

"How very absurd."

"Yes, perhaps."

"What do you call him?"

Tristram laughed warmly as he answered. "I call him Uncle."

"That's sweet."

"Valeria...this opal has a magic that I don't understand." Tristram continued earnestly.

He took her hand and placed the jewel in her palm and held it there.

"Look closely at one of the colours, Valeria. Look at the light blue fragment in the centre with me..."

Valeria gasped and trembled as sensations flooded into her from the opal.

"Our first picnic!" She cried. "When you fell into the river trying to retrieve my hat...you were so good natured, even though I laughed at you mercilessly..."

"It is the first of the best memories of my life..."

"Michael...It was as if I was actually *there*...but I was seeing it through your eyes!"

"I told you that it was magical. It came from the opalised fossil of an ancient creature that no naturalist has described before. Uncle's family were gold miners and they unearthed it in the red desert country. Uncle said that a debt to the spirits could be paid with something sleeping in its bones."

Tristram gazed into Valeria's eyes, expecting to

see her usual, cool incredulity. However, her eyes were wide in wonder.

"Go on." She whispered eagerly.

"Uncle carved this opal out himself. He said that it fell from the skull like a tear into his hand. And then, in the strangest twist of this tale, he gave it to me after we had been friends for a few years. I rode to see him tonight. It is a long journey to his house and my horse is quite indignant with me."

"Vernon is like that, even on short rides." Valeria grinned.

"I made the trip so that I could ask him if I could give this opal away to my beloved...it seemed the proper thing to do, somehow. He laughed when I asked him and said that while the opal cannot be taken away, it can certainly be *given* away."

"Michael, you're not giving this to me?" Valeria was astonished and moved. "No, Michael. It's too much!"

"Please accept it. You have my heart in your hands, Valeria, and no one can steal it from you. It will always find its way back to your line..."

Valeria trembled and put a gentle hand on his chest, then up the side of his neck and caressed his face. All the while she stared into his eyes with a peculiar coalescence of bliss and sadness. He kissed her hand and then they embraced. He smelt her hair and relished the feel of her body as she held him tight. They kissed and to Tristram's wonder, who was at an age when girls were the enemy; he was not repulsed by the kiss. Instead he was aroused. A wild and strange desire possessed him entirely. It was absolutely animal. Tristram did not understand it all; it was as though he wanted to devour her and embrace her all at once, and that it would excite her if he did so. Their kissing became deeper and gratuitous. Their hands moved over each other's bodies in gentle, sensuous caresses. Their breathing changed, becoming deeper and more rapid. Suddenly Valeria groaned and kissed his neck with a carnal indulgence. Her warm, moist kisses sent tingles of delight across every inch of his skin. She then began to unbutton his shirt. Tristram ran his hand smoothly from the back of Valeria's neck in spiralling caresses towards the back of her thigh. Then he slid his hand under her dress. His fingers massaged their way up the back of her thigh, over her round buttock, up the small of her back, then around her ribs to the front of her body. Finally, he fondled her plump breasts. He kissed his way slowly across her face, then down her neck, then across her collarbone, then down her chest until he had her erect nipple between his lips. He rolled his tongue gently and rapidly around the areola, massaging her bosom with his lips. Valeria shuddered and sighed. She began to gently bite Tristram's neck.

Tristram was lost in sensation, and a wondrous change occurred in his perception. He became two people at once, both in an intense euphoria...

. . .

Suddenly a savage, tumultuous cry shattered the moment, and the boys were brought back instantly to the fireside.

"Whoa! Was that from the opal or the bush?" Asked Pyran.

There was another tortured roar from the dense shadows of the surrounding forest. It shred the night air.

"Was that a man or an animal?" Whispered Tristram.

"I dunno...but I reckon we should get back into our tent. Right now!"

There were no more cries as they scurried back into their tents and into their sleeping bags.

Neither boy said anything to the other as they both lay awake, their minds a whirl of thought. Of everything they had experienced that night, they reflected little on the cruel witch doctor and his ungodly torture of the kangaroo. Neither were they apprehensive about the clamorous, woeful cries that they had just heard from the bush. What haunted them most was the carnal, electric craving that pulsed in their veins as they relived the passionate moment with the exquisite Valeria MacAllister.

STEWART'S TALE

Magpies warbled, yellow dawn filtered into the tent, and bacon and eggs sizzled into the cool air. Such were the sensations that enticed Tristram and Pyran from their dreamless sleep into a new day.

Pyran rubbed his eyes. "Boy, what a night."

The night's anxieties melted away as they slipped out of their tent into a clear, crisp morning, and wandered across the dew-soaked grass to the fire.

"Good morning, boys!" Beamed Stewart in his deep nasal drawl, as he turned the bacon and eggs over in the pan. "The only thing better for breakfast than porridge with honey and cream, is good ol' bacon 'n' eggs. You fellas look all rustled up; did yer have a tumble with some night horses?"

"Night horses?" Scoffed Pyran.

"No? Well, yer must've been fightin' with somethin'. Look at the pair of yer! You're not like me. Yer don't wake up already scrubbed up 'n' handsome, the way I do."

"Maybe you didn't have the night we had." Tristram smiled.

"Hmm? Oh no, I have a rough night every night, Tris. Your grandmother is forever beltin' me up through the night – but you get used to it after forty years of marriage or so."

The boys chuckled.

"Grandma is far too nice to do that." Pyran grinned.

"Oh don't be fooled, Pyran. Your grandmother might look all timid and polite and everything, but she's got a terrible temper. She's not a gentle soul like me."

"How come she's still in bed, then, eh?" Said Pyran suspiciously, "I reckon *you* beat *her* up."

"Good heavens, what a terrible thing to say to yer poor ol' granddad! The only reason Jack's not up yet is she is exhausted from beltin' me up all night...*Yeah.* It's *true.* You gotta believe me, boys. I declare meself non-guilty."

Saffi approached the fire, fresh faced from a good night's sleep.

"Good morning, Saffi!" Stewart bellowed.

She grinned. "Good morning, Granddad."

"Has it made your day to see me?" He beamed.

Saffi smiled shyly at the happy old man.

"Well?" Boomed Stewart charismatically. "I think it has. It makes most people's day to see me. I'm a delightful character..." He patted his round belly." But yer can see that I'm unloved and neglected. Look at the condition I'm in, eh? Oh! Look out! Here comes Jase – good morning, Jase!"

Little Jase giggled, the sunlight golden in his curls. "Mornin', Granddad."

"Breakfast ready yet, Granddad?" Pyran asked.

"You bet it is – my timing is perfect. Grab a plate, boys. You too Saffi – gosh you look pretty this mornin'. You've got my good looks, I reckon. I wish people would say pleasant things about *my* appearance, Saff. You know what me mother used to say to me? She said I had a good build, but a cheap head. A cheap head! That isn't very complimentary, is it? Eh?"

"I think you're handsome, Granddad." Smiled Saffi.

Stewart chuckled. "Yes, but you're one of the few women that think so. But they can't all have your good taste, eh? No... Hey Tris, why don't you go and wake ol' Warrick up? He'll want to start a row if we don't take him with us."

"OK...where are we going?"

Stewart's eyes twinkled.

"I thought us kids might sneak away an' do some fishin' before the day gets too bright. What do you fellas reckon about that?"

"Radical!" Exclaimed Pyran.

With that, he and Tristram eagerly went to stir Warrick.

After a hearty, savoury and oily breakfast, Stewart and his grandchildren were tramping through the bush towards the stream in an opposite direction to the one they had travelled yesterday.

"You were up early, Granddad." Remarked Tristram, as they walked.

"Well, Tris, yer gotta get up early to go fishin' in these parts. Yer see, the early bird gets the worm, but we want that worm for fishin' bait – so we've gotta get up even earlier than the early bird."

"But Granddad, I saw you get these worms from our garden before we left." Laughed Saffi.

"Struth, I've been caught out. I should've known you wouldn't miss a trick, Saff. I wish I was as clever at villainy as your grandmother. She's always got an *exterior* motive! And I never see it until it's too late."

Soon they had found a promising stretch of the stream. A shallow run poured into a deep groove around a slight bend, over which a young wattle had fallen into the water, creating some snags. The forest was tall, fresh and vibrant about them.

"You fellas know how to go about trout?" Asked Stewart. He was unusually quiet.

"We usually fish for bream and mangrove jack up our way." Retorted Warrick.

"Well, listen up then." Drawled Stewart. "Trout are finicky things, so for a start, yer gotta be quiet. So, don't go shoutin' an' hollerin' all over everywhere and everything. Keep quiet. Agreed?"

"Yes, Granddad." They answered in unison.

"Next: yer see how that fast water comes off that shallow area an' then into this deep hole? Well, I reckon there'll be a fish or two in the slower movin' water of that eddy. Yer see, they're lazy like most people, and don't want to waste energy tryin' to stay put in the fast current. So, they haul up in the slower water and rush out an' grab beetles 'n' frogs 'n' things as they go past. Understand?"

"I reckon." Said Warrick eagerly as he took a rod and some worms.

"Righto then, Warrick. Catch a big one. Me, Tris, Saffi 'n' Pyran will have a red hot go for Big Scale, eh?"

"What about me?" Jase asked anxiously.

"O' course we're gonna need *you*, Jase! We're gonna use you for bait if Big Scale comes along."

Saffi caught the first two fish, much to the chagrin of Pyran and Tristram. They were two pan-sized rainbow trout, and while Stewart had cast and baited the hook for her, Saffi had managed to hook and land the fish all by herself. Stewart killed them for her and described how he would cook them in butter for her lunch. It was one of the best mornings of her childhood, and she positively beamed in the glow of Stewart's exuberant praise.

Pyran caught a small blackfish, a curious little fish with a blunt face and olive body. Jase managed three small brown trout with a lot of help from Stewart, but they threw them back to fight another day.

They heard the odd report from Warrick as he appeared for more worms – apparently a couple of big fish took his bait but didn't stay hooked.

It was nearly two hours before Tristram got his fish. It was a large brown trout. He got a lot of fuss and praise from the others, but he knew that they were merely relieved that he was now no longer the only one in the group without a fish. As Tristram removed the hook from its mouth, he noted that it was a male on account of the large jaw. The slime on its body, and the sheen of its scales and spots were radiant in the sunlight. It gaped helplessly at him and rolled its bright, golden eyes.

A thought pierced Tristram as he held the animal. *This creature is at the point of death. I can kill it, and the beautiful colour will fade, the eyes will dull, and the scales will fall off. Or I can let it live, and never see it again. Either way, I can't look at it forever...*

"What's it gonna be, Tris? You wanna eat him? He'll be good tucker."

Stewart observed Tristram closely, well aware that the boy was in deep reflection. To his surprise, Tristram suddenly smiled at him, and reaching into his pocket, pulled out the opal. He stared at the fish and Stewart saw the opal glow briefly in his hand. Delighted, Tristram then placed the trout gently into the water, and let it swim away.

"Saffi will let me have a little taste of her fish, won't you, Saffi?"

She nodded at her brother.

Stewart grinned. "Lucky he wasn't my fish, Tris."

"You're bloody mad!" Cried Warrick as he neared the group.

Tristram responded with a tranquil grin.

Warrick smiled and shook his head at the others.

"You're a strange one, cousin. Ah well, I reckon it's nearing lunch-time."

"Getting hungry already, Warrick?" Asked Stewart. "It's only ten thirty."

"I don't want to fish anymore. I reckon they're off the bite."

"But Tristram just got a fish!" Cried Pyran.

Warrick shrugged with a slight grin. "Yeah, but that'll be the last one."

Stewart chuckled. "I reckon you're old enough now to head back by yourself if you want to, Warrick. Just keep an eye out for snakes. You kids can go with him if yer like, I'm gonna stay for another forty minutes or so."

"OK." Rejoined Warrick, "Who's comin? I'll need help getting the barbie goin'. Are any of yous good at making' a salad?"

"I am." Said Saffi.

"Righto. Pyran? Jase? Tristram?"

"Yeah, we're comin'." Said Pyran.

"Actually, I'll stay with Granddad." Rejoined Tristram.

"Fair enough, let's go." Ordered Warrick, and with that had most of the rods and was on his way.

Saffi lead Jase along, even though his instinct was to stay with his brother.

Pyran struggled internally about whether he preferred food or more interesting company.

"Fine, I'm stayin' with you." He sighed finally. "But if I get too hungry, I'm off."

When the others were out of ear shot, Stewart looked coolly at the boys.

"So, fellas...what were the pair of *you* all excited about last night?"

The boys exchanged guilty looks.

"What do you mean?" Pyran asked levelly.

"Oh...last night I thought I heard a bit of excitement by the fire..."

Tristram gave Pyran a look which said, 'leave the talking to me'.

"We heard noises last night too...a kind of roaring from the bush."

"That's right." Concurred Pyran eagerly. "We did. It woke us up."

"Yeah?" Drawled Stewart as he eyed the boys thoughtfully.

"Yeah." They both answered.

"Huh...well I reckon I've got a theory about that..." Stewart murmured as he filled his pipe with tobacco. He lit it and put it languidly to his lips.

"Well? What was it, Granddad?" Tristram asked quietly, as Stewart puffed contemplatively.

"The roarin' you heard last night is quite understandable. Bit surprisin' how loud it turned out to be, considerin' how far away it was – but grief has a way of sorta magnifyin' everythin'." He turned and looked Tristram right in the eye. "It was your father, Tristram."

"Dad made those sounds?"

"Yep...he was just doin' what a man has to do sometimes. Did the same thing when me own father died. Just went out onto the farm and let all the anger and grief out in the isolated paddocks. Can't lock it up forever."

The three were thoughtful for a moment, as the stream continued babbling. Tristram could hardly believe that those awful cries came from his own father. His wonder turned melancholy as he realised that he would one day have to do what Russell did himself.

Soon Stewart broke the silence again.

"Well, that explains the roarin'...but we're still in the dark about the excitement I heard about the fire." He said it without looking directly at either of them.

Tristram finally decided to confess.

"Me and Pyran were looking at the opal."

He watched Stewart's face and wondered anxiously where this was going to lead. Stewart did not change his serious, ponderous expression.

Finally, he said. "A lot of disturbing memories in that opal, aren't there, boys?"

They were startled by his knowledge.

"How did you know?" Tristram asked in awe.

"Yer remember, Tris, how I said that more than one person's history is associated with that opal? Well...one of those histories is my own. Why don't the pair of yer sit down on that log there an' I'll fill yer in on a couple of things."

The boys did as they were told and sat in eager anticipation as Stewart began his tale.

"The opal was given to me nearly thirty years ago when I was on a fishin' trip up at the Murray. It was an odd sort of an affair, boys. I'll never forget it for as long as I live...

I was up there by meself – which was unusual for a start. Usually I went with a bunch of fellas I'd known since high school. But anyway, I was up there fishin' away an' I met this ol' fella who was amblin' along the river. Well, I'm a sociable sorta fella an' we got talkin' an' he decided to sit down and join me. I remember he had a well-brought up sort of English accent which was nice to listen to. He seemed a bit lost or distracted or something, but at the same time I reckon he was glad of my company.

Anyway, the fish were bitin' well – we had a lot o' yellow belly and redfin...but the prize catch o' course is the ol' Murray cod. By the end o' the day we hadn't caught a single one – at the time, that was very unusual. I know it's the norm these days, but then... well, it was very mysterious...

Later that evening, me an' this ol' fella – Gerald was his name – were sittin' about the fire on the bank, wonderin' why we hadn't caught a cod. It was a beautiful, warm night an' we were enjoyin' the conversation."

A tenderness suddenly softened Stewart's hard features – a rare sight.

"Yer know...there was a sorta kindness and a deep sadness about this ol' fella that really got to me. I reckoned at the time, listenin' carefully to his silences, that he had a strange story in him. I woulda tried to draw it out of him, but I noticed he was sick lookin' and sorta breathless and haunted. I began to worry that he wasn't gonna last long. I was about to offer to take him to the nearest town when all of sudden he gets this wild look and takes off into the trees like a scolded cat...

Well, I thought, he's an old fella, maybe he needed to suddenly take off and have a wee or somethin'. I sat there and waited, and after a few moments I hear the snap of leaves and twigs an' things, an' I thought to meself 'poor ol' fella, here he is, back again' – but no...it was another strange ol' fella...and he was *black*."

"The witch doctor..." The boys breathed.

"He was sorta half hunched over in this big, dark green trench coat, and he had a green floppy hat. He wore big long leather boots that came up over his trousers to his knees. The strangest thing about him though, was his walk. He sort of bowed at every second step, so that he sorta seemed ta strut like a cocky does. Anyway, over he comes an' looks out at me from under the brim of his hat. He had these angry, inky black eyes an' he says, "Have you seen an old man by the name of MacDougall?"

And I sat there startled, 'cause I was a MacDougall. Not only that, he didn't sound at all the way I expected him to. He spoke with a perfect, clear voice like a sophisticated Englishman or something.

"Well?" He asked in a threatening way.

Well, I puffed meself up an' I looked him in the eye an' said "*I'm* a MacDougall."

He stared at me and I stared right back at him. I was younger then, yer see, an' never backed down to anybody, especially not to a grizzled old character like this.

Anyway, he suddenly smiles an' says "You're not da MacDougall I'm lookin' for' in a nasal sorta *aboriginal* accent. I began to wonder if I was goin' mad.

"So, brother," He says in his aboriginal accent again, "Caught anythin'?"

"A few." I said.

"No cod, though, eh?"

"No" I said surprised. "How'd you know that?"

He just sorta smiled again, and as he did, I thought I saw the fire reflected in his eyes, the way it does in a dog's eyes.

"Dey don't bite when da season's like dis." He said.

And I said, "Oh yeah? Why's that?"

"No flood for a while, mate." He said, "No flood, no spawnin'. No spawnin', no feedin' up."

He let me ponder that for a moment an' then he said. "There is one sure fire way to get big cod, no matter what's goin' on, mate."

And I said, "Oh yeah, what's that?"

And he gave me this cold, cruel look and a smile that made me shiver all over, an' he said "*snakes heart.*"

I just sorta laughed at him, an' said that I didn't have a snake handy – and then! The ol' bugger reached into his pocket and pulled out this bloody tiger snake!

"What's the matter, kordah? It's only a little fella...sleepy, too." He says.

"It might only be little, but it's still just as poisonous." I said, sorta glarin' at him an' feelin' around for me fishin' knife.

"Hmm. That's very wise..." He says with this funny sorta thoughtful look, an' then he added "...and I reckon ya got more nerve than most white fellas... and I can see by ya eyes dat ya spend a lotta time in da bush. Hmm. Tell ya what, white fella. I'll do ya dis one favour, eh?"

And right before me eyes he cracks this snake like a whip and the head snapped clean off and flew hissin' into the fire. Then with his bare hands, he tore the snake from the neck down, blood spurtin' everywhere, and *ripped the heart out*. Then he looked at me with this mad smile, threw the body of the snake into the fire and held the heart up in front o' me. I could see it was still beatin' – I'll never forget it for as long as I live.

"Give us ya hook, mate." He says.

Without thinkin' I handed me line an' hook to him and he threaded this beatin' snake's heart onto the hook an' said "Put 'er in close to da bank, kordah."

Well, curiosity had the better of me, so I did as he said and sure enough, within about a minute I had a fairly decent sort of a cod.

"Well, I'll be buggered." I said. "I had me doubts, mate, but you've proven something. Thank you."

"No worries." He smiled. And then he turned to hobble off, but then stopped and turned his head over his shoulder to look at me. I had a sort of sick feelin' when he did that, because his neck turned just a little bit further than it shoulda been able to. Not only that, his black eyes shrank in the fire light – an' I realised then that the black was his pupils, not his eye colour, 'cause he had these sorta orange eyes, like an emu.

"One good turn deserves another, brother." He said. "Ya see an old MacDougall, ya give us a coo-ee, eh?"

And with that he hobbled off into the shadows of the trees.

Well, for a few minutes I sat there sorta unsettled an' thinkin'. I had the cod there, still alive...but I just couldn't bring meself to eat it, knowin' that I caught it on snake's heart. So, I threw it back and was kinda relieved to see it gone. I could smell the burnin' snake flesh – it actually smelled quite tasty – an' I watched all the flesh burn away from the skeleton in the coals... I reckon I sat there for about an hour.

Suddenly I hear twigs snappin' again and out of the scrub comes this ol' fella, Gerald.

"You handled that well, my friend!"

He was all energetic an' enthusiastic an' I didn't know what to make of it."

Here Stewart paused awhile, grinning to himself and taking an extra long puff of his pipe.

"You know, boys, life is a funny old thing. People

say it's a small world an' all that – but some coinci-
dences really rock yer boat. Now I got a question for
you two. Yer see, the opal that yer holdin' there in yer
hot little hand, Tristram, tends to throw up two old
memories more than any other that are found in it.
By the noise I heard you makin' last night, I reckon
you saw that poor ol' kangaroo bein' tortured by this
ol' witch doctor. Am I right?"

"Yes." The boys were astounded.

"It was the most awful, scary thing I've ever
seen." Pyran murmured.

"Yeah...I haven't seen much that would top it."
Conceded Stewart. "But the second memory...well, I
dunno that you boys would understand all of it." He
searched their eyes in turn.

"You mean the memory with Valeria MacAllister, don't you?" Asked Tristram finally.

Stewart sighed. "Yep, that's the one. I tried not
look at it again after the first time I saw it, and I suggest you boys do the same."

"Why?" Frowned Pyran. "It wasn't scary. It
was..." Pyran suddenly blushed. "It was odd, that's
all. Weird... In a nice sort of way."

Stewart gave a gentle laugh. "One day you fellas
will understand this better, but the sensations in that
memory are really only for grown men and women.
You'll feel them again one day with someone special
– but that memory is sorta private. I reckon it was
meant only for Michael and Valeria – and we should

respect that. Having said that, Michael tells a bit of a story in that memory that has some bearing on our own story. Yer see, this ol' fella Gerald...was the only son of Michael and Valeria."

He watched their faces and grinned slightly when the penny dropped.

"Whoa!" Exclaimed Pyran. "So, he woulda had the opal...and given it to you. Wow."

"That's the bottom line, Pyran, but there are a few more details to clear up. Yer see, stories in real life are never clean-cut sort of affairs, yer know? In real life, there's a sorta tangling of history and mystery and falsehood. There are credible bits in the story that just aren't true – as well as incredible things that no one in their right mind would believe – but really happened. Now listen up, fellas. I dunno what's true or false in this story exactly, so I'm just gonna relate it to you as Gerald told it to me.

For a start, Gerald explained to me that he was not really a MacDougall – he was a Dubrelle, after his father, Michael Dubrelle. He was travelling under a false name, and he chose the name of Mac-Dougall, after my very own great grandfather, Dougal MacDougall."

"*Dougal MacDougall?*" Snorted Pyran incredulously.

"They were a proud clan, the MacDougall's."

"Why did Gerald choose the name Mac-Dougall?" Asked Tristram.

"I'll get round to that in a moment. For now, you must know that both Michael and Valeria were killed by the witch doctor just after Gerald turned ten years old."

"Shit." Pyran said, and then remembered his company. "I mean, um...that's horrible."

Tristram recalled the sorrowful face of the ancient Chinese man, as with cruel triumph, he waved the blood covered opal in the old man's face...with fresh horror, he realised that the dead woman was Valeria MacAllister.

"The witch doctor slit Michael and Valeria's throat right in front of their little boy." Stewart continued. "An' he told poor young Gerald that his name was 'Dinewan' – an aboriginal word meanin' 'emu'... anyway, he took the opal from Valeria, and he took the boy with him into the bush."

"Wait a minute!" Tristram interrupted, "How old is this witch doctor if he was around when your *great grandfather* was alive and yet, he met you thirty years ago?"

Stewart stared hard into the boys. "You've both seen the opal's magic. Yet you find it incredible that a witch doctor, wrought with magic, can't also live an incredibly long life?"

"Sorry." Murmured Tristram. "Please continue, Granddad."

"Now Valeria had a cousin, Cameron MacAllister. And Cameron had a best friend, none other than our own ancestor, Dougal MacDougall. Both of these fellas were employees on Michael's father's farm. When they heard about the death of Cameron's cousin and her husband, they were absolutely wild. But when they heard about the kidnappin' of Gerald – well! They left the farm an' were off into the bush after the old witch doctor. Michael's father and their employer, Melvin Dubrelle, went off with them. This much I learned from Gerald, but he was babblin' an' excitable an' getting sicker by the minute."

Here Stewart paused again to refill his pipe. His face was anguished. He puffed a couple of times and then sighed.

"He died that night, boys, without tellin' me everythin'. Obviously, my ancestor Dougal, Cameron and Michael's father Melvin were successful in re-trievin' Gerald and the opal. But the actual story Gerald never got a chance to tell me. What he did say was this: Dougal MacDougall had protected him and remained true to his word. After that, Gerald went all pale an' incoherent– I heard word of bush-rangers an' somethin' about a monster."

"A monster? What kind of monster?" Tristram asked.

"Well, yer see, that's sorta the frustratin' thing about this story – he didn't get a chance to tell it all properly. He mentioned this monster and bush rangers an' it was all garbled and incoherent an' everything. I kept askin' him, but he just went pale and repeated 'don't talk about the monster' – an' I dunno whether he meant the witch doctor or some other creature. The answers are written down in an account done by Melvin Dubrelle soon after the adventure – but it was stolen by Cameron's son, Andrew MacAllister, an' it remains an heirloom in the MacAllister family. Hmpf...Gerald said many times to be wary of the MacAllisters because they think the opal is rightfully theirs. There was some treachery apparently.

Anyway, finally, with his dyin' breath, Gerald told me that the opal will find its way back to the right family line, and that *MacDougall blood* would see it through...*yeah*..." Stewart ruminated. "Those were his last words exactly in fact. He said, "beware of Dinewan, beware of MacAllister...and Mac-Dougall blood will see it through."

Stewart let the story hang in the fragrant air of the bush and tobacco smoke. A sudden breeze animated the eucalypt canopy above them.

"I reckon we should head back, fellas." Stewart murmured quietly.

As they walked solemnly back through the forest to camp, Tristram asked.

"So how did Granddad Toby get the opal?"

"Well, Tris, I gave it to him because he reminded me of Gerald. Yer see, I dunno whether the opal is rightfully a MacDougall heirloom, or whether we're just custodians of it, yer know? Me sense of honour says that we're just lookin' after it until its rightful owner show's up. I never had a word of trouble from any MacAllister – an' only once or twice was I ever worried about that ol' witch doctor. Sometimes I thought I saw him lurkin' about the various farms I been on – the last time in Queensland, about ten years ago – but I never had a confrontation.

Then, eleven years ago, I met yer granddad Toby – a nice, quiet Englishman, whose son was to marry me youngest daughter. He said that one of the things he always wanted from Australia was one of her opals. Well, as I got to know him, and I saw that he was a thoroughly decent fella, I decided to give him the opal. Then lo and behold, it comes back to not just his family line, but mine."

He looked triumphantly down at Tristram as they walked.

"What makes me the rightful owner of it, Granddad?" Tristram asked quietly.

"It was given to you, so it is yours, Tris. Be grateful, look after it, and then one day you can pass it on." Stewart answered.

They maintained a reflective silence for the rest of the walk back to their camp.

MEMORY OF A MONSTER

As all the family savoured their lunch and waved the acrid smoke of the fire away from their faces, they exchanged news of their morning. Stewart let the children tell of their success and delighted quietly in their wonder and exuberance. Mary showed the children a crimson rosella feather that she had found.

"See the pretty blue and crimson?" She asked them quietly. "Feel how soft it is. Doesn't that feel nice?" She brushed Jase's grinning face tenderly with the feather.

"Did ya get a bird, Jack?!" Boomed Stewart encouragingly, as if the gentle old lady were a triumphant cat.

A laugh ran around the family.

"I'm gonna have to check her for animals before we go back." He added. "You kids know she used to leave a saucer of milk on the veranda at the farm for the stumpy tailed lizards?"

Mary chuckled delightfully. "They were dear little things and they looked just like pinecones."

"They ate all our bloody strawberries, Jack!"

"They didn't eat that many...we couldn't have eaten them all, anyway."

"How did you end up a farmer's wife, Jack?" Smiled Stewart.

"You can't win them all." Russell quipped.

"She even looked after this ol' huntsman in the kitchen." Stewart continued unabated. "What did you end up callin' 'im, Jack?"

"Bronson." Mary answered, and her face softened into sweet pity at the memory. "When spiders get too old, they start to eat their own legs, you see? So, when I noticed that Bronson wasn't moving much and began to eat his own leg, I plucked a straw from my broom, and placed a little particle of minced meat on the end and fed it to him. I think he was grateful."

Hester and Holly laughed raucously as the others smiled.

Russell and Karl had been fly-fishing all morning and had enjoyed it immensely. Both of them had a couple of strikes but were unsuccessful in actually landing a fish. They had even ventured back to the pool that they were all at yesterday and tossed a line in without result.

"We didn't spend too long up there, though. Did we Russ?" Karl remarked.

"No." Russell agreed. "The place was unnaturally quiet...it didn't feel right to fish there, for some reason."

"At first the place looked good for a cast, an' the sun was shinin' an' everything." Continued Karl. "But then I noticed that there were no bird noises at all. Or insects. There was no wind. Just the sound of the stream pourin' into the pool...I said to Russ, 'Oi, this place is a bit spooky, eh?' And we decided to get out of there." Karl suddenly looked sheepish as he felt the mocking grin of Hester and Warrick.

"I felt a bit scared there, actually." Pyran admitted.

"Did you? So, did I." Tristram added.

"Me too." Saffi joined in.

"There was some sort of bad vibe at that place. I could feel it too, kids." Holly rejoined.

"You're all bloody mad." Scoffed Hester. "The place was beautiful."

"Isolated places always feel a bit spooky to you city folk." Stewart opined. "But after a while, yer realise that isolated places are the best places in life. They give yer a real chance to think. Yer notice more, too. Yer see and hear birds and animals yer never noticed before. Yer smell things. There's nothin' better in all the world. I love the bush. I *love* this place."

"I don't mind this place either," retorted Hester, "but it could do with a bloody kiosk."

The talk turned to lighter matters, of fishing tales and childhood memories. Pyran asked Stewart to tell of his encounter with Big Scale, but the old man declined, saying that he was saving it for the campfire that night.

Later that afternoon, Pyran and Tristram went for a stroll along the edge of the clearing of their campsite. They had deliberately sneaked away while Saffi and Jase were talking with Mary, so that they could be alone.

"Hey Tris, have you ever been kissed by a girl?" Pyran asked suddenly after a few moments of idle silence.

"No." Tristram answered as they walked. "I was nearly hugged by one once, but I climbed a tree and stayed up there 'til she went home. Have you?"

"Oh...you know...*once.*" Pyran admitted embarrassed. "But I *was* outnumbered."

"Was it gross?"

"Oh hell, yeah. I thought I was gonna throw up. I woulda punched her, but ya can't hit girls, eh?"

"Yeah."

"Yeah...kissing is just one of those disgusting things, eh?" Pyran spat some phlegm into the bush as he said it.

"Yeah. I dunno why adults go on about it." Tristram rejoined. "I mean, think of all the germs. I might hug a girl – you know, if she was hurt or upset or something – and it would have to be pretty major – but kissing? Nup. That'd make me sick."

"Are you gettin' a stiffy?" Pyran asked suddenly, with a mad grin.

"No!" Tristram laughed.

"Be honest." Pyran answered. "I am. Talkin' about girls does it to me every time. Weird, eh?"

"I s'pose I am getting one, now you mention it. And you're right, it does happen when I think about girls."

"At first, I thought we get stiffies because of the weather or somethin, ya know? I always wondered why we get 'em. Often, I can get one when I'm havin' a bath, just by thinkin the right way. And they're real useful in pissing competitions. Don't tell Mum, but when I stand up in the shower, I can reach all the way to the basin when I piss with a stiffy."

"That's revolting!" Gasped Tristram.

"What?" Grinned Pyran. "I always mop it up with a towel afterwards. But you know somethin'? You know what Warrick reckons stiffies are for?"

"What?"

"*Sex.*" Pyran whispered.

"Sex? Nah...how would that work?"

Pyran stopped walking, looked around furtively and then leaned towards Tristram.

"Sex gets girls pregnant."

"I know *that*. Where does the stiffy come into it?"

Pyran giggled lecherously. "You're gonna love this. It's funny *as!*"

"Well?"

"Warrick reckons *ya gotta stick ya dick in them.*"

"No way!" Tristram roared in incredulous horror.

"Shhh!! Not so loud! I told ya it was funny!"

As the cousins relished their hysteria, the opal gained a rosy fragment of colour in Tristram's hand. It had Pyran's laughing green eyes, his long orange fringe, and a bright white smile among the gum trees.

When the mirth had abated somewhat, Pyran asked Tristram seriously. "Do you get a stiffy whenever you think about that memory...you know...the one with Valeria MacAllister?"

"Yeah..." Tristram frowned. His newfound concupiscence did not sit comfortably with Witness dogma. "I know that's wrong, but I can't help it."

"Wrong? Why is it wrong?"

"It's not exactly...well...*right*, is it? The bible says we should watch our thoughts and that we have to be married before we can have sex. Seeing as it'll be years before we get married, it doesn't seem wise to start thinking about it now." Tristram didn't realise it, but he was parroting a respected Jehovah's Witness elder. "Still..." He resumed, as his own thoughts drove his words. "I haven't stopped thinking about that memory since we looked at it."

"Me neither. I've been thinking about that memory all day, you know? I just don't get it. We were *kissing* in that memory – but it wasn't disgusting. It was nice, eh? It's got me thinkin'...maybe girls are gross, but women...full grown *women*...are actually pretty good. I reckon...well, I reckon those two were about to...you know...*do it*."

Tristram looked sternly at Pyran. "I know what you're thinking. You want to look at that memory again. I want to as well, but I think it's wrong. I don't think we should."

Pyran blushed. "Fair enough. I s'pose you're right. I was just curious, see?"

"Yeah...that's cool. I suppose we'll find out one day anyway, eh?"

"Yeah."

After an embarrassed silence, their conversation returned to that of the other memories of the opal, and the tale told by Stewart. What was that Gerald had said about bush-rangers? How was Cameron MacAllister killed? And what was that about a *monster*? They had asked Stewart repeatedly, but he was unable to give them a satisfactory answer.

"I've told yer all I know about it, boys." Stewart had said. "If there are any answers, they'll be written down in the account by Melvin Dubrelle...but I can't see us ever gettin' a chance to see that thing."

"God!" Pyran exclaimed as they walked, throwing a stick into the bush. "It seems that life is just full of things you're not allowed to know!" A thought struck him, and he looked into Tristram. "Doesn't mean we can't find out if we want to, though...I mean...maybe..."

"We should look at the opal again?" Tristram asked. It was the only possible source of illumination. "Surely Granddad or my other Granddad would have told us if any other memory shed light on the story?"

"Not necessarily – I mean they're both pretty... well...no offence, but...they're not the type to explore that sort of thing, are they?"

"Mmm. You may be right."

"Besides, lookin' at the opal shouldn't be so scary in daylight, eh?" Pyran offered.

"Yeah...but I dunno which colour to look at, you know? Besides...we've been warned not to look at the rusty red colours...we now know why..."

Tristram's answer was unsatisfactory to both of them. There was a restless pause as they each searched for an argument that enabled them to look into the forbidden colours of the opal again.

"This story is gonna bug us for the rest of our lives." Pyran concluded bitterly. "Pity we aren't brave enough to look into the opal. Sure – *it's probably scary* – but we survived that other horrible memory."

"You're right. We've got a choice, haven't we? We can show a bit of guts and get an answer – or spend the rest of our lives wondering. What's life for, if it isn't to answer questions, anyway?"

That was reason enough for both.

"Let's do it!" Pyran exclaimed, slapping Tristram on the back.

"I'll find a memory that scares me a little – and then I'll tell you which one and we'll look at it together, OK?" Tristram announced.

Pyran agreed and Tristram once again let his mind glide over an ocean of sensations...a red flash made his heart skip a beat and he pulled his gaze away instantly.

"You found it?" Pyran asked, as nervousness tempered his curiosity.

"Yeah." Tristram answered his face pale. "But I think it might be even more awful than the one we looked at last night."

"Will it answer any of our questions, do you think?"

"I don't know. There's only one way to find out."

Enough had been said. Tristram pointed out the colour and the boys braced themselves.

"One...two...three..."

Tristram was triumphant but anxious. He gripped the opal in a tight fist, and neither Mr. Dubrelle nor that old witch doctor were the wiser. The old Chinaman would never know, either...

Fortune really did follow the brave, Tristram mused as made his way through the trees. He had sweated from his long and frantic ride. The night air chilled him. His hair was thick and long, and it bounced on the back of his neck as he jogged. His calves were scratched from his passage through the scrub. The moon rolled above him through the ominous clouds and twisted eucalypt canopy.

The opal was rightfully his. Valeria was *his* first cousin, *he* her only next of kin – and while he loved Gerald, he felt certain that the lad had been killed by the bushrangers. Dougal had probably died defending him. He felt a terrible rage and grief, as well as guilt – but he had the future of his family in his fist. The opal would buy him land. His wife Alison and bairn Andrew would never want for anything.

He turned behind him to look at his son Andrew, a lad about Tristram's age, waiting beside their horse. The boy was anxious, watching him as he jogged towards the billabong. He was a good lad and had been very brave throughout this whole ordeal.

Dinnae worry. In a few hours, we will be safe and rich, my lad.

Finally, he slowed as he approached the billabong. At last, a chance to drink.

There was an unnatural silence and rippled reflections of moonlight on the white tree trunks. He knelt by the billabong and stared morosely into its still water...

What have I done? I have betrayed my friends... will I ever see them again?

He suddenly felt tired, overwhelmed and wretched. Tears formed in his eyes, and his chest felt constricted. A sob escaped from him.

Not now, man. Bear up now. Look at your future.

Tristram opened his hand and stared into the opal, glowing in the moonlight.

He let out a long, heavy sigh.

That's it. Relax and concentrate on the task at hand.

A minute or so went by, then slowly, it dawned on him...

There was no sound at all but that of his frantic breathing. The hair on his nape stood on end as clouds covered the moon...

He felt stalked. He listened with every inch of his skin for the faintest sound – a twig snapping or the parting of undergrowth...there was nothing but his frenzied respiration and pounding heart. He expected the witch doctor to appear suddenly from the trees, his orange eyes ablaze, pointing a yellowed bone and a nasal curse at his very soul.

He waited. Utter silence set his nerves shrieking.

Suddenly, as the clouds rolled and revealed the moon, he saw them. Large, bright white eyes staring up at him from under the water...

It happened in an instant. The water parted as the large shape behind the enormous eyes leapt out towards Tristram. He felt the shock of long teeth spear through his rib cage with a sickening crunch, as the animal took him by the head and chest. The opal fell from his hand...

Tristram and Pyran were screaming and running together through the bracken. They recognised each other, and their panic came to an end.

"Jesus Christ!" Pyran managed as he caught his breath.

"Oh my god! I can't believe what just happened!" Tristram answered...then he realised that he was no longer holding the opal. "Pyran!"

"What?!"

"I've dropped the opal! Shit! Help me find it! Oh shit – how far did we run?!"

"I dunno – hey I reckon we were standing by that big, thick tree over there!"

"Let's go!"

They ran back to the tree as a new fear possessed Tristram. After a short search Pyran smiled.

"Here it is, mate."

Relief washed over Tristram.

"Thank God...I don't think I can take much more of this stuff, Pyran." He said as he accepted the opal.

Suddenly the relief Tristram felt was linked to the finding of his baby daughter safe and sound.

Tristram looked into his cousin, bewildered. "This is such a strange opal, isn't it?"

"No shit, Sherlock!"

"Pyran, I think we should just go back to-"

His sentence ended abruptly as a new presence arrested their attention.

The old aborigine seemed to have emerged suddenly and silently from the thick trunk of the gum tree. He stood staring at them, elderly but sinewy, in dark green pants, a navy woollen jumper and an olive, floppy hat. He smiled.

"G'day." He said in a rattling, nasal voice.

The boys looked at each other, screamed and pelted away towards their camp.

STEWART AND BIG SCALE

"THAT WAS VERY immature of *both* of you." Holly scorned. "And you ran off and left poor Saffi and Jase with no one to play with. I'm totally embarrassed by your behaviour. Oh God, here he comes."

"We'd better run for it!" Shouted Tristram.

"Shut your mouth." Holly snapped and glared into Tristram. "Now you listen to me. I know this man. It is *not* the witch doctor from the *opal*. That is just a story – and it's about time you grew up. You're a big boy now; you're too old to be spooked by *fairy* tales. His name is Fred and he is a friend of mine. I've known him for years and we get along very well. But now – well, you've insulted him, I'm sure. He'll think that you're racist. He'll think that *I'm* racist, and that I have taught you to be scared of aborigines."

"Ease up, Holly." Russell interjected coolly. "*We*

might know him, but they don't. They're only kids, and Fred *is* a stranger to them."

Holly did not answer him as Fred was now within ear shot.

"Hello, Fred!" She beamed. "Fancy seeing you out here."

The old aborigine smiled at her and looked Pyran and Tristram up and down, his eyes twinkling with amusement.

"G'day, Holly, Russ. I think I scared ya little fellas dere."

"Yes, I'm sorry about that, Fred, they've been listening to stories about a witch doctor and well, you know how overactive kids' imaginations can be."

"Yeah. Dey did da right thing. I coulda been a bad stranger, or a mooki man, eh? Or maybe...the ol' *mirachy*, eh?"

He looked playfully at the two boys, who were frowning at him nervously.

"What's a mirachy?" Pyran asked.

"Da *black mirage*. Haven't heard aboud 'im, eh? Good for you. It always backfires ta tell children about da mirachy. Dey won't go to bed wid out da light on." He chuckled to himself, as he watched their anxiety become curiosity. He then turned to Holly and Russell. "Thought I'd come an' say g'day, seein' as ya saw me yesterday. Don't want ya ta think I was snobbin' ya, eh?"

Holly smiled. "I did see you, Fred. So, did Tris –

you haven't met Tris, have you? Fred, this is my eldest son Tristram, Tristram this is Fred."

"Hello." Tristram said.

"You're da boy dat's always findin' frogs, aren't ya? Holly's told me a lot about ya, mate. Sounds like ya woulda made a good tribesman, eh?"

"And this is my nephew, Pyran."

"G'day." Pyran said. "Sorry we ran off, but ya scared the hell out of us."

"No worries, mate. Dat's why I came over, ta put ya at ease."

"We did see you yesterday evening, Fred." Holly confessed. "But I thought that you might have come here to get away from people, and so I thought it best to leave you be. I wasn't being ra- you know, I wasn't being snobbish."

"I know ya not a racist, Holly. I didn't come down an' see yas last night 'cause I thought it was a family thing, unna?"

A few more pleasantries were exchanged, Holly babbled far too much, and her forced chuckle grated on Tristram's nerves. Fred found it charming, however, and did his best to put Holly and everyone else at ease. Russell joked with Fred as he did with all his acquaintances, and soon Fred was invited to tea with the rest of the family.

Hester had her reservations about Fred at first, as they all sat about the fire after their meal. However, as the night wore on, and they exchanged stories and jokes, she was impressed by his good nature, and the way he listened carefully to any person who was speaking. Stewart and Karl regarded Fred with affable curiosity. Mary took a kindly interest in him, as she did with every person who crossed her path. Fred enjoyed Mary's observations about the habits of birds and insects.

The topics of conversation rolled smoothly into one another, and they were all intrigued by Fred's knowledge of bush tucker. Of course, they all knew already about witchetty grubs and kangaroo flesh, but they were amazed at some of the bush cordials that could be made with grevillea and myrtle flowers.

"Meself, I prefer the simple things." Stewart drawled. "I like the idea of a bit of fire-cooked kangaroo flesh, or fish or wombat or anything. Simple things. Not these sorta delicate, airy-fairy, fancy things yer pay a thousand dollars a head for in every city restaurant."

"Oh Stewart, don't exaggerate!" Mary sighed.

"I've told you a million times not to exaggerate." Russell quipped.

Eyes rolled.

"Whose exaggerating?" Bellowed Stewart. "Yer get these giant plates with a single mouthful of raw meat covered in grass and flowers – Jack, I could get that for you after *five minutes* in the garden."

"It's the culinary experience, Dad." Hester rebuked. "It's cooked by excellent chefs with supremely developed senses of taste."

"Maybe so but they don't have to send me bankrupt for a *third* of a meal, just 'cause it looks arty. Nope – those in the restaurant business are all con artists and thieves."

"Oh God!" Sighed Mary and Holly.

"Dad, you're a tight-arsed, silly old bugger!" Hester shouted jovially, though her eyes hinted at heart-felt criticism. They all chuckled.

"Tea was good tonight, Russ." Fred observed.

"Thank you." Russell answered.

"Yeah, it was good, Russ." Hester added. "You really are quite good in the kitchen, Holly's very lucky."

"It was beautiful – but again, too fancy." Stewart opined.

"Here we go." Russell mocked. "What do you care, you miserable old bastard? It didn't cost *you* anything."

"It didn't cost me any money, but I nearly died *waitin'* for it." Stewart teased. "I mean, yeah, it was cooked beautifully, an' it melted in the mouth and had every herb an' everything. But it wasn't ready *now*, yer know what I mean? When I'm hungry out in the bush, I get a good steak with a few mushrooms and some onion; whack it on the barbie and she's ready to go in moments. But with your stuff Rusco – is it ready yet? No. I wait another half hour – is it ready yet? No – an' more time goes by an' it smells delicious an' I still can't get anywhere near it – no – not ready yet. And by the time you've finished cookin' I'm *dribblin'* and *delirious...*"

"Oh, will you cut it out?!" Hester shouted, laughing. "If you're going to dominate the conversation you should at least tell us something interesting. I want hear about your encounter with Big Scale."

"Yeah!" Exclaimed the children enthusiastically. Suddenly the attention of the family was eagerly centred on the old farmer.

"Big Scale?" Asked Fred.

"A big fish that fights every fisherman on earth and keeps their hook." Answered Holly. "Every fisherman must face him one day."

"I see." Smiled Fred.

"We all have to face our own particular monster at some time or another in life." Began Stewart. "Whether it's a fish or a bull or a dog...sometimes, the monster we have to face is a man...and fairly often, that man is the very same fella we see starin' back at us from the mirror."

"Just tell the bloody story, Stewart." Russell scoffed.

Stewart chuckled. "Fair enough, then. Now yer all remember Rusco's story yesterday. It was well told, an' he was right to point out that all the cleverness in tryin' ta catch him was me own."

There was an audible sigh from Russell.

"Well, me own encounter with Big Scale happened the very next day." Stewart continued. "Yer see, Big Scale saw Rusco put the cod on the anchor the day before, so he knew that technically he was fightin' with Russell. He now knew he had beaten Rusco, but he didn't know how he'd go with me. That's how I knew he'd be back. Well, I was up all night thinkin' about how to tackle him. Remember, that we had to travel all the way back along the river from Mildura to Swan Hill – a fair old hike, so I had plenty of time to think. Now, I wasn't gonna let Big Scale off without a bloody decent fight. Yer see kids, there hasn't been an animal on this earth yet that could beat me – and I was buggered if I was gonna let Big Scale be the first.

Here's what I did: I got another anchor and used a whole sheep for bait – there was one newly dead an' fly blown in a nearby paddock. I got some good, triple weave rope, and tied it very securely to the anchor and around the sheep. Next, I tied the other end of the rope to Rusco's car."

"Awesome…" Grinned Pyran. Bright young eyes watched the old man with wonder as adults smiled. Stewart had them in.

"Just as the sunlight began to creep across the paddocks, I had everything ready. I was havin' me pipe, an' a good bowl of porridge with me honey and cream – yer need a good breakfast to tackle a big fish – an' ol' Rusco was havin' a coffee, watchin" the river.

Suddenly it got all quiet. The birds stopped chatterin', an' the sheep stopped bleatin', an' even the leaves of the ol' red gums stopped rustlin'.

"Here he comes, Rusco" I said, before we even saw him. Yer spend enough time in the outdoors, yer soon learn to read the signs of nature. Sure enough, there he was about two hundred yards down the river, just cruisin' along. Again, we watched his dorsal fin stand up straight, and again he dived.

"GET TO THE CAR, RUSCO!" I shouted, as I suddenly realised that Big Scale had launched straight into the fight! He grabbed the sheep – and the rope was coilin' off the bank at a million miles an hour into the river!

Well! Rusco throws his coffee into the air, *leaps* over the campfire, *kicks* the billy over as he does – an' jumps into the car just in time. He started the engine an' put 'er straight into fifth gear. The rope went horribly taught and I felt sure it was gonna snap. The tyres were screechin' an' the engine was revvin'! It felt like the whole world was in a panic.

"Put 'er into first or second, Rusco!" I shouted. He did just that and slowly but surely, we pulled the big bastard in. Boy was he mad! His giant head broke the surface – an' it woulda been as big as Holly's little Mazda 323. And his eyes! I will never forget those giant, golden, lidless eyes – they rolled and reflected the sunlight, and he was starin' straight into me very soul. Well, I stared back!" Stewart was sincerely fierce with his narrative and his eyes blazed with determination.

"Didn't you want to run?!" Saffi exclaimed.

"*Run?!* Never! Not in this situation, anyway. Yer must never run from any big animal – it invites it to chase yer. If you can definitely out-run it to safety – maybe it's worth a go, otherwise – stay put and look prepared to fight – an' most likely you'll bluff it into not attackin'." Stewart rejoined.

"Did you get him to the bank?!" Pyran asked, his eyes bulging.

"You bet yer boots we did! And didn't he make a fight! I grabbed a crow-bar an' it was on! I whacked him and belted him, and he lashed with his tail and tried to maul me with all the rusty hooks in his mouth! Oh! Kids, we fought for hours!" Stewart gave his tale a lift with wild and exaggerated gestures.

"So, he how did he get away?" Asked Tristram in total disbelief that his granddad could lose. The fight was vividly real in his eyes. He saw the elephant-sized fish thrashing through the yellow grass on the muddy banks of the mighty Murray river. He caught the flash of hooks in the giant mouth; he heard and felt the impact of Stewart's hits with the crowbar. He saw the bright, silver flesh bruise with each belt, and saw scales the size of dinner plates fall to the ground in the morning light. He heard the screaming car engine and he watched Stewart dodge the taught rope and the wide whipping tail. He saw his grandfather sweat, as he glared into the huge malevolent eyes of Big Scale, his robust build rigid with rage, and his jaw clenched in defiance...

"Well, Tris..." Stewart sighed bitterly, "It happened this way: with the rusty hooks in his mouth, Big Scale savaged the rope and finally snapped it in two. O' course, Rusco was sent flyin' in the car across the paddocks with the elastic force of it all. It took him half an hour to drive back – going at full speed.

I grabbed the snapped end and tried to hold Big Scale on the bank – I was exhausted from the fight, so I could only hold him for forty minutes."

The adults scoffed at Stewart's playful conceit.

"Don't laugh – alright, it was more like five minutes. See, yer gotta remember that all me life I've done the work of three men – until recently. (Sheep are a lot stronger than they used to be). Anyway, the hook suddenly pulled out of his mouth and the giant fish began to roll slowly back towards the water. In a last effort to finish him off, I lifted the crowbar for a final belt. I could see he was exhausted, an' I honestly thought I could have him. But, with a sudden surge of energy, which all fish seem to have at the end of a fight, he whacked me fair in the face with his giant tail and knocked me unconscious."

"So, you lost..." Pyran sighed, disappointed.

"Well, Pyran, when I woke up, I thought so. The trees around me were all splintered and broken and snapped – the riverbank where we fought looked like a ploughed field...when Rusco finally showed up he said "Look at your nose!"

Now, you kids don't know this, but I used to have the longest nose in the Mallee and Wimmera country. Yer grandma has pictures. Well, Big Scale flattened it into the wide spectacle yer lookin' at today."

The children were utterly convinced. His nose was irrefutable proof of the encounter.

"However," Stewart continued with a twinkle in his eyes, "I found something on the bank that made me decide that I didn't really lose, after all. In fact, it made me realise that Big Scale and I will fight again. It was a draw, yer see, kids – *because he didn't get to keep me hook.*"

The family laughed and applauded the tale.

FRED'S WARNING

OLD FRED MORRIS had listened with child-like joy to Stewart's tale, but a sudden change in the breeze alarmed him. He looked into the forest from whence the breeze came. His nostrils twitched, and the aborigine elder was forcibly reminded of his aim in visiting the family. It was a very distinct odour – wet, oily fur, which was tainted with pungent clay made rich with decaying leaf matter.

He searched the trees on the edge of the clearing but could not detect the bright white eye shine of the animal he feared. However, he knew that it was watching them from the bush.

"Oi Fred..." Began Pyran but was instantly reprimanded by Hester.

"Pyran! Don't be so rude! You say, 'excuse me, Fred'."

"Sorry. Excuse me, Fred?"

"Yeah, mate?" Fred answered, polite but distracted.

"Can you please tell us about the mirachy – the black mirage? Me and Tristram have been wondering about it since tea-time."

"The mirachy, eh? Mmm...better ask ya mum if it's alright first, eh?" Fred answered languidly – then suddenly he saw a segue to his purpose. "Although... yeah...it's a little bit spooky, but I reckon ya look like brave children – ya won't have too many nightmares."

A knowing look from Fred elicited the approval of the parents. After a thoughtful sigh, the old elder began his narrative in a deep, nasal voice.

"I often see in da classroom, kids sittin' around, listenin' ta fairy tales, unna? Stories wid dragons, an' princesses, an' trolls, an' goblins, an' all that. I like dem stories, eh? Dey make ya think about things ya never seen before...well, when I was a little fella, we never had books or a classroom – but we had *stories*. An' dese stories were told sittin' around da fire like we are now, or around a billabong, or on da long walk up da mountain for da Bogong moffs. Dese stories don' have any fairies, or goblins an' that – I reckon dose creatures wouldn't survive in our bush. But we got *magic* – an' *ghosts*, an' *monsters*. We got things out here in our land dat a white man born in a bed won't often recognise – but I seen things, unna? I was born ta da *ground*, not ta a bed. I was raised in da bush."

Here Fred paused as a haze seemed to lift from his deep brown eyes, and rich reminiscences softened his harsh wrinkles. He stubbed his cigarette out, and instead breathed in the smell of the fire and the night. The terrible animal watching from the trees had departed – probably because it had sensed Fred's awareness of it. The elder relaxed and savoured the air. The odours he caught were a mix of real and imagined – wattle blossom, ti-tree, grevillea, myrtle and the smell of fresh fish cooking on the fire. His wide flat hands began to register a thousand textures – soil, bark, fur, fish flesh. He tasted the sweet abdomen of ants, the nutty flavour of the witchetty grub and the feathery crunch of the Bogong moth. Fred suddenly remembered his audience and smiled sheepishly.

"Sorry – I gotta lotta good memories, eh? I know ya asked me about da mirachy – an' I'll tell ya aboud 'im – but there other things out there more interestin', unna? First of all, there's da great father spirit, Mungan-ngaen. Dat's 'is name in da Kurnai tribe, which is me own tribe. Lotta other tribes call 'im 'Baiame'. You white fellas know 'im as God – Holly, ya know 'im as Jehovah, eh? It's important dat ya respect Mungan-ngaen – an' I tell you kids dat now, 'cause later you'll want somethin' comforting ta think about after I tell ya what else is out dere, unna? Such as the ol' mirachy...

Da *Black Mirage* as early whites called 'im.

Huh...hard to explain what dis spirit looks like – he's very tall an' thin, an' is arms an' legs stretch like a daddy-long-legs spider...he's a shadow dat walks upright, instead o' layin' on da ground like every other shadow...he *hates* human beings.

Not a good idea to talk aboud 'im, cause dat makes 'im come around ta spook ya, see? You'll know 'im when he comes. First, there's a *warm* breeze dat comes through da trees...often ya get spooked by it in summer when walkin' about at night – but dat doesn't mean he's come. Summer's warm at night anyway, eh? But in winter – watch out! A warm breeze is probably da mirachy comin' ta get ya...

The breeze is warm at first, 'cause of 'is anger – it makes da wind hot...but when he arrives, when he is *very close* – the air becomes still and *cold*...da way it always does when somethin' wicked stalks a human soul..."

His serious eyes had both the children and the adults hypnotised, and the suspense hung thick in the pause of his narrative.

"I can see dat ya respect what I'm sayin' – dat ya believe in da mirachy, an' dat's good. Ya woulda made good tribesman...ya see, back before white man came, we didn't have electric lights to chase da spirits away. We couldn't hide in buildings or drive away in a car. All we could do at night was stick together by da fire, Mungan-ngaen's protection for his people...an' tell stories..."

After a suitable pause, Warrick asked "Are there any spirits out here? Is the mirachy in the forest?"

Fred smiled. "Nah, mate. Da mirachy is a poor spirit, really. He hides about in da town ta torment da wicked fools dat wander da streets drunk in da night. He breathes down the necks of young boys an' gives a good fright is all, unna?"

"So, you only have to worry about the mirachy at night, then?" Pyran asked eagerly.

"Dat's right. In the day, he crawls into da thin cracks of da world where all shadows go when night's over. But da mirachy – nothin' for you children ta worry about, unna? Just the name of Mungan-ngaen, da great father spirit, is enough ta send 'im away from ya."

Tristram nodded to himself as he recalled the psalm: *Jehovah, your name is like a watchtower...*

"But before ya relax too much...there's somethin' else I wanna warn you all about, here tonight...all o' ya woulda heard of 'im – *da bunyip*."

The children didn't answer, they were simply enchanted by the old man. Holly mistook it for ignorance.

"You kids went to my school fair last year – the 754 twilight fair – you saw the big bunyip costume the grade sixes wore."

"*That*," interjected Fred with supreme disgust, "looked *nothin'* like da bunyip! *That* was a Chinese dragon – I tried ta tell 'em dat an' dey wouldn't listen.

Dey reckoned dey knew better. Well, dey've never seen da bunyip – I *have*. He's not a big furry koala dat gives lollies ta kids, unna? He's not a big colourful snake like da rainbow serpent or da *Chinese dragon*... he's da most dangerous thing in da bush. He's older dan da ol' stone Nargun down dere in da Den o' Nargun – an' he's more terrible dan any mirachy. Mirachy is just wicked – da bunyip...da bunyip is *thoughtful*..."

Fred was genuinely agitated as he spoke.

"You really have seen the bunyip, haven't you, Fred?" Holly murmured.

"Yeah...but only a coupla times...always up at *my* spot..."

"*Your* spot?" Holly asked.

"Yeah...most black fellas have a special spot dat belong ta just them, unna? At least dey did have... anyway, my spot, which I won't tell nobody nothin' about – I seen 'im...and he knows I'm scared of 'im, even though I'll never let 'im sneak up on me..."

"Excuse me, Fred?" Tristram interjected politely and seriously. "What does the bunyip look like?"

"Dat's a good question...for a start, he's *big*...when he's on all fours, he's about as big as a four-wheel-drive, unna? But when he stands up on his back legs, da way a kangaroo does, he's nearly twice as tall as dat...

His fur is a mix of grey and light brown, unna? It's fairly long 'n' shaggy, an' from a distance through da trees his back looks like dat of an emu...He's got a long, heavy tail for balance an' he's got long ears, too, like a kangaroo, but dey sorta tuck away beside 'is head – prob'ly ta keep da water out, unna? Because dat's where da bunyip usually stays – hidin' under da water waitin' ta ambush things dat come down for a drink...but da bunyip also hunts on land. When he's in da bush, he's always movin' *slowly*...and *quietly*. He *stalks*...Not a bird makes a noise when da bunyip is about. Even the trees hold deir breath – everythin' stops and listens in *fear*..."

"What about his face?" Asked Warrick.

"Dat's da worst of all...da bunyip has a big head, with a wide mouth dat comes away from da face, with a nose as big as a bull's. Behind 'is leathery lips, he has long, sharp teeth, each as long as boy's forearm...but da worst, da very worst! Are his *eyes*...dey look almost too big for 'im – dey make 'im look sorta owl-like. Dey're about da size of head-lights – an' dey look like dey're takin' in da *whole world*, not just *lookin'* at it, unna? The colour of 'em is just like dat of kangaroo's, an' wombats an' wallabies – sorta dark, chocolate brown. But dey reflect more dan any other animal's eyes. In the moonlight, dey look bright white – da scariest thing of all ta see in da shadows of da trees at da edge of a clearin'. I seen dat once when I was a boy. Da other time, when I was a man, about twenny year ago, I saw him at da edge of a clearin' just as da sun was settin'. I was about two hundred yards away, on da opposite side of da clearin'. He was stalkin' a wallaby dat was feedin' near da trees, see? Then suddenly, he turned his head and looked right at me. He stood up and his eyes caught the dyin' sunlight, and reflected it right into me soul...I'll never forget dose eyes, glowin' like live coals amongst da shadows of da bush, as the first stars were comin' out..."

Fred allowed the vivid image to suspend itself on the smoke of the crackling fire, as the insects made their song to the stars. A thousand wonderful and frightening visions pirouetted through the children's minds. Even the adults sat nervous and spell-bound, waiting for more. This was the moment Fred had crafted for himself, and he now took full advantage of it.

"I'd tell ya more...but I've only seen da bunyip twice before yesterday..."

"Before *yesterday*?" Asked Karl in amazement.

"Yeah...dat's one of da reasons I wanted ta come an' talk wid ya all, unna? See, I saw somethin' last night dat bothered me...somethin' dat really worried me, unna?

First of all – I know ya all went for a walk in da bush yesterday – an' dat's good. Da more white people dat fall in love with da bush da better for its survival, unna? But I reckon ya went to a place ya best have left alone."

"The pool an hour's walk away from here." Holly breathed.

"Yeah..." Fred sighed. "Ya see, I only just worked out dat he lived there, see? I didn't know where he slept, only where he hunted – an' dat's where I saw 'im last night. I watched 'im come to da edge of da clearin – a couple o' hills away from here – where a mob o' kangaroos were feedin'. Da moon was full an' bright as ya know, an' I could see 'im stalkin' a big, male kangaroo. He was *so quiet*...an' he got *so close*... His huge eyes were focused on his kill...an' da kangaroo diddin know nothin' aboud 'im bein' right behind it...but den...you know what? *He didn't pounce.* He could of, but he *didn't*... Ya see, dere was a change in the breeze, an' I saw 'im sniff. I watched 'im consider da scent...and den...*I watched 'im change 'is mind.* He crept back into da bush and not one of da kangaroos in da clearin' ever knew he was dere.

Well, I got nervous den, an' a bit suspicious, 'cause I reckoned he could smell your camp, unna? So, I followed 'im very carefully, at a fair old distance...an' sure enough...I saw 'im watchin' your camp last night. When ya all went ta bed, he circled da camp, an' came within about fifty yards of ya tents...but lucky for ya all, he was nervous about da cars an' da tents, an' o' course da fire – so he didn't come any closer dan dat...an' den... dere was a fierce cry from the bush – an' den another...da bunyip listened, den slowly crept back into da bush, an' probably back up to 'is home in dat pool..."

The children were absolutely pale, and this concerned Russell.

"Well, Fred," He began seriously, "That was a terrific story – but the kids are not going to be able to sleep tonight."

"Why not?" Fred answered simply. "In all me life I never heard of da bunyip takin' people asleep by da fire or in a tent. Da bunyip never attacks a group of people, an' he never attacks in da *middle* of a clearin'. As I said, he's an animal dat ambushes from da trees or from da water's edge. Now you children all listen. Da bunyip fears da Great Father Spirit. If ya ever worried aboud 'im – just call on Mungan-ngaen, or Baiame, or Jehovah or whatever ya call 'im – an' you'll be right. An' be good children, an' don't wander by yaself in da bush. *And...* never, *ever* go back to dat bewdiful pool up yonder there...OK?"

The consent was unanimous, and Fred smiled. Hester grunted as she thought that she had detected smugness in that smile, but both Holly and Mary saw the truth. Fred was tremendously relieved.

"What if we see the bunyip and it isn't our fault?" Pyran asked quietly.

Fred looked hard into the boy. "I don't reckon dat's ever goin' ta happen, mate. But...if ya find yaself face ta face wid da bunyip – don't run. Like ya granddad said, runnin' from a big animal invites it ta chase ya. Stand strong an' face him. Call on Mungan-ngaen. If ya run, dat'd be da end of ya."

All of the children, especially Tristram, took the advice to heart.

The elder then pacified the adults somewhat by telling the children stories of a lighter nature. He spoke of playful water spirits and other sprites that haunted the limestone caves of the region. He also told them of the tuckonies, a tribe of tiny people that he had heard about from another aboriginal population further north. By the time he had finished his tales, the children were relaxed and happy enough to go to bed.

"There's been a change in the sleeping arrangements." Hester announced as the children prepared to head for their tent. "Pyran, listen to me. Saffi and Jase are going to sleep with you and Tristram tonight, as Warrick wants to stay up later and sleep with the adults."

Pyran glanced at Warrick, who was straight-faced.

"Fine." He shrugged.

JASE'S WANDER

BEFORE HE WENT TO SLEEP, Tristram stared with tired anxiety into a yellow fragment of the opal. He wanted a happy thought to banish the nightmares of the last two days...

It was Friday night, and a little boy watched the television. He was two years old, with hair that was auburn, fine and shiny. There was a squeal of mirth and clapping as the toddler tried to sing along with the Muppets...

"Dut da der dut, ta-dut da... Dut da der dadut da..."

There was the delicious, savoury smell of salt, oil, and butcher paper. Friday night was fish 'n' chip night.

Suddenly Tristram chuckled and a deep love embraced him from the inside. The chuckle was husky and familiar. It was Toby's. Tristram was looking at himself as a baby with his grandfather's eyes. The realisation was strange, beautiful, and sad.

Two-year-old Tristram grinned at Kermit the frog, and then his eyes widened with wonder at a big shaggy monster Muppet with large, rolling yellow eyes. He turned and beamed at his grandfather.

"A monsder!"

"Yes," Tristram answered with his grandfather's light, pleasant voice. "A *monster*."

"I wan' do see a monsder one day!"

"Really? Most kids are scared of monsters."

A frown from the child. "Why?"

Tristram grinned at the boy's innocence. "Mmm. Children always ask such good questions."

The toddler did not hear the response as Gonzo fought with Miss Piggy...

Tristram fell asleep as his eyes slipped away from the memory...

The opal was the most precious thing in the world, and as long as he had it with him, he would never feel alone or disconnected from the ones he loved.

· · ·

Outside by the fire, Holly hugged herself and smoked. Fred had departed, and everyone else but Russell had just gone to bed.

"What's on your mind, darl?" Russell asked quietly.

"Huh? Oh...just Fred's stories."

"They were rather *vivid.* I wish I had heard the one about the bloody bunyip before the children did. That'd spook any child."

"The stories were good, darl." Holly murmured. "Fred came here deliberately to tell them. I think there really is a monster out there that wants to eat my children."

"*Holly.*"

"I'm serious."

"OK." Russell nodded respectfully. After a thoughtful pause, he added "You know, Hol...last night it was me who made those cries..."

"I know. You did the right thing."

"Yeah...but you know what else? I had a feeling that I was being watched as I came back into the clearing."

"Maybe it was your father."

"No...I felt cold all over. I told myself it was just the night air. But after Fred's story...well...I don't know."

"I think there is something out there. That's why I am going to sit up and watch the camp."

"I'll stay up with you, if you like."

"Thanks…"

"We're going home tomorrow, anyway…we'll have a good sleep tomorrow night."

As Holly and Russell kept a vigil by the fire, the children slept deeply. The night wore on without alarm or incident. Finally, after hours of whispered conversation, dawn stretched over the hills. The magpies and currawongs announced the onset of day, and the parents felt it safe to go to bed.

As Russell and Holly snuggled into their sleeping bag, little Jase was wide awake and looking at his sleeping brother. He had seen Tristram look at the opal the night before and draw comfort from its universe of experience and sensation. Jase needed comfort himself. The camping trip was almost over, and Tristram and Pyran had spent most of the time together away from himself and Saffi. Jase loved Tristram and looked to him for guidance in this time of bewildered sadness. Maybe Tristram would let him look at the jewel again when he woke up…maybe he would see Granddad Toby in there.

Tristram was dreaming as morning approached.

· · ·

Wide, white eyes stare up at him from under the water. There is the nasal singing of children. His wonder turns to alarm in an instant – wide, white eyes before the instant of death!

The water parts and the teeth have him. The spirits of the children scream and run through the trees, and Tristram's spirit joins them as it flees panic-stricken from his twitching corpse. Children's eyes wide in terror – their pleasant lullaby revealed for what it really is – a warning, a scream warped by an evil magic.

The old witch doctor laughs, orange eyes ablaze with horrible triumph.

"Didn't ya hear boy?" He says and he looks exactly like Fred. "MacDougall blood will see it through."

Jase was shaking Tristram gently. Tristram started awake, his blood hurtling through him, his nerves on fire. He recognised his little brother.

"Jase." He breathed, as he came to himself.

"Good morning, Tris." Jase whispered. "Were you having a nightmare?"

"Yes."

"What about?"

Tristram considered the dream, as its awful spell was shattered by the reassuring light of dawn, and the wide hazel eyes of his curly haired little brother.

"Just about the mirachy, Jase. Nothing serious." He whispered and relaxed into the warmth of his sleeping bag.

"I was dreaming too." Jase said, but Tristram was only half listening. Sleep beckoned to him again...

"It wasn't a nightmare..." Jase whispered, looking at his brother who had now closed his eyes. "It was about *ducks*."

Jase was disappointed at Tristram's lack of interest.

"Tris?"

No response.

"Tris?"

"Mmm?"

"*Tris?*"

"What?!" Tristram was awake again, with an impatient glare.

Jase blinked and bit his lip. He wished that Tristram would just listen to him, the way everyone else in the family did. He didn't understand his brother's aloofness, and the way Tristram and Pyran had avoided himself and Saffi. Why couldn't he play and talk with him? Didn't he love him? However, little Jase was too young to articulate these feelings. All he could do was shyly ask for what he wanted.

"Can I look at Granddad Toby's opal again?"

"No." Was the flat response.

"Please?"

"No."

"Please?"

"Not now, Jase. Go back to sleep."

"*Please*, Tris?"

Tristram was now awake and furious. "*Jase*," He whispered harshly through gritted teeth, clutching his brother's pyjamas and pulling Jase violently towards him. "*I said 'no! Now leave me alone and go back to sleep!*"

Tristram shoved the shocked little boy away from him and turned his back on his brother. He was immediately sorry, as he heard a gentle sobbing behind him, but he was determined to ignore it.

Within ten minutes, Tristram was back to sleep.

Outside the tent, little Jase sat in silent tears. Out of the three children, he was the quietest. He rarely complained or cried, and when he did, it was always in gentle sobs. He took everything his family said or did straight to heart, and any criticism or harsh word from Tristram was especially painful. Toby's death was not real to him – but the tragic change in his family permeated every cell in his sensitive soul.

The sun was not yet above the trees, but its light was warm and green in the forest. Another bright day. Jase dried his tears on his sleeve and thought about the ducks.

Suddenly he thought he saw one at the edge of the forest. He squinted, but the shapes were indistinct as the light came into his eyes. Was that a duck or just a tussock of grass or bracken?

The shape moved again, and Jase was nearly certain that it was a duck. He heard a distant quack, but it was so faint that he might have imagined it. He decided to go over for a closer look.

As he wandered closer, he saw that it was indeed a most beautiful duck, just like the ones he had seen in the opal. If Jase knew the species, he would have told any who would listen that it was a mountain duck. It waddled comically across the grass and wagged its tail feathers, which made Jase grin.

It was closer to the edge of the forest than he had previously thought.

Jase wanted to get as close as possible to the friendly looking duck, but just as he got to within about five metres of it, it waddled slowly away...*into the bush.*

Jase stood at the edge of the forest in uncertainty. The gum leaves glowed, the bracken shone with dew. How far would the duck go? He would follow it a little way.

Minutes later, Jase had wandered after the duck a good distance into the forest and totally forgotten himself. Always, he almost got close enough for a satisfactory look at the bird – then it would turn a corner. When he heard the babbling stream, Jase was suddenly alarmed by how far he had come. The duck stopped still and looked quizzically at him.

Jase turned back, but the bush looked shadowed and forboding. He turned to the amiable duck again, and saw an inviting, sunlit path. He was anxious and undecided.

Suddenly he heard his mother's voice through the trees, perhaps just a few metres ahead of him on the track.

"Mummy?" He called in his soft voice.

He listened but heard only the stream.

"Mum?" Jase called again and walked further along the track.

Jase...said an indistinct voice that may have been Holly's. It could have come from his imagination.

"Mummy?" He called again, walking rapidly even further along the track until suddenly he was standing beside the stream.

In the distance, again he heard his mother. Where was she?

The duck had begun to waddle along the path beside the stream. Jase squinted up the stony river and blinked nervously. *The duck was heading up to that scary pool...*

The thought was interrupted as Jase saw a figure turning the corner, about a hundred and fifty metres ahead of him. He didn't get a good look, but the transient phantom may have been Holly.

"*Jase.*" Called a more definite voice, and Jase was now certain that it was his mother ahead of him.

He shrugged, smiled and then wandered happily after the duck along the stream towards his doom.

THE TERRIBLE RUN

TRISTRAM HAD SLIPPED into a new dream, as his little brother wandered along the stream...

Joan looks lovely as she sleeps in their bed, and the Sunday morning light bathes her face through the curtains. But something frightens him.

He turns to look into the large mirror on their dressing table.

Tristram is Toby Jones – tall, strong, healthy... and seriously alarmed. His light blue eyes hold Tristram's gaze intently in the mirror, his eyebrows are raised in urgent care.

"Jase." He whispers at Tristram.

· · ·

Tristram sat bolt upright and looked about him. He met Pyran's eyes and Saffi's eyes – they were wide awake.

"Jase." He said. "Where's Jase?"

"That's just what I asked Pyran." Saffi answered, her blue eyes anxious.

Fear sliced a black hole in Tristram, and the warmth of his body was sucked into it. Clutching the opal, he leapt out of his sleeping bag and the others followed him out of the tent.

"I don't see him anywhere, do you?!" Tristram asked in a panic.

"Maybe he crawled in to sleep with your mum and dad?" Pyran offered. Saffi ran to check.

"No." She said frantically as she peered into their tent. She was going to wake them but was distracted as Tristram and Pyran dashed past her.

"Where are you going?" She shouted after them. Saffi decided to pursue the boys.

The three of them stopped at the edge of the forest, panting.

"You don't reckon he'd go all the way to that pool by himself, do you?" Pyran asked.

Every fibre in Tristram's body screamed in the affirmative. He looked into the eyes of his sister and saw that she agreed with him.

"Yes." He said. "You think so too, Saffi. It's enough for me, I'm going after him. One of you should wake Mum and Dad." With that he ran down the track as fast he could.

Without a word Pyran followed him.

"Wait!" Saffi shouted, then joined them in the desperate pursuit.

They hurtled through the bracken, and descended gullies of towering tree ferns. Sunlit verdure was infinite either side of the fleeing children. They ran through the lactic acid and their lungs stretched painfully to keep breathing. Finally, they arrived at the stream.

A frantic search up and down the stony mountain river.

The curly haired little boy was nowhere to be seen.

As Tristram stared into the fast-flowing waters, a dark resignation suggested itself.

Why run? It has been done. You know what you will find there. A floating fragment of his pyjamas. His blood upon the rocks where he was taken. And the stream will flow on and on...

"No!" Tristram shouted in hot, terrible grief and hatred. He snatched a rock from the stream and ran, a new energy speeding him along the river. Bewildered and frightened, Saffi and Pyran followed.

Tristram hated himself as he remembered the hurt in his little brother's face earlier that morning.

How will he look just before the monster takes him? *Run faster!*

The bends of the stream seemed endless as they leaped over logs and rocks and ducked under branch's – but on they ran. The stream babbled as usual, and the sun relaxed into the bright blue day, oblivious to their terror and desperation.

Suddenly, they were around the corner and there it was. The beautiful, haunting pool – and at its edge, his attention totally absorbed by the blackness at the bottom of the pool, sat little Jase.

"JASE!" Tristram shouted as he bounded towards him, expecting a huge shape to leap from the water any second. The child came to himself as though a hypnotist had snapped his fingers. Jase was shocked by the fierce, terrified energy of his brother as Tristram threw the rock in his hand at the water directly in front of him. In seconds, Tristram had Jase in his arms and carried him away from the edge of the pool.

Relief, wonderful relief as the children crowded together amongst the trees. Tristram thought he was going to cry as he hugged the bewildered Jase tightly.

"I'm sorry I yelled at you, Jase." He whispered in his brother's ear.

Pyran was moved, as was Saffi who was on the verge of tears.

"Why did you come here, Jase?" Saffi asked angrily. "You scared us to death."

"I dunno..." Jase answered tearily. "I was following the duck an' then Mum called an' so I came here...but she wasn't here..."

"What duck?" Asked Saffi.

"There was a duck an' I followed it – but it's gone now."

"Wait a minute!" Pyran interjected, looking thoroughly spooked at Tristram and Saffi. "*Aunty Holly called you?*"

"Did she?" Inquired Tristram urgently. "Did Mum call you?"

"Yes."

Saffi looked fearfully at Tristram.

"Mum was asleep in the tent. I saw her next to Dad before we ran here."

"Are you sure?"

"Yes."

Beats of silence.

"Jase?" Tristram asked slowly. "Are you *really* sure you heard Mum calling you?"

"Yes!" Jase shouted confused and upset. "I saw her when I was over there." He pointed vaguely downstream. "I yelled to her, but she kept walking an' I ran an' called an' she still kept walking...an' then I got here an' she wasn't here. I said Mum? Mummy? An' she didn't answer...an' then I went to the water, cause that's where the duck went...an' then...an' then I got scared...an' I couldn't move..."

The little boy cried and Saffi, Tristram and Pyran held him and comforted him.

"It's alright, Jase. You're safe now."

But the children were far from safe. Startled by the fierce splash of the rock, something had retreated into the deep blackness. It watched the edge of the pool and waited for the men with spears...

"God, I never thought I could be so scared in broad daylight, eh?" Pyran said to be light-hearted. "Scary stuff like this is supposed to happen at night, or during a storm or something."

A child talking. It sounds relieved, brave in the company of men with spears. The monster listened from the cold centre of its stony underwater den...

"Let's get out of here." Suggested Pyran.

"Good idea." Tristram agreed.

No grown men's voices...just children...just children...

It crept stealthily up the stone floor of its lair. A gentle spring from powerful back legs, a swish of a long tail, and the animal had its eyes, ears and nose at the surface of the water...

Tristram felt the predator's gaze as the children turned their backs on the pool and began to leave. He turned...

Wide chocolate eyes were watching them at the surface of the water, in the shadow created by the recess in the wall at the back of the pool. They disappeared instantly, in a way that would make a casual observer doubt and forget what they had seen. Tristram knew better.

If ya ever face da bunyip – don't run. Fred had said.

Run?! Stewart echoed in Tristram's mind. *Yer must never run from any big animal. It invites it ta chase yer.*

It invites it to chase.

What chance did they have of outrunning this monster? Tristram knew they couldn't just walk away.

Pyran noticed that Tristram had stopped walking with them.

"Tristram?" He asked nervously. "You comin' or what?"

Think fast. Tristram's mind was a whirl of surreal horror, yet his intelligence spoke through the clamorous scream of alarm. *The others must go and I must stay and distract it.* He shut his mind to the consequences of that action.

"Yeah...I'm comin'..." Tristram said as he struggled internally. "But I have an idea...just to be safe... um...I think Saffi and Jase should walk ahead a few metres."

"Why?" Saffi frowned in annoyance. "I can't believe you want to avoid us again after what's just happened!"

Pyran was dumbfounded. "Why should we split up?"

"Saffi..." Tristram began, then beckoned to her. "Come here."

With an angry frown of suspicion, she obeyed, and Tristram whispered to her and Pyran.

"I think there really is a bunyip in that pool...and I think that it will follow us."

Pyran and Saffi exchanged fearful looks before Pyran answered.

"Then we should stay in a group. Fred said that the bunyip never attacks a group."

"That's right." Saffi agreed. "We should stick together!"

"*Saffi.*" Tristram urged. "I don't think an animal the size of a bunyip is gonna be scared by four small children, do you? If it does attack, it will catch Jase for sure as we run away."

If Saffi had a rebuttal, terror had made it unutterable.

"If you walk ahead with Jase and Pyran," Tristram continued, "I can watch you from behind and yell if I see it coming."

"But it'll kill you!"

"I'm the fastest runner here and I won't let it sneak up and catch me."

"But..." Saffi nearly sobbed. "Fred said *don't run...*"

"And Granddad said run only if you have a chance of outrunning it. Out in a clearing I'd have no chance – but how would it catch me through the trees? It's too big to fit through the narrow trunks – that'll slow it down. Saffi, this is the best thing to do. Walk ahead with Pyran and Jase. It'll be OK. It won't take that long to get back to camp and we can see heaps in this daylight. It won't be able to sneak up and catch us."

"I've got a better idea." Pyran said solemnly. "Saffi and Jase can walk ahead – and I'll walk behind beside you. That way, if it follows us, you and I can take off in different directions, and it won't know which one to chase."

The idea was considered over racing heart beats.

"I agree with Pyran." Saffi concluded with determination. "You are not going to walk by yourself, Tristram."

"Fine." Tristram conceded, somewhat relieved. "Now take Jase back to camp as fast as you can. When you get around that corner, we'll follow you.

Don't wait for us. Trust that we are following. Get to camp, then get Mum and Dad and Uncle Karl and Aunty Hester and tell them to come into the bush to meet us. Got it?"

Saffi hesitated before reluctantly assenting.

"Aren't they coming with us?" Jase blinked anxiously as Saffi led him away.

"Yes, but they want to talk about something private." Saffi answered.

Jase looked Saffi right in the eye. "Are we in danger?"

Saffi hesitated. What could she tell him?

"We will be safe if we hurry up. Don't worry about Tristram and Pyran, they are big boys and they will be just fine. OK?"

THE BUNYIP

"WHEN SHOULD WE FOLLOW?" Pyran asked as Saffi and Jase were about to disappear around a bend.

Tristram did not answer. He was trying to commit the image of Saffi and Jase's departure to heart.

Two blonde haired siblings, hair golden in a bright blue morning. Hand in hand they walk away by a beautiful mountain stream, that courses through soaring gum trees...

Tristram frowned miserably. Though it was just in front of him, he couldn't capture all the detail indelibly in his mind. In minutes, Saffi and Jase had turned a corner, and Tristram thought that he might never see them again. Why hadn't he tried to give more of them to the opal? What was left to give the opal now? His eyes swept rapidly over the scene, trying to hold it all.

It was impossible. His life was a cascade of picturesque moments slipping though his fingers...

"When should we follow them?" Pyran asked again.

Tristram swallowed and his lips felt numb at the answer he had to give.

"We can't...it will come out of the water and attack. I saw it in a dream. And I saw it watching us just now...we have to face it."

Pyran considered Tristram with bewildered dismay.

"How are we going to do that? What should do we do? We should get a stick...some rocks."

Pyran began to scan the scrub frantically for a weapon.

"Pyran," Tristram interrupted with a surreal calm. "The bunyip fears the name of the great father spirit. Jehovah will be on our side. All we have to do is pray."

He got on his knees and bowed his head. Pyran joined him.

Large nostrils twitched at the surface of the water, near the recess in the wall behind the pool. Sunlight was reflected from golden ripples onto the underside of overhanging rocks. Dangling ferns glowed bright green. The monster relished the scents of the children

against the eucalyptus. Long ears folded out and pro-
truded from the water's surface. The animal considered the soundscape...

Filter out the rushing stream and what is left?
Heartbeats. It always listened for heartbeats first...

Naturally, the loudest were the children's. The
monster considered the rhythym and volume of their
heartbeats and compared it to what else was usually
nearby. The children's heartbeats were not as rapid as
those of the birds perched silently in the twisted, ma-
jestic canopy of the forest. It could deduce the species
from the sound of its heart. It could hear seven kook-
aburras, twelve currawongs, three magpies and a
sleeping powerful owl. In the scrub, the signals were
not so clear, but it could hear superb blue fairy wrens,
whistling fly-catchers, and other small birds. In the
trees nearest the pool it detected mice-sized bats sleeping, as well as a group of brush-tailed and ring-tailed
possums in various dreys and hollows. The monster
could also hear grubs gnawing in the wood, and spiders creeping under the bark.

It listened for the reptiles next. They had the
slowest heart beats, and they were the hardest to listen
for. Snakes, lizards and goannas were easier to hear in
the warmer months when they more active...

What else? There was usually a koala asleep in a
nearby tree, but the monster could not hear its heart
now. Nor was its scent on the wind...

Suddenly it detected another smell. A man! There was another man in the forest...this must be a trap...

It inhaled deeply, then duck-dived silently into the still blackness at the centre of the pool.

The boys had finished praying and now stood resolute, facing the pool.

Tristram glanced at the opal and saw that the red fragments of the opal glowed, giving it a maroon appearance.

"Let's go." Tristram breathed.

To his suprise, he walked quite steadily with Pyran to the large rocks at the edge of the pool.

Every second spasmed with vivid detail. The rustle and crunch of twigs and gum leaves under their bare feet. The brush of bracken fern on their legs. The warm rocks with their feathery lichens. White ripples of sunlight on cold, clear water. The mossy, earthy smells and eucalyptus fragrances of a reticent forest. The air, absolutely still.

Water cascaded tentatively into the pool and bubble trails departed swiftly across its solemn depth. There at the water's edge, they stood staring at their reflections.

The bunyip watched in wonder...

· · ·

Pyran and Tristram felt the monster move closer to them. Their skin prickled at each silent, menacing step. The massive paws barely disturbed the mud and silt that caked the stone floor in the permanent eddy of the depths.

"Something horrible is coming." Pyran murmured miserably.

The monster salivated, as it moved from the still water and felt the fresh current wave through its dark grey fur. Look how close they are. What about the man? The animal reflected on the recent scent...it was a familiar man...an old man. How far away was he? It closed its enormous eyes to aid concentration...a breeze had brought the scent...he wasn't close. The eyes opened again, and a cold, wild hunger caused the pupils to dilate...

The opal grew unbearably hot in Tristram's hand, but he couldn't let it go. Shrieking phantoms of terror rushed through his veins. A cold vapour filled his soul. The warmth of his blood was being sucked into a freezing vacuity in the opal. A cruel whisper tickled its way up his spinal cord.

MacDougall blood will see it through.

Moments of stinging suspense...and then, in a

smooth, silent movement – at the very edge of the light under water – the monster's face appeared.

Pyran and Tristram instantly wet themselves.

Two golden eyes glowed up at them. They were about twelve feet under the surface and were alight with savage hunger. How long had those intense eyes been watching them before they had seen them?

The children were paralysed by the thought of the huge, furry, muscular bulk that must be tensed, ready to lunge behind the enormous eyes.

The bunyip inched forward, the light still bright in the viscous *tapetum lucidum* of its eyes, until the outline of the animal was clearly visible. Now, the children could see its strange, dark and oily fur. It was thick and littered with sticks, leaves and mud. They could see its massive front paws, with long stained claws, that each could have clutched a cow's head. It was still at least eight feet under the water's surface.

It moved slowly forward another three feet, its huge head leaning keenly over the front legs. The eyes flashed white as it moved, and then suddenly stopped reflecting the sunlight. Now they were held by a pair of rich chocolate eyes. Each pupil was a universe without stars.

Why don't they run? The monster reflected. *Strange, unnatural children, with pale skin and discoloured fur...*

At that instant, as the animal paused to consider

its unusual prey, Tristram suddenly found himself in the calm eye of his cyclone of terror. An echo of clear thought rang through his mind.

The bunyip is thoughtful.

Though his mind didn't articulate the impression into words, Tristram realised that the bunyip was not merely a predatory animal...it was also somehow *sentient*. At that revelation, Tristram began to try and fathom the presence behind the bunyip's dark eyes.

The bunyip noted the change in Tristram's expression and halted its movement.

What is happening?

Taking Pyran's trembling hand, yet holding the gaze of the predator, Tristram took five measured steps back away from the water.

The bunyip responded with a censuring tilt of its giant head.

As Tristram made no further movement, but seemed to be waiting, the bunyip moved its large, long back legs forward past its front legs, the way a kangaroo moves when on all fours. Remaining on all fours, the enormous animal moved forward again and finally came out of the water. As its head broke the surface it snorted air and water explosively from its nostrils.

The children were terrified anew, and Tristram's thoughts were shattered into frenzied panic once more. The size of the animal was daunting.

Suddenly they were hit by the reek of ancient

mud, that was rich with the decay of plants long extinct.

The chocolate eyes were intense and predatory again, and the beast looked ready to pounce once more. The large, bull-sized nose twitched. Long, bone-snapping, flesh-tearing teeth rasped together behind black leathery lips. The long ears were tucked behind the monster's sagittal crest in preparation for the kill.

Tristram and Pyran felt an impending sense of doom, akin to the instant before a snake strikes dead its prey.

The beast inhaled sharply, its body tensed, its eyes widened, showing the whites – Pyran fainted and collapsed under his panic to the stones – and then, in the heart-beat before it struck, Tristram shouted with all the faith and fear in him.

"JEHOVAH!"

The child stood rigid and glaring in front of the startled monster and in his hand, the opal flashed like an azure beacon.

Angered, the bunyip raised itself upon its back legs and towered over them. It spread the long sharp claws of its mighty front paws and glowered at the boy. A thunderous rumble emanated from the beast. It had all the intensity of a bushfire's terrible roar.

Tristram remained defiant, his courage as strong as his faith.

"JEHOVAH!"

What is this noise? A challenge? What is the child holding?

The animal stared at the glowing opal and suddenly an intense connection between itself and the boy was formed.

Both Tristram and the bunyip gasped, as though they were breathing air into their lungs for the very first time. Tristram uttered a tumultuous cry. A billion neurons fired, the shell of his mind shattered, and his very soul exploded into a fresh universe of perception....

It was a fossil that no naturalist had described before...

The opal fell from the giant skull like a tear into his hand...

· · ·

The bunyip had been challenged many years ago, on a bright morning, just like this. It was a smaller animal then...

A child ripe for the taking, crying scared by the pool. A lunge and a successful kill. Suddenly, a tribe of aboriginal men with fire and spears. It kills two of them in one lunge, its claws piercing through their chests as it slams them to the stones and leans all its weight onto them. It then lunges again and grabs three more screaming men, pulling them into a crushing bear hug. It carries them into the water and drowns them. Spears fly as shouts echo. It is grazed three times and pierced twice, as it holds the three squirming men under the water. With a savage roar of pain, it leaps from the waters again and savages more men. It tears the other shrieking, fleeing men to shreds with its terrible claws and teeth. Blood is sprayed over the rocks and bracken. Bodies fly and thump against tree trunks.

In the stillness that follows, it moans over its bleeding wounds...as days crawl by, the injuries become infected and the animal is dreadfully sick...

What is this? The monster remembers experiences it never had.

A man...sick, dying...A man old, yet too young to die, gives a tear with his memories in it to a child...this child...

. . .

A powerful grief, and a tremendous and sad love pierced the soul of the bunyip. It exhaled sharply...

Family...love...stories...a giant fish...wonder, absolute wonder...a beautiful fish in the paws...released unharmed...

Tristram was crying at the emptiness he felt. He was alone...crawling in the dark...injured...sick... hungry...alone...

The bunyip missed a man called Granddad Toby. It loved a family it had watched under the stars in a clearing, but not understood. The mystery of their babble was elucidated, and the monster watched Granddad Stewy fight with Big Scale. It relished the stories, the jokes, the hand running through its fur, the warm food in its belly, and the smiles of its family...

A tear swelled in its left eye and glistened like the opal.

Voices echoed over the powerful loneliness that sank into Tristram's stomach and dragged at his heart...

. . .

"I dunno whether it's a MacDougall heirloom, or were just lookin' after it, yer know?"

Sucking at my mother's milk, warm and safe.

"A debt to the spirits could be paid from something sleeping in its bones."

Chased away and bitten. Alone.

"It fell from the skull like a tear into his hand."

I am alone.

"MacDougall blood will see it through."

The bunyip was being moved by a galaxy of experience that it had only vaguely perceived before...

A shock of sensation, at the smells, the sounds and the majesty of the bush. The stars. The rushing stream. It imagined. It was in awe of life. It felt connected to others... a hundred lifetimes whirled through its subconscious. A sea of emotions swayed over the planet of its heart.

Two blonde haired siblings, hair golden in a bright blue morning. Hand in hand they walk away by a beautiful mountain stream, that courses through soaring gum trees.

Tears obscured the bunyip's view of the opal, and the spell was broken. It was breathing rapidly. Its eyes were wide in pleading wonder.

Tristram was crying on his knees with heartfelt sorrow for the bunyip.

Pyran stirred suddenly and started awake. Confused, he looked from Tristram to the bunyip.

In that instant, a powerful bitterness overcame the monster. It yearned for the sensations it had just experienced, as it felt love fading from its soul like some transient daydream.

Sorrow...emptiness...loss...tremendous loss.

Tristram saw it all in the miserable, wet eyes of the bunyip, and he could not bear it.

The boy and the monster looked into each other and found understanding. The bunyip bowed its head sadly, and Tristram's heart swelled with such pity that he thought he would never be happy again.

Before he knew what he was really doing, Tristram held up the opal before the bunyip in an open hand.

Trembling and bewildered, the monster considered the jewel, and then the face of the boy. Then, it stretched out its massive front paw to humbly accept the gift.

As the opal fell from his hand into the giant paw, Tristram felt as though he had just dropped his soul into a bottomless well.

Long black claws closed over the opal. The bunyip closed its eyes with gratitude.

With its other paw, it extended an index claw, and tenderly collected a tear from its enormous eye. The tear glistened in the sunlight as it hung suspended on the claw, and the bunyip let it fall gently onto Tristram's face.

For as long as he lived, Tristram would always feel the melancholy splash of that salty baptism.

The ominous bulk of the bunyip then turned to look upon Pyran. The eyes considered his flesh and it salivated anew. It drew its colossal head in close and sniffed the child, its exhalations lifting his orange fringe from his terrified face. Pyran whimpered as the eyes held him with murderous desire...then, soft grey lids with long lashes lowered over the eyes in thought.

With a solemn look at Tristram, the great beast raised itself to its full height again, then slowly and deliberately, it turned back into the water.

The long, heavy tail followed the curve of the animal in front of the children and with one kick of its back legs, the bunyip disappeared into the blackness at the centre of the pool.

LIFE GOES ON

WHEN THE FAMILY found Pyran and Tristram, they were talking peacefully with Fred beside the stream. When questioned later, the children were reticent about their morning.

Saffi and Jase were monumentally relieved and overjoyed to find them safe. They asked repeatedly about the bunyip.

"There was nothing there after all, was there Tris?" Pyran answered quickly.

"No." Tristram answered flatly.

"I was watchin' dem from dat hill over dere." Fred interjected languidly. "Dey were good fellas... dey were careful an' respectful of dat place."

A conspiratory look was exchanged between Pyran and Fred, but Tristram was expressionless.

"So, what have you been doing?" Holly asked

coolly. "You scared your brother and sister half to death."

"Not to mention the worry Holly and I – and Hester and Karl and your grandparents have been through." Russell added angrily.

"We're sorry." Pyran said simply and dejectedly.

Tristram remained silent and melancholy.

Something about their defeated faces troubled the adults, and their anger seemed to melt away. Even Hester, who was usually quick with reprimand, felt unable to yell at Pyran.

"What happened to you this morning?" She asked tenderly.

"Dey had a bit of a fright, dat's all." Fred answered for them. "It's me own fault really, for tellin' dem stories last night. For what it's worth, I'm sorry. But da boys are alright, now."

"Ah well." Stewart drawled. "All's well that ends well, I reckon. We've had a good little trip away, and I don't think we need to spoil it now. I reckon we should head back, have some breakfast and be on our way."

As they all wandered back to camp, Stewart relished the smell of the forest and the sunlight, whilst Mary silently said her good-byes to the twittering birdlife. Hester, Karl and Warrick looked forward to the creature comforts of civilisation. Holly felt obliged to be entertaining because Fred walked with them, and Russell helped her out by interjecting with playful witticisms.

Intriguingly, Pyran joked and played with Saffi and Jase. His was a soul that accepted a cycle of punishment, and he had learned to relish the period of relief in between.

Tristram trudged morosely along with them. He had thrown the colour of his life away. The forest was now merely the grey corridors leading to the gallows of the rest of his life.

In a swirling moment of chatter, Fred placed a hand on Tristram's shoulder.

"Remember what I said, matey." He whispered warmly. "Ya behaved like a true warrior today...an' like all true warriors, ya mourn for the sacrifices dat ya made...but listen, little brother..." He waited for Tristram to look into his deep, smiling eyes. "Ya see da sunlight through da trees? It's all yours, mate. Never stop lookin'. Can ya smell da gum leaves? Mmm. Never stop smellin'. And do ya hear dat all around ya? It's da voices of ya family, unna? Still got dem, brother. Never stop listenin'."

With that he gave Tristram a gentle squeeze on the shoulder and left him to reflect.

The hidden valleys and clearings of the forest were haunted by the bunyip long after the family had left the evergreen high country. Few other people camped in the monster's territory, and those who flew over the hilly landscape never noticed the animal as it stalked through the bush. Even the locally famous pilot Ben Buckley, whose eyes were keen and whose ancestor had seen the bunyip, never glimpsed the animal. We rarely see that which we are not looking for.

The bunyip floated in thought for days after its encounter with the boy. The cold clear water, which flowed from a myriad of underground caves, animated its thick shaggy fur as it cruised slowly though shafts of sunlight. Its wide eyes were totally absorbed by a bright azure opal in the centre of its massive paw.

It was a universe of experience and sensation.

MELVIN DUBRELLE'S ACCOUNT

The tale that follows was written in 1865, by Mr. Melvin Dubrelle. It details a fantastic adventure that took place near Fiery Creek in Ararat some years earlier. It has a direct connection to both the Opal and Tristram Jones.

THE BRUTAL MURDERS

My grandson Gerald was a timid, gentle boy. He had inherited those qualities from his father and my only son, Michael...and Michael's gentle soul could only have come from my own dear departed wife, Edith. May the Good Lord rest their souls.

Gerald was barely seven years old when his parents were brutally murdered, and he was kidnapped by their killer. My tale will be that of his rescue, and the terrible and fantastic perils which we had to overcome to effect it.

The following narrative is sad and true, and parts of it shall distress God-fearing folk, let the reader be fairly warned. It is set in the Australian bush, which is a wonderful and frightening place. Amongst her eerie eucalyptus trees wander monsters and ghosts that rival those that are said to haunt the darkest European forests. In all my peregrinations, never have I seen such singular landscapes, flora and fauna, that so ignite the imagination and haunt the soul. Our parrots have colours spawned of an opium pipe hallucination. Painted iguanas hide amongst the tree trunks, decorating those twisted pillars of the bush like grotesque gargoyles – how their sudden animation quickens the pulse, and how their delicate patterns do delight the eye! Horrors lurk under the dry, curled bark of our trees – poisonous spiders innumerable. Venomous serpents we also have in abundance: some with bright coppery scales; others pitch black, with a belly as bright and red as a desert sunset. Still others have stripes that resemble those of the tiger himself, and his bite is just as fatal.

Yet, these monsters share the land with other creatures benign as they are bizarre. The echidna, our own answer to the English hedgehog, is a peculiar fellow indeed! He wanders about in search of ants with a long beak and sharp yellow quills upon his back. He shares the day with large emus, that comically wander our waving yellow grasslands amongst mobs of graceful kangaroos. At night – by Jove! What a wondrous parade of animals do haunt the forest! A fellow could be forgiven for the fabulous conjecture, that a rich child's soft toy menagerie had come to life and commandeered the bush. How endearing in appearance are our possums, the ring-tail and the brush-tail, and the little sugar-glider – who spreads his furry cape and flies amongst the tree-tops! And what of our robust wombat, or his charismatic cousin, the little koala, who slumbers among the gum leaves? However, I hasten to warn the reader: beware of disturbing our sleepy koalas, for they have sharp claws and an ursine temperament indeed.

It should be noted that not every soul who spies this Eden is as affected with awe and wonder as I. Verily, as the country is besieged by gold fever, the scenery is ignored, nay, lamented and scorned, as men assault Victoria in the hunt for precious metal. Melbourne, our young state capital, has emptied her populace into the gold fields of our western district. Indeed, only recently, Melbourne's police force was reduced to a mere two men! Here they are in droves, with high hopes and heavy tools, tearing the earth apart with a demon's lust. The law is stretched and ambiguous, with yesterday's defendant as today's officer. Bushrangers incite fear amongst the diggers. By Jove, what a state the country is in!

Yet, this turmoil affected me and my own only lightly. My farm had and still has, its fair share of drifters and swagmen, but these folks are mostly honest men trying to get by in a hard world. There is always wood to be chopped and sheep to be sheared, and so it well behoves me to feed a fellow who is willing to work. Indeed, if the good Lord hast made us in his own image, then when gazing upon our own reflection, we are in fact peering into the very countenance of our own heavenly judge. In that case, may all men see a charitable and benevolent fellow when they peer into the looking glass!

Amongst my permanent staff were two men, to whom I owe a debt that can never be repaid this side of heaven. They were Dougal MacDougall, and Cameron MacAllister.

These recondite Scotsmen were ere side by side, whether they were out in the paddocks herding or fencing or sitting down at the dinner table. They were as hard as men have to be out here, yet there was always a twinkle of humour in their eyes and a dry jest upon their lips. However, for all their similarities, these two men were not mirrored souls. To begin with, Dougal was handsome, but Cameron was supernaturally striking. Dougal was over six feet tall and broad, with long russet-brown hair – of true highland warrior stock. However, Dougal's proud, muscular appearance and saturnine countenance were softened somewhat by a spiritual gentleness. A phrenologist would easily conclude from Dougal's high forehead, keen hazel eyes and prominent nose that he was a man of shrewd intellect and strong character. Cameron, on the other hand, was lither, with a roguish, playful animation. Everything about his appearance was pleasing and symmetrical. His eyes were wide and azure with cheerful flashes of light. He had a strong jaw and an aquiline nose. His raven hair played over his shoulders in luxurious locks.

Cameron was a man for the ladies. In fact, it was rumoured that he had had his way with more than one of the ladies about the district, without too much consideration of their marital status – or his own, come to that. Cameron married young to a rather plain, lachrymose girl called Alison. With her, he fathered a son called Andrew, who was approaching Gerald's age of ten years.

Dougal and Cameron were recommended to me by Cameron's own cousin, the beautiful Valeria Mac-Allister. The family resemblance was unmistakeable, both being uncommonly fine specimens of human folk. Cameron and Valeria both caught the eye of the opposite gender, and often their poor hearts as well. My own son Michael fell in love with the dear girl, as we all did. Valeria was a rare gift upon the earth.

My eyes moisten as I think of Valeria, and my own gentle child Michael. I was forever reprimanding Michael for his childish optimism and dreamy ways. Edith was ever protective of the boy, and to my chagrin encouraged the wild flights of fancy to which he was prone. True, Michael did not shy away from his chores, but his notions were always whimsical and impractical. I remonstrated with him on many stern occasions, that his romantic idealism would put neither food in his belly nor cloth on his back. However, he was incorrigible, and in truth, I think that made him all the dearer to me.

It is said that the Lord protects fools – and I

often quoted this to Michael whenever the contrast betwixt he and Valeria was remarked upon. For whilst Michael was winsome and carefree, Valeria had a level mind and a practical nature. Yet, I concede that they complimented each other perfectly. Betwixt the twain the sum of human virtue was in abundance, with one the balance for any deficit in the other. How sorely my old heart misses them both.

It was Dougal who found them away off in the bush, attended by a gruesome pack of dingoes. With an anguished roar and one shot from his rifle, Dougal saw off the dreadful mongrels. His rage was heard three miles away back at my farm. A chill crept into my very soul when I heard that piercing, tumultuous sound. With one alert look, Cameron signalled to me to be upon my horse and away after him to the source of the distress.

When we arrived, we found Dougal there on his knees, weeping. Soon we joined him in the most awful grief, for our loved ones lay slaughtered before us.

An eternity passed within half an hour, and slowly a most detached coolness overcame the three of us. We began to examine the terrible scene and form plans for the bodies.

Suddenly, as Dougal knelt beside the body of Michael, his eyes fell upon something that sent him into a new rage.

"Look! There is more afoot here!" He growled, his keen hazel eyes ablaze with suspicion.

"I'm with ye, Dougal!" Cameron exclaimed, as his azure eyes fell upon what had so agitated his companion. "Nae tyke ever slit a man's thrapple!"

"What are you saying, men?" I thundered wildly.

Dougal was quick to elucidate. "See here, Mr. Dubrelle. Ye mark the cut about the thrapple there? T'was nae tyke's tooth that made such a cut, sir. That ye can well ken. Bloody murder has been done here!"

"There's more here, Dougal!" Cameron shouted. "I ken young Gerald may yet be alive! Do ye not mark his footprints there!"

"Aye, right you are man, there they are in sooth. And I'll wager those other prints are those of our enemy. So, it is kidnapping as well, is it? Damn me if his blood will not be upon my dirk by morning!"

"There are no horse tracks, men!" I added, hot blood simmering in my veins. "The scoundrel was on foot! How many men were involved do you think?!"

Dougal, Cameron and I scanned our surrounds wildly, and finally concluded that there were only two sets of prints: those of a man and our Gerald.

"The poor child!" I wailed.

"With respect, Mr. Dubrelle, sorely as it distresses us, we cannae afford to grieve whilst Gerald remains unrescued and his kidnapper unpunished." Dougal opined in a firm but gentle tone. His face was hard, but his eyes still had a tender concern in them.

It was always a marvel to me how Dougal reconciled two such contrary qualities in his personality and manner. Even his voice, which was deep and guttural, also had a quiet and mellow timbre, like a low note on some old wooden instrument.

"He's right, sir." Cameron added in his contrasting, bell-like voice. "We must hie back to farm to fetch water and supplies and be away after them."

Dougal had fetched our mounts as Cameron continued to try and comfort me. I set my inflamed emotions aside and focused my resolve to the hunt before us.

"Right you are, men." I concurred. "We are away this very minute!"

Hurriedly preparations were made back at the farm. Cameron saw to the horses and supplies, whilst Dougal and I saw to the hands and family. Trusted men were sent to fetch Michael and Valeria. Awful wailing could be heard from the women inside the house.

I chose for this adventure, the best horse I had. His name was Vernon, and he had been with us on the farm for six years. He was a chestnut gelding fifteen hands high, with a white star on his forehead. Vernon was an obedient but proud horse. Sensing my distress, he allowed me to saddle him and tighten the girth without his usual mischief of inflating himself.

"We will return successful." Dougal announced resolutely, as he saddled his own horse, a roan gelding called Bronson. Then he espoused his clan motto. "*Buaidh no bas*". It means 'conquer or die'. He said it without arrogance or rage. It seemed that he thought his motto were as unavoidable and binding as every other law of nature.

I knew that Dougal meant those words with his very soul, as I spied a sword in a sheath upon his back.

"Is that a sword you have there, Dougal?" I asked respectfully, showing my surprise at his possession of such a weapon.

"Aye, sir, that it is. An old family possession. Cameron has one much the same. For sooth, Mr. Dubrelle, when my grandfather passed mine down to me, he dinnae ken that it would ever be used in battle again but find some safe harbour on a mantel above a fireplace. Until this very hour, my mind was in sympathy with his."

Suddenly a lyrical, youthful voice called out behind us. It was none other than Gerald's playmate and Cameron's son, Andrew. He was a tanned, skinny boy with his father's raven locks and sapphire eyes.

"I'm comin' with ye." The boy announced resolutely. Seeing him nearly brought tears to my eyes again, as I thought of Gerald. Oh! My poor boy! His laughter was fresh in my ears from breakfast that very morning. Suddenly the clearest image of him accosted me. His rosy cheeks, and bright blue eyes, and the morning sun golden in his curls. Yet, I mastered my feelings and looked sternly at little Andrew.

"Nae, lad." Cameron answered him. "You are to stay here and see to your mother."

"Gerald is my friend. I will not stay here when he is in trouble." Little Andrew rejoined.

"You will mind ye father's words and hie back inside." Cameron glared.

Andrew seemed uncertain and anxious. Yet he did not move. "No." Said he, finally, bracing himself for rebuke.

"No?" Cameron rejoined with incredulous anger. "Is this how you respect your father, then?"

"I respect you father, but I respect my duty to my friend as well. It is a matter of honour, sir."

Cameron sighed, yet the faintest twinkle of pride danced in his brilliant eyes. It was mirrored by Dougal. Cameron turned in the saddle to his comrade.

"This is your doing, Dougal."

Dougal grinned. "He has a strong sense of honour, Cameron." He then addressed Andrew. "Now see here, lad. Ye have honour and courage, that we well ken. Yet there is more needed in battle than a brave heart and a good cause. One needs strength in his arm and wisdom in his head – and ye are too young to possess either. Mark your father's words and stay inside. And remember that part of honour is obedience to ye parents."

"I can help ye." Andrew answered. "I know what he looks like. I saw him just the other day."

"You dinnae ken what ye speak of, Andrew." Cameron barked dismissively. "We ha'e no time to waste, now do as yer told!"

"It was a black man. He had dingoes with him." Andrew persisted.

We stared at him astonished.

"When did you see this, Andrew?" I interjected.

"Two days ago, at the edge of the bush over there." He pointed towards the southwest paddocks.

"Why did you not say anything about it before now?" I asked hotly.

Andrew looked pale and embarrassed. He bowed his head and his long dark fringe covered his eyes. "I dinnae say anything...because it was a secret between Gerald and I."

"Gerald saw him and the dingoes, too?!" I exclaimed.

Andrew nodded sadly. "Aye, sir. We dinnae ken any danger. He spoke with us and let us pat them. He said around here, the blacks call them warragul. I'm awful sorry, Mr. Dubrelle. But I thought it would be alright, because Gerald was going to take his parents to meet him." Suddenly Andrew began to sob bitterly.

Our hearts softened at the sight.

"Bear up now, lad." Dougal soothed.

Suddenly his eyes lit up with a new conviction. Dougal frowned and exhaled as a case made itself in his mind. He turned to me.

"Mr Dubrelle, I believe it prudent to take the boy with us. He is a good lad, as ye well ken, and he'll give us no trouble. Is that not so, Cameron?"

Cameron hesitated, but eventually nodded to his companion.

"Why do you suddenly wish the boy to come with us?" I asked searchingly.

"I ken it is best." Dougal answered gently, but resolutely.

Dougal was a strange and spiritual soul – but a man of sagacity, whom commanded obedience – even from his superiors. I trusted his judgement even when his speech was ambiguous.

"Very well." I conceded. "You shall come with us, Andrew. I know you can ride a horse by yourself, but I want you to ride with your father on his horse. And you must heed instruction, do you hear?"

We thundered back to the scene of the atrocity, taking great care to avoid the exact place, so as to spare Andrew the gruesome sight. We quickly identified the tracks and followed for about half a mile or so, until they intersected with a rough dirt road that wound through uncleared scrub.

"Their tracks do not continue through the bush but disappear into these going along this road." Cameron concluded, after carefully examining the scene before us.

"I'm agreed." Dougal murmured seriously, his eyes narrow in thought. "A company on horseback, not long passed through. The marks are clear, as this is a disused road. I'll wager there were other men waiting with a horse for the kidnapping murderer. I dinnae ken how many. They went this way not more than a few hours hence – and we must be away after them directly! Andrew, ye must stay close to Mr. Dubrelle and if there is trouble ye must stay with him and leave the fighting to ye father and me."

Without another word we spurred our horses down the track. I remember the queer, forboding feeling that accosted me as we clattered along that winding tunnel of eucalyptus trees. Ominous dusk was now less than an hour away. The trees were full of shrieking white parrots, the little corellas, and their calls reverberated around us like a battle cry. After half an hour or so of heavy riding, Dougal suddenly signalled for us to slow down and finally stop.

He turned to face us, and his eyes were wide with a wild longing for revenge.

The sun had only just set, and finally silenced the birds as the first stars appeared.

"Until we know the number of our enemy, we must err on the side of caution." Dougal opined with quiet command. "They must be near here setting up camp for the night, as ye can well conclude from that lonely column of smoke o'er yonder. However, if we thunder along our present course, the clattering of our hooves will soon be within ear shot of them, and they will likely set up an ambush."

"There's sense in such reckoning." Cameron agreed. "If we should be outnumbered, it is better that the surprise be on our side."

As he finished speaking, Dougal had dismounted and approached me.

"Let us find a secluded camp near here, Mr. Dubrelle, and tie up the horses. Cameron and I shall advance on foot as scouts and try to get an estimation of them."

I concurred with his notion of setting up camp and keeping Andrew well out of danger. However, I remonstrated with him on the point of who should stay with the boy.

"Dougal, whilst I do not doubt the courage of Cameron and yourself and know that your love for Gerald is without question, he is my kith and kin. I cannot sit idly by a campfire, when I could be out effecting his rescue. Nay belay your objections, men. I will have my way in this."

"With submission, Mr. Dubrelle, I am loth to confound your will, sir. But pray, who is to watch over the lad, in case of wild dingoes or a back-tracking bush-ranger?" Dougal answered mildly.

"You or Cameron can well answer the need, Dougal. I would not choose betwixt you for company on this venture, but I will not replace one of you in the office of minding Andrew."

"I can take care of myself." Andrew interjected indignantly.

"Andrew, stay out of this." Cameron warned.

"But I can fight." The boy pleaded.

"Ye will stay here and that's final."

"I'm coming with you!" Andrew shouted stubbornly. "And you can't stop me!"

Before he could blink, Andrew received a mighty clout on the back of the ear from Dougal.

"Ye will mind ye father's words and hold ye tongue!" Dougal growled.

Andrew was in shock at first, and then he began to bawl.

Cameron and I sighed, but the discipline was warranted.

Dougal's features softened at the sight.

"Listen to me, Andrew. It hurts me to see ye grieve so bitterly. But it is better ye cry now, than me cry later."

"I just want to help." The boy wailed petulantly.

Andrew's light, childish voice awakened a sudden paternal protection in me. How his strong conviction contrasted with his vulnerable little body! As I eyed his scrawny frame, I was reminded suddenly, and unpleasantly, of my own particular physical inadequacies for battle. Whilst I considered myself a healthy and sanguine fellow, I was well beyond my prime in vigour and strength of arm. The tobacco pipe had long ago left me short of breath, as I frequently discovered after the mildest physical exertion. Even then, as I stood beside my horse after the evening's frantic ride, I could feel my legs quaking underneath me, and the muscles in my back tensing painfully.

The two Scotsmen considered me in my tired and conflicted rumination with patient compassion. It was Cameron who finally breached the impasse.

"Ye are a man of brave and powerful spirit, sir. I would be a fool to opine otherwise. Yet, with submission, sir, it is powerful limbs needed for the battle ahead, and whilst I dinnae doubt ye possessed such in your youth, it is Dougal and I that possess that advantage now. And before ye offer rebuttal, sir, pray consider this. The office of minding Andrew is of no small import – to me, particularly, as he is my own bairn. Do ye not think it just, sir, that as I gang in pursuit of your kith and kin, ye stay here and look to the safety of mine?"

So were the shrewd and diplomatic words that persuaded me.

"Very well." I concluded most reluctantly. "May God be with you, men."

VISITORS IN THE NIGHT

IT WAS one of the longest nights of my life. My body protested fatigue, whilst my mind hurtled through a thousand nightmares. I looked for comfort and clarity in the campfire, whilst little Andrew stared wistfully through the canopy at the stars. Neither of us breathed a word.

Gradually, though, a sort of peace descended upon us. It was totally involuntary. The human soul cannot stand forever in the hurricane of agitation, but must eventually, for some time at least, step into the eye of the storm and take a moment's ease. The horses had settled, and the crickets and frogs of the bush soothed us with their ancient lullaby.

For some indefinite time, both Andrew and I fell asleep.

· · ·

Suddenly, I was very conscious of my thirst. I awoke instantly and took in my surroundings. The fire was very low. Andrew was shivering as the crispness of night began to settle upon us. Blearily I searched for some fuel for the fire, and found a dry, leafy clump of scrub. I set it upon the coals, and the flames leaped up and suddenly threw a wide, bright circle of light about our camp.

What I saw astonished me.

We were surrounded by glowing green and yellow eyes.

Dingoes. Maybe a dozen or more of them.

How silent and intense they were!

I realised with a shiver that they had been watching us from the shadows us as we slept. Furthermore, until I had stoked the fire, they were totally undetectable.

Why hadn't the horses stirred? I looked over to where they were tethered. They had moved closer together and their ears were back – but they were not particularly distressed. Vernon, my proud, strong steed, was likely a calming influence on the other two.

The dingoes continued to stare eerily.

I noticed one in particular – old and scrawny he was, with bright orange eye shine. Unlike the others, he sat perfectly still and stared right into my very soul.

As much as it unnerved me to take my eyes of this

old fellow, I reached for my rifle. When I turned to face him again, he had gone. I loaded my weapon and the other dogs stirred nervously. Suspiciously they eyed me, as I glared at them, carefully considering which one to shoot first.

Then, at some unknown behest, the dingoes suddenly trotted away with haste into the bush and were gone.

No sound remained to comfort me, but that of the crackling flames.

A lonely hour went by, and it was time for me to stoke the fire again. I watched anxiously for those horrible, glowing eyes, but nothing was revealed as the shadows retreated away from the leaping yellow light.

"What is it?" Asked Andrew sleepily.

"Nothing to worry yourself about lad, I was just stoking the fire."

"That's good. I'm freezing over here, Mr. Dubrelle."

"Well then, Andrew." I smiled, grateful for his company. "It's time for you sit with me by the fire and have a cup of tea. I'll fetch the billy and the water. We'll have a nice brew while we wait and try to get our spirits up. We'll need to be refreshed for what may await us later in the night."

We sipped our tea and stared into the flames,

both of us lost in our own private ruminations. In the distance we thought we heard shouting, but we could not be certain.

Then we heard rifle fire. We both tensed.

"Now lad, don't fret." Said I. "That sound may be that of our victory. We'll wait a while and see if they return before we decide what else to do."

Finally, our companions materialised wraith-like from the shadows of the bush. Our relief was short-lived, for Gerald was not among them.

"The battle's not over yet, but we have news." Dougal announced.

Then to my astonishment, an old Chinese man stepped into the fire light.

THE BUSHRANGERS' TALE

DOUGAL RECOUNTED to us the adventure upon which he and Cameron were recently engaged. I shall tell it now in my own words.

As the two Scotsmen advanced stealthily upon the camp, they heard a tremendous commotion. There were shouts and jeers and drunken laughter. As they stole ever closer, they soon saw what the ruckus was about.

Bushrangers.

They were a group of five outlaws. Their clothes ragged and filthy, and their beards long and unkempt. There they were drinking and sharing out the loot they had recently acquired from some unfortunate district.

Our companions considered the group of

scoundrels carefully before Cameron whispered to Dougal.

"They are criminals, but are they our quarry?"

Dougal considered the group carefully, then his keen eye fell upon something that boiled his blood.

"Aye, they are our quarry." He rumbled. "Do ye not mark that cap upon that man nearest the fire, there?"

"Which one? Oh aye! Look at that. His cap is a size too wee for him, Dougal." Cameron answered coolly.

"Aye...Tis Gerald's cap and that's no mistake. But what have they done with him? I dinnae see him among them."

"We'll not have our answer hiding here. Shall we wait until they sleep, or shall we surprise them now?"

Dougal drew his sword. "I'll have my answer sooner rather than later, Cameron."

A sudden shout arrested their attention.

"What the devil is happening over there?" Cameron breathed.

A new figure stepped out of the shadows. He was an old Chinese man, most likely from a family of gold miners. His stature was short, yet dignified, with a tanned, serious face and shining, black almond eyes. His white beard was long and neat.

It soon became evident to the Scotsmen that this character was a prisoner. The men stood about him jeering and threatening him with rifles and mining implements.

"Tell us where ya family's minin'!" A lanky, and dark-haired figure demanded, before calling him names that decency forbids me to repeat.

"He probably doesn't speak English, Ted." A gaunt, sneering red-head answered. "But I wanna hear 'im say somethin' anyway, eh? I like a good conversation. Go ahead chink. Don't be shy now. Say something. My name is Roy O'Leary, a gunner for the infamous gang of the Dingo. Ya heard of the dingos? 'course ya have. Who hasn't, eh boys? What's your name? Say somethin'!"

The old man remained coldly silent.

"He'll either *say* somethin' or *scream* somethin'." Another brooding ruffian announced, drawing a stock whip. His cronies laughed derisively, as this criminal stepped centre stage.

Dougal described him as 'a lupine predator, with malice towards the weak, but mere petulance to the strong'. Later I saw the fellow myself and sympathised highly with that description. He was a dirty blonde with cruel grey eyes and he had a wiry, skulking aspect. The pitiable school bully allowed to grow into a man, without the proper correction of the cane.

"Do ya hear that, chinko?" The one called Roy leered. "This here's the leader of the pack. Hank Hammond. *The* Dingo o' Fiery Creek. He wouldn't think twice about guttin' an old chink. So why don't ya show 'im how well ya can speak English, eh? Tell us about the gold. We know you chinks are good at findin' our gold..."

"Enough talk." Growled Hank. "Stand aside whilst I whip this chink to within an inch of his life."

The old Chinese man stood his ground with quiet dignity. His black eyes considered his persecutors with a patient contempt.

Just as Hank raised his arm to strike with the whip, he felt cold steel beside the tender skin of his neck, just under his scraggly beard.

"Put the whip down, there's a good doggy." Cameron crooned laconically into the Dingo's ear. By Jove, how his brilliant blue eyes must have sparkled!

"You're a dead man." Muttered Hank sourly.

"We're all dead men, sooner or later. Which shall it be for you?"

"You're outnumbered, friend." Hank smirked. "Five to one."

As he finished speaking, Dougal strode out from behind a tree. The nearest bushranger turned just in time to receive the full force of Dougal's right fist. The wretch fell to the ground instantly and remained still.

"Now it's four to two." Dougal announced matter-of-factly.

Hank glared at Dougal petulantly. "What do you want with us? We got no quarrel with you men."

"Is that so?" Dougal growled menacingly, his hazel eyes piercing. "Well it so happens that *we* have a quarrel with *you*..." Dougal drew his sword and pointed it squarely at Hank's heart. "If ye speak one false word, man, I'll run ye through. Now...ye slavering companion there has a cap that belongs to one of our lads. Ye best have a good explanation as to how ye come to have it."

"I dunno what you're talking about." Hank answered defiantly. He then yelled as the point of Dougal's sword cut half an inch into the flesh of his bosom.

"Don't vex him." Cameron warned. "And don't vex me either. A wee cut like that to the thrapple and ye're at hell's gate, man."

Hank, petrified now, began to babble to the Scotsmen. "We never harmed the lad, did we boys? Honest, sirs, we didn't touch a hair on his head."

"Explain...*fast*." Dougal glowered.

"It was an old coon, ya hear? A crazy old nigger with a funny walk. We had nothin' to do with it. We found the two of them on the road. We tried to rescue him! Didn't we, men?"

"A LIE!" Roared Dougal.

"The TRUTH!" Hank wailed. "We're thieves — there's no denying that! But we haven't kidnapped no one yet!"

"And why would a cowardly loon like you care to rescue a boy?" Cameron asked with incredulity.

"We didn't think it right that no black should get away with kidnappin' a white!" Hank protested.

"How did he get away from ye, then?" Dougal barked. "There are five of ye to one old black. Don't tell me he bested the lot of ye!"

"On my mother's grave I swear that we tried to rescue the lad. But that old nigger – and this is the lord's own truth – that old nigger is magic. He could kill a man with a word, we seen it with our own eyes!"

"What a pathetic wretch ye are! Cameron, there'll be hemp about this craig before sunrise."

"Wait!" Called Ted, suddenly. "Ease up, men, ease up. He's tellin' the truth. Let me speak, I'll tell you what happened."

"Out with it!" Cameron growled.

"Alright...easy now, and please listen." Ted implored insipidly. Hygiene and nutrition may have made a comely fellow of this wayward lad – if only his phrenology had not predisposed him to criminal vice. Whilst his pale face was an open and honest one, he had a weak and undeveloped chin, which left him susceptible to unwholesome influence. His blue eyes hinted at a once potentially keen intellect too, but a lack of proper education had depreciated this original virtue to mere cunning. It was clear that he hid his eyes, the window to the soul, behind his dark oily fringe, that men might not mark the shadow of sin within them.

"First of all, we found that cap along the road, see?" Ted began. "And we knew it had only just recently been dropped there, so we thought we'd trot along the road a bit faster and see if we could get a glimpse of who left it."

"Ye were hoping to rob somebody else, as likely as not." Dougal interrupted with a sardonic grunt.

"I'll not argue with that, sir. We are what we are. But let me finish our tale. Sure enough, after a short ride we spy this old black hobblin' along the road and he had a small boy with him. We thought it mighty strange, and as we came near, we realised that somethin' wasn't right with the lad. He was in a kind of trance or somethin'. He didn't answer us when we talked to him. He just stared, with his eyes facin' forward and empty, and his mouth was hangin' open. We surrounded them, and they stopped."

"And then?"

"And then, Hank says to this old coon 'what's this all about? What are you doin' with this young boy?' And the old black was just starin' at the ground, and we couldn't see his eyes, see? They were hidden in the shadows of his hat. So, Hank asks him again, and we got off our horses and walked right up to him. I had me rifle pointed square at him, as did Red and Ben. We had him surrounded. Still he didn't say nothin'. Hank was just about to knock him one when we heard this quiet sort of *hissing* noise..." Ted paused, measuring the effect of his tale on his stern audience.

"Hissing noise?" Cameron prompted.

"Yeah..." Ted continued in earnest. "We all looked to each other, wonderin' what it was...and then it happened. He lifts his head and stares at Hank with these bright, *orange eyes*..."

"Orange?" Dougal questioned.

"Bright orange." Ted shuddered, his eyes wide with fearful conviction. "I swear on my mother's grave – they were orange. Lads?"

The other bush rangers nodded seriously.

"Continue, then." Dougal commanded.

"Well, as I said he looked up at us with these orange eyes and says 'how nervous your horses are'... Sure enough, as soon as he said it, our horses started to get mighty restless and flighty. The whites of their eyes were showin', their ears were back, and we had trouble holdin' them. Then Roy says 'you're the one who should be nervous, mate'. The old coon just smiled, and his orange eyes kept rolling about like a bird or somethin'. Then he said somethin', I dunno, somethin' else about our horses..." Ted looked to his companions.

Another bushranger interjected. "He said 'horses are such sensitive creatures. They feel...but they don't *know*...horses simply...*wisely*...*react*.'" Dougal noted that this criminal had a thick Irish accent.

"Yeah, that's it." Ted nodded. "Red's got it right – he spoke just like that."

"Sort of with a well-to-do accent." Red added humbly.

"Yeah...yeah, that's it."

"A black with a 'well-to-do accent?" Dougal repeated incredulously.

"It is the truth, sir. Really strange to hear that from an old coon, you know?" Ted rejoined earnestly.

"Go on, then." Dougal barked.

"Well, after the nigger spoke, the hissing got louder and louder. Suddenly Roy's horse screamed and reared up. Then the old coon leant forward and said "They know what the hissing noise is...""

Ted seemed to struggle with the rest of his sentence.

"Well?" Cameron demanded.

"We dunno how...but suddenly we all saw that the bush around us was crawling with hundreds of snakes. None of us got a good look at any one snake in particular...it was as though the ground was just *crawling* with them, but you could only ever see them out the corner of your eyes. We weren't sure if we were seein' things or what...but we were powerfully scared. The horses all started to scream, and then Roy's horse up and bolted. We had just enough time to get up on the other horses, with Roy up with me on mine, before they too just bolted down the road after

Roy's horse." Ted waited patiently for the facts to make their mark in the Scotsmen.

Dougal looked hard into Ted, then he turned to Cameron. Cameron shook his head.

Dougal considered the wretch before him, and then the other bushrangers about him. They were all silent and pale, as their campfire crackled and the insects sung.

In that moment, Dougal felt the ring of truth and got goose pimples.

"You can doubt my character, and you can doubt my words, but I see that you don't doubt my fear." Ted added finally. "We were right scared of this old nigger, and that's the Lord's truth, plain and simple. We had no reason to go back to him."

Cameron chuckled derisively. "He takes us for a fool, Dougal." Suddenly he pushed Hank forward to the ground and sauntered past him to the unconscious bushranger. He reached down and retrieved Gerald's cap. "I'll take this, if ye dinnae mind, man." Said he and placed it upon his head. "What now, Dougal?"

Dougal sighed and sheathed his sword. "We find this old black. Speak up, men. To which direction was he headed when ye left him?"

Ted looked uncertainly to the red-haired ruffian. "We dunno, do we Roy?"

Roy seemed reluctant to answer. There was a petulant defiance in his eyes.

"Well?" Cameron barked with a laconic grin. "Speak up, lad! Did ye ken where the old black was headed or no? Out with it!"

Roy grimaced, attempting to smirk, but unable to hide his fear. "We reckon he was headed north."

"How so, then?" Dougal demanded.

"I dunno." Roy mumbled. "Somethin' to do with bein' a coon, I s'pose. Hank'll tell ya."

Hank looked sourly at his companion and then slowly stood up.

"There's this landmark a ways from here, see? Near Fiery Creek. Every year, about this time of year, all the blacks assemble there and trace out a strange shape. It's about thirty feet long, and ten or so wide. Some say it's a symbol to be read by the spirits in the sky...others reckon it's the outline of some sacred creature that died there a few years ago."

Dougal exchanged a grim look with Cameron, before he barked one final command to the motley crew. "Listen now and listen well! Henceforth ye are to depart the district – for very soon ye shall be reported to the authorities, and they will come hot upon ye heels with a length of hemp for every craig among ye. There is nae disputing this directive, and any skulduggery will be met with swift death. Furthermore, ye are to let the old Chinaman be free to gang about his way. You!" Dougal pointed at Hank. "Ye shall guide us to where these blacks are thought to congregate."

A tense silence followed Dougal's speech. No man was ready to either oblige or oppose him. Cameron stepped decisively forward to breach the impasse.

"C'mon Doggie!" Cameron clapped. "Rattle ye dags, my wee tyke. Ye have a new master now. Hop to it."

"I'm not goin' anywhere with you." Hank protested, suddenly.

"Then we shall run ye through. Do ye ken the district will miss ye?" Cameron rejoined.

Before Hank could answer, a quite whisper of voice interjected.

"I will show you where they go."

All turned, astonished, towards the old Chinamen.

"Yes." He announced with regal composure. "I speak English."

OUR NEW UNCLE

"That signalled the end of the discussion. We gave those bushrangers a final warning to be gone by sunrise and made our way back here with our new companion." Said Dougal as he concluded his tale.

"We are humbled and grateful to have you, Sir." I announced sincerely to the Chinaman. "May I inquire as to your name, friend?"

Cameron answered for the old fellow. "He dinnae gang by any name, Mr. Dubrelle. We have already well established that." A mischievous smile played upon his handsome face.

"No name?" I expostulated. "Come now, gentlemen, don't be absurd. These circumstances are trying enough."

The Chinaman answered me in a quiet but assertive voice. "A name is rope around soul. I have left all rope behind." He smiled at me suddenly, and it was a beautiful, disarming smile. "You may call me Uncle."

An involuntary laugh escaped my lips.

"Uncle, you say!" I exclaimed. "By Jove! I am far too old to have an uncle! I'm too old to have a mother and father, come to that!"

I was attracted to this unaccountable old Chinamen from that moment on. A decent, wholesome wisdom, coupled with a humble self-possession, seemed to exude from the very centre of the man. His eyes were astonishingly dark, but it was a pleasant darkness, akin to a warm summer night. It seemed that tiny stars shot across that night when ever a smile was hinted at upon his lips. Wrinkled as he was, he was yet hale, lean and hygienic. There was a marked contrast betwixt his body and soul: whilst his countenance bespoke a lifetime of cares, an eternity of peace was his.

"Very well." I conceded, pacified somewhat by the good nature of our new companion. "I shall call you Uncle, if it pleases you as much as it suddenly pleases me." A chuckle escaped me then and took me by surprise. I was so weary.

"What about the bushrangers?" Little Andrew asked with awe.

"Yes, what of the bushrangers?" I inquired eagerly. "Surely they did not submit to your authority without protest?"

Cameron chuckled. "Dougal here, has a commanding presence. They dinnae stir a foot to stop us. Aye, they fired a few shots into the air with their rifles, but it was an empty, cowardly gesture. As best as we ken, they were in no mood to follow us back here."

"Well." I sighed. "We'd best start on our way. Uncle, I understand you must be sorely tired, but we must move in all haste – my very own Grandson is in mortal danger. When this horrible adventure has concluded, I shall reward you as handsomely as I can."

My new-found old Uncle made a submissive bow and added solemnly. "I too am in fear for the boy. However, he is not in danger now. I know where he is, and we cannot reach him now. I suggest rest."

"Rest you say!?" I bellowed. "Absolutely not! I demand to know where my grandson is, right now!"

Old Uncle raised a placating hand. "I understand urgency. I want to find grandson quickly too."

"Is that so? You want to find my grandson quickly too? Why is that? What is he to you? No, we shall not delay!" I thundered.

The Chinaman suddenly approached me and looked right into my eyes.

"Your son, Michael, was a dear friend to me." He said with deep melancholy. "It was I who gave him the opal."

I was astonished at this development. A connection snapped into place for me.

"You were friends with Michael! You are Uncle – *the* Uncle. Yes, I have heard of you! You are a solitary hermit who sometimes traded with Michael and some others on the farm!"

Old Uncle inclined his head with a shy smile. "Yes."

"In fact, you gave us some seeds recently, some lovely greens."

"Yes. I have small garden."

"Oh! Why have we not met before?" I expostulated with shame.

"I prefer not to be with people." Old Uncle answered seriously.

"But surely our paths have crossed before now? Cameron, Dougal?"

"He looks a little familiar." Cameron shrugged. "But how are we tell one Chinaman from another? They are like sheep, ye cannae tell them apart."

"Cameron!" I rebuked.

He laughed defensively. "Why can I tell ye? Tis how it is."

"I have not seen him up close, but I do recall Michael had an old friend in the bush, who is Chinese." Dougal added.

"Well, Uncle, I am much relieved to know that you are indeed a true friend of this family. But tell me, how can you be so certain that Gerald is safe? And where he is being taken?' I asked.

Old Uncle nodded understanding.

"The black man can not harm the boy yet. He will take him to where the monster died many year ago. That is day ride from here. Now, many black people camping there, and the old black man is afraid of them. Therefore, he will wait until they leave, which is not tomorrow, but day after. Then he will approach where monster died and try his magic."

"Magic?!" I scorned.

"Tis nae magic to us, Mr. Dubrelle." Dougal answered. "Cameron and I have already spoken at length with our new Uncle. This old black is after something wee Gerald has. However, he cannae take it from him at present due to superstitions peculiar to the black race. Tis the old black's belief that the death place of the monster is where a spell can be broken."

"The death place of the monster!?" I expostulated.

"Aye, Sir. I am sure ye have heard of it." Dougal began.

However, the answer came to me and I interrupted him.

"Gerald is being taken to the Bunyip of Fiery Creek!"

"Aye, that we ken, Mr. Dubrelle." Cameron answered. "That is why we suggest that we heed our new Uncle's advice, and rest here for the remainder of the night. Tomorrow we shall make for Fiery Creek and lay in ambush for this old black."

After much deliberation and discussion, it was just this plan that our company settled upon.

By Jove, what a day had passed! Two brutal murders, a frantic ride, bushrangers, a witch doctor and a bunyip! Each seemed more fantastic than the last!

Could the bush-rangers have really been spooked by the magic of a witch doctor? Or being ignorant and vulgar, were they merely inflamed by their suspicious and over-active imaginations? It seemed highly probable to me, that an uneducated criminal would be more than usually susceptible to paranoid delusions.

Finally, what of this sacred site – the Bunyip of Fiery Creek? Was there ever such an animal in existence – or was this too, merely folk-lore and legend?

Our camp talked over these things long into the night.

Eventually, despite our restless souls, sleep came upon us all, with a little help from a pungent, foreign tea brewed for us by our strange new Uncle. Even so, we slept but a few hours, and it was a fitful sleep at best.

THE HEIRLOOM

AT THE SOFT hint of dawn, magpies warbled mellifluously, and currawongs echoed through the scrub with their uniquely pleasant calls. I stirred in my warm swag, with the chill of night upon one side of my face and on the tip of my nose. With consciousness, came a sudden and awful remembrance of where I was. Before I arose, however, I overhead a startling conversation betwixt two very familiar voices.

"Dougal hear reason. The opal by rights belongs to my cousin's next of kin." I heard Cameron implore. "Tis nae bonnie lad's trinket – tis the wealth of my ain family."

Dougal answered in a soothing, but firm timbre. "Tis better we secure the lad first and consider the proper owner of the opal second."

"Dougal, there's nae disputing that. I just want to know whether I can count on ye when the time comes, to back the just cause."

"The just cause is that the opal shall pass onto its owner's next of kin – which is clearly young Gerald."

"And if wee Gerald should, may heaven forbid, be unable to claim his inheritance?"

"Then perhaps it should best reside with the boy's grandfather."

"Pah! Tis nae muckle sense in that, Dougal! Inheritance should gang to the next generation, nae the one e'en closer to the grave. Ye ken that as well as I."

Dougal sighed. "I dinnae understand ye heatedness, Cameron. Tis all speculation."

"We have a real chance to track down a better future for a' families, Dougal. Do ye nae ken? If wee Gerald is nae found alive, sure as hell we'll find this old black with his dirty hand upon this opal. Run him through, and the fortune is ours – as by rights it should be. I'm tired o' workin' like a tyke, with nary a pair of pennies to rub together."

"Calm down, Cameron. The stronger the words, the weaker the argument. If Gerald be nae longer with us, then perhaps the opal should be given to ye – but I'll nae gang into dispute with ye against Mr. Dubrelle over it. To my mind, ye eagerness for this opal is unbecoming. If the boy is alive, and I ken he still is, the opal is his, and that is final."

"Tis nae final, Dougal. I hope Gerald is alive, and

that we are permitted to confiscate the opal from him and put it to proper use. But make nae mistake, I will look after wee Gerald – he shall want for nothing for as long as I live."

I heard Dougal tense and then rumble through a whisper. "Cameron, ye are a disgrace."

"Spare me ye lecturing tongue, Dougal. I do what I ken best for my family."

"Ye do what ye ken best for ye own self." Dougal rejoined flatly.

"How dare ye?" Cameron gasped.

"Ye always do things that ye well ken make ye poor wife Allison cry."

"Dinnae bring her into this, Dougal. I warn ye."

"Ye dinnae have a pair o' pennies to rub together, because ye have drunk them all away – or given them over to other pretty faces. And some of those pretty faces belong to other men."

"Enough, Dougal!"

"And what about those other men, Cameron? Do ye not call some of them friend by the light of day, after sleeping in their bed with their wives when they're away at night?" Dougal continued with controlled contempt.

"All men are sinners. I have prayed for forgiveness." Cameron returned petulantly.

"Ye have prayed for opportunity – but it is the devil that has answered ye."

"Now see here, Dougal!" Cameron growled.

"Dinnae protest just rebuke, Cameron!" Dougal barked over him. "What will ye do, man? Call me a liar? Strike me down? I speak the truth, and it is ye own wickedness that has ye so inflamed. What of this opal? Why this sudden interest? Did ye nae ken wee Gerald possessed the thing?"

Cameron did not say anything, but his anger and shame shouted at Dougal through the silence.

"Nae..." Dougal began again, in a somewhat calmer tone. "Ye dinnae have knowledge of the opal in wee Gerald's hands. But know of it ye did. When it belonged to our poor Valeria."

A sudden pain gripped the two of them, as it did me who was listening in shock to this conspiracy.

"I dinnae wish any evil upon Valeria and Michael or poor wee Gerald." Cameron suddenly continued, suppressing a tremendous grief. "But aye, the opal was known to me. Valeria and I had a special bond, long before she fell in love with Michael, as ye well ken. The opal, was like an engagement present. The day after Michael had given it to her, she showed it to me. Aye, Dougal, it is like nothing ye have ever seen before."

"Aye, maybe so. But is such a trinket worth your honour?"

"Ye dinnae ken the thing, Dougal. Neither do I. It is something... wonderful. When ye look into it, ye feel the strongest joy and the strongest sorrow all at once. Valeria said to me, that the thing is like a tear of

God, that washes away despair and renews the love of the soul. Oh, aye, I felt that Dougal, as I gazed into that beautiful opal."

Dougal grunted noncommittally. He was probably as uncomfortable as I to hear such emotive and feminine dialogue from a man such as Cameron.

"Make nae mistake, Dougal." Cameron continued in a sterner tone. "Tis nae just poet's babble. Tis the Lord's own truth. The Holy Grail would not move a man more."

"And would ye sell the Holy Grail too, if ye came to possess it?" Dougal returned sardonically.

"I'll not speak any more of it to ye, man." Cameron answered petulantly. "But I shall expect more understanding from ye, when we recover the opal, and ye can look into it with yer own eyes."

Suddenly I heard both men tense. Somebody was stirring.

"Good morning, Dad. Good morning, Mr. Mac-Dougall." Little Andrew began sleepily.

"Good morning, Andrew!" Cameron rejoined heartily. "How long have you been awake then?"

"I don't know. I woke up when I heard you and Mr. MacDougall arguing. Is everything alright?"

"Of course, it is! Ye well ken how Dougal and I are wont to disagree. This morning is nae different from any other time. Is that not so, Dougal?" Cameron asked brightly.

"Aye, tis so, Andrew. Dinnae concern yourself.

The older the friends, the hotter the arguments." Dougal returned with a smile in his voice.

"Well, gentlemen!" Cameron announced. "Now that the best man among us is awake, we shall see about cooking breakfast."

THE RIDE TO FIERY CREEK

WITH A TIN CUP of steaming tea in my hands, eucalyptus in the air and a brightening morning, some of my strength slowly returned to me.

"Well, gentlemen. What is next?" I asked rather flatly. Perhaps it reflects poorly on me, but the conversation that I had overheard that morning had began to stir a great anger in me, that somehow strengthened my resolve.

The two Scotsmen considered each other.

"We shall follow the directions of our old Uncle to where the bunyip lay at Fiery Creek." Cameron answered with a shrug.

"And where is our fine old Uncle?" I asked, suddenly aware that he was not about the camp. "Don't tell me the old fellow has crept away in the night?"

My other three companions merely gave a knowing smile.

"He's still around, Mr. Dubrelle." Andrew answered brightly.

"Where?"

"Have a look behind you, through the trees in the clearing over there. He has been there since sunrise."

The three of them gave a gentle chuckle.

Sure enough, when I turned around, I spotted our Uncle. By Jove! What a peculiar spectacle!

"What on earth is he doing?" I expostulated.

Our Uncle appeared to be doing a slow, purposeful dance, the likes of which I had never seen. At first his posture seemed absurd – his legs were wide apart, and bent at the knees, whilst his palms were open, face up at his hips, and his shoulders were straight. Suddenly his legs moved in harmony with his arms, as he traced some invisible course around him. At times he would raise a leg on one side of his body, only to turn and do the same with his leg on the other side. At times his hands were open, at other times he would do specific gestures with his fingers.

"It's called Tai Chi." Andrew smiled. "I asked him while you were having breakfast, Mr. Dubrelle."

I continued to watch, and my confusion and bemusement slowly turned to wonder. The precision of his movements and their unending flow, one into another, began to charm me. I suddenly realised that what I was looking at was something highly practised and special, with an antiquity I could scarcely fathom.

Finally, our Uncle stopped, arriving smoothly to an upright and relaxed posture. His eyes were closed, and he exhaled slowly. After a moment, he opened his eyes and walked resolutely towards us.

"I am ready." He smiled quietly, with a pleasant bow.

The morning and afternoon that followed was upon reflection, a very pleasant affair. Despite our fears for Gerald, and our grief at yesterday's horrible scandal, the sun shone warmly upon our backs. The old Chinaman sat serenely in the saddle behind little Andrew.

The boy chattered away at our old Uncle, and he listened with gentle patience and quiet smiles. Our old Uncle wore none of the care and woe that so marked itself on all our faces.

"So, my new-found Uncle," I began, "How did you sleep last night?"

"Good, thank you." Old Uncle returned. His eyes were as dark and shiny as a sparrow's.

"That is remarkable. I slept rather badly, I must say. So, tell me...what brought you to the western district?" I thought my tone pleasant and congenial, yet the old man's expression saddened.

"I came with my family for gold. Like many Chinese. We seek gold to pay off debt in China. To make fortune for our house. We come to *Dai Gum San.* The Big Gold Mountain."

"Did you find what you hoped?" I asked.

"We find what we seek. But gold without can destroy riches within." Old Uncle answered and turned his sad dark eyes upon me.

"The love of money is the root of all evil." I conceded.

Old Uncle seemed impressed by the saying. "That is wise."

"The scriptures, my dear friend." I returned, piously. "Have you read them?"

Old Uncle shook his head.

"You should. They improve a man's hopes and character."

Old Uncle inclined his head politely.

"Uncle, please do beg my pardon, but I believe the time has come for you to tell me everything you know about the opal that you gave to Michael." I asked him resolutely.

Old Uncle considered me briefly, then spoke.

"I was mining for gold with my nephews. I had a wife and child, but they died many years ago. I lived with my brother and his two sons. When my brother died, he left his fortune to his sons. They were not good men. Soon, all fortune gone. With what is left we come here and seek gold. We mine deep and we work hard, but we did not find gold. Nephews fight and no longer work together. Much shame and sadness. Then my family divide and go separate ways. But the night before we all go, I had a dream about a dragon. Dragon long dead, and he had died with one tear in his eye. A crying dragon..."

Sad reflection filled Uncle's pause.

I prompted him to continue.

"Why do you think the dragon was crying?"

"I think...Dragon regret. In the dream, at his feet, I saw a giant gold nugget. The dragon, far from home, died with the gold he craved at his feet...and a single tear in his eye. So sad was he, that when he died, and his flesh disappeared, and he was only bones in the hard ground, still a tear remained."

"That is quite a dream. It is beautiful in some way." I said.

"In the dream, truth." Uncle replied.

"How do you mean?"

"In the morning after dream, I take a pick and dig some more. I found a large bone. For many days, I dig and find more bones. I dig with great respect. My nephews come back, and we all dig. I did not tell them about my dream. Then one day we find large gold nugget. This nugget...biggest ever found. We think, over two thousand troy ounce. We were all very happy. My nephews build special cart to carry nugget and they take it away. But I stay."

"Why did you stay?" I asked, though I felt I knew the answer.

"We found nugget, but still I have same dream." Old Uncle continued, reverently. "Dragon lie with tear in his eye. Family found gold, but we had not found all bones. The skull was still in rock. I wanted to dig up skull. I dig slowly and with much respect for many more days. One day, the old black man come, and he threaten me with bad magic. He say that dragon skull is bunyip skull. He say bunyip must stay in ground. I told him of my dream. Old black man was very interested. He told me that the bunyip tear contains great magic and that he will let me dig for it. So, I dig more and carefully bring the skull out of the ground. The skull was as big as a whole sheep and very heavy – I could not move it. I see opal in the skull. In the corner of one large round eye. It was shaped like a tear. I sat and thought about how to re-move opal. Then a storm come. Much rain and thunder. Lightning flash and the wind blow strong. I tapped the opal once...just once...with a small pick. The opal came loose, and it fell from the skull like a tear into my hand."

Through-out his tale, Old Uncle seemed to be reliving a most moving memory. At the end, he was holding his hand out as if to catch the jewel, and as his hand closed over, tears formed in his eyes.

"Uncle, that is a fascinating story." I replied. "But if the opal was so precious, why did you give it to Michael?"

Old Uncle wiped his eyes and continued. "I feel

magic in the opal. Strong destiny. The black man came again and demanded that I give him the opal. He pointed a bone at me and cursed me. But I would not give him the opal because he threatened me. My family left me alone, and they did not care for me anymore. They had biggest gold nugget ever found. I decided that I would keep the opal until I knew what else to do. I wandered the land, and I meditated. I focused on the opal, and in it, I saw the world. I came to understand through meditation and through my dreams that the opal was the world. I was an old man...and I am still an old man...what should an old man do with the world?"

"A deep question." I nodded thoughtfully.

"My nephews took the gold, and I hear nothing more from them. I don't want to know what happened to them. The price of that gold was so high that it made a dragon cry. And I had his tear. In tear, wisdom. Hard learned wisdom. One day, I got sick. For days, I could not move, and I starved. Then your son, a young man on horse, found me and gave me water. He gave me food..."

Here Uncle's tears welled anew. He wiped them away.

"You see?" He continued. "Years later, it makes me cry. I cry a little then. I had not had any kindness for so long, and here a stranger cared for me so much. So, we became friends. And one day, I thought I should give him more than my tears. I thought, I should give him the best tear that I have. I gave him the dragon's tear. I gave him the opal."

I am not lachrymose in the slightest, nor were my saturnine Scottish companions. Yet, all of our eyes moistened at his tale.

"Thank you, Uncle." I murmured. "Truly...thank you very much."

After sombre moments of reflection, I broke the silence again.

"So, Uncle, how far away is this magical place to which we are going?" I asked.

"We shall get there before night time. We will not be alone. The old black man will be watching us."

"And how are we to flush him out?"

Cameron answered the question. "We will lay in wait some distance from the spot, and when we have a clear shot, Dougal shall take him right between the eyes with his rifle."

"No!" I returned firmly.

"No?" Cameron returned, surprised.

"No. We are we not murderers, Cameron. We will follow the law."

"Mr. Dubrelle is right, Cameron." Dougal rejoined. "There's nae excuse for murder, lest it be in hot blood."

"No, Dougal – even in hot blood we shall not kill if we can possibly avoid it." I replied sternly.

Old Uncle nodded sagely. "For revenge, first dig two grave."

"Listen men. We will apprehend this fellow, and he shall be tried by the law. He is only one man. An old, black man at that. He will have neither wit nor weapons to match us." I announced.

Oh, by Jove! How those arrogant words would come back to haunt me!

THE DJAPWURRONG

THAT EVENING AS DUSK FELL, we literally stumbled right upon the sacred site that was to be the key to the success of our adventure. What a queer and sudden forboding came upon us!

The sun had set only moments ago, and as rosy dusk eased away the bright blue sky, and the white corellas screeched among the trees, all five of us were in a fatigued trance. We stood in a wide, grassy clearing, and by the sound of frogs we knew that water was not too far away.

There it was – the Challicum Bunyip – the legend of Fiery Creek. Or rather – the very spot where the mystical beast is said to have perished.

Few people had ever come there, since it was discovered nearly fifteen years previously.

"Djapwurrong." Mused Old Uncle.

"Pardon me?" I rejoined.

"The black men are from Djapwurrong clan. Every year they come. Every year they take spear, and trace shape in dirt and dig up grass. They dance sacred dance, and then sleep by two fires." The old Chinaman bowed reverently. "Here is where a monster died."

The shape had been traced very recently. The turf had been meticulously removed, and there were hundreds of footprints in the dust. I noted that there were two large campfires that had burnt out quite some distance away, in opposite directions. The fires were well over three hundred yards apart and were still smouldering.

The shape was most peculiar and ambiguous. It was about thirty feet long and approximated the shape of a fat necked emu or a seal, depending upon the angle at which it was viewed. In fact, it was entirely arbitrary as to which end of the shape was the head, as the stumpy legs appeared to come out from close to the middle of the animal – if indeed they were legs, and not flippers or some other appendage.

"Do you really think a bunyip died here, sir?" Little Andrew whispered in awe.

"Oh yes." Old Uncle replied. "This is sacred place. The men of Djapwurrong are wise. They show respect."

"I'm not so sure that I believe in the likes of a

bunyip." Cameron opined. "One might just as well believe in kelpies and banshees."

"The world is greater and more mysterious than ye and I shall ever ken, Cameron." Dougal returned. "Besides, if a man believes in an almighty god, or that certain gems have mystical properties, then, Cameron: there ought to be room in that man's imagination for an animal like the bunyip."

Cameron was visibly chagrined but said no more.

"In China, there is dragon." Old Uncle began. "He is fierce, strong, wise. Dragon live in mountains, away from men. Here, there is no dragon. Here there is bunyip."

Suddenly everybody tensed.

"We are no longer alone." Dougal announced harshly.

They appeared about us like shadows that had learned to stand upright and become independent of their source. I did a quick count – there were over thirty of them, and they all carried spears. They were aboriginal men of ages varying between about fifteen and forty. Their movements were smooth and silent, but not overtly hostile. Serious faces considered our party as they approached.

"Djapwurrong." Old Uncle observed, as if the approaching men were no more interesting than a flock of birds.

Suddenly, Old Uncle bowed and began to speak in a peculiar, nasal dialect.

He was given an answer, and after some exchange the men began to smile and laugh. One man in particular, a young fellow perhaps twenty, came up to our old Uncle and started to do a peculiar dance.

Andrew leaned into me and whispered excitedly. "Look Mr. Dubrelle – he is trying to do Tai Chi!"

As soon as Andrew had pointed this out, I recognised the movements immediately.

"By Jove, lad, I think you're right. So, our Old Uncle is a friend of these people."

Cameron made a disgusted scoff and spat.

The Djapwurrong and our old uncle conversed for the better part of half an hour. It was an amiable, and yet serious discussion that we were witnessing. I had encountered aboriginal men on my travels before, when I was driving oxen through the bush to the east. I had found that their favour was easily obtained with trades of flour, tea and tobacco. I rummaged through my pack to procure these things, but that proved unnecessary. The affair was concluded suddenly, and the men waved good-bye to us as they left hurriedly across the clearing and into the bush. Old Uncle bowed solemnly as they left.

"Well, Sir?" Dougal asked the old man keenly. "Was that a fruitful meeting?"

Old Uncle turned to him seriously, then to me and Cameron. "Djapwurrong were going to stay one more night here. But they are afraid."

"The old black?" Cameron asked.

"No. Another bunyip has come to this place." Old Uncle answered matter-of-factly.

"What?" We expostulated, almost in unison.

Old Uncle turned placidly and pointed west across the clearing. "Bunyip live in swamp. That way."

"How casually he points it out." Cameron sighed, raising his eyebrows. "One might think the existence of a bunyip no more fabulous than that of a horse."

"Oh..." Uncle smiled, then laughed gently. "No... many more horse than bunyip!"

Dougal took a practical approach with this new information. "Tell me, Sir – is the bunyip dangerous? Shall we gang from this place right away?"

Old Uncle became serious at once. "Bunyip like dragon. Bunyip watch...bunyip think. Bunyip is hunter."

"Very well, man, but what shall we do?" Dougal barked impatiently.

"Bunyip afraid of fire." Old Uncle answered calmly. "We can stay here and wait for old black man."

"Did those blacks say anything about the old black?"

"Yes. His name Dinewan. He is not from Djap-wurrong. He is magic man. And he has boy. Some of them think that he has summon bunyip. Others think that bunyip summon him."

Cameron gave a derisive sigh. "More magic?"

Old Uncle inclined his head. "Maybe not magic. Maybe just man. Maybe just beast."

"But you think that this old black man will come to this spot? Are you certain about it?" I asked earnestly.

"Yes." Old Uncle replied. "This spot magical for him." He then turned to eye Cameron seriously. "Maybe not magical for all men – but magical for old black man."

"How do ye know?" Cameron asked suddenly with suspicion. "Have ye known him before now?"

"I trust Djapwurrong." Was the rejoinder, and Old Uncle's dark eyes were resolute.

"Well, I *don't*." Cameron glowered menacingly.

"Cameron..." Dougal sighed.

"I've muckle reason to doubt the blacks, Dougal! That ye well ken! 'Twas only a few years ago that they murdered Ronald MacAllister near Port Albert!"

"Aye, murder has been done – by men both black and white. But this tribe is likely no relation to those who murdered Ronald, Cameron." Dougal rejoined.

"Besides," I added with indignation "the revenge killing at Warrigal Creek, done by none other than the men of Angus MacMillan, amounted to over a hundred and fifty bodies – women and children among them. It was an appalling massacre."

"Dinnae slander MacMillan, Sir!" Cameron protested.

"Don't speak so haughtily of what you don't know, Cameron!" I shouted back with sudden ferocity. Both men were startled into silence by my expostulation.

"I have a reliable account, from a credible witness who saw the massacre with his own eyes!" I continued hotly. "If those men involved had done to *animals* what they did to those poor souls, they would be hanged! Now, enough of this. Uncle, do you really trust that the Djapwurrong have told you the truth?"

Old Uncle nodded. "Yes."

"Then it settled." I announced. "We will set up camp and wait here."

THE MEETING WITH DINEWAN

OUR PARTY WAS SEPARATED into two camps. This was done at the behest of Old Uncle, who suggested that we follow the lead of the Djapwurrong tribe and maintain the two campfires that they had left to burn out. Old Uncle related to us that the Djapwurrong light two fires to represent two bright burning eyes, that watch over the spot where the bunyip had perished, and over to the swamp which was beyond the trees.

In the light of day, it appeared that either camp could see the other across the clearing, but this proved not to be so. The strange shape of the Challicum Bunyip was in fact traced at the top of a gentle rise, with each campfire parallel to it about a hundred and fifty yards away. Hence, when sitting about at either fire, the rise obscured the other camp.

It was arbitrarily decided that Cameron and me would camp by the western fire, with Old Uncle, Dougal and Andrew tending to the fire in the east. Our horses we turned loose into the clearing, knowing that they would not stray too far away.

Under different circumstances, our evening camp may have been considered a very pleasant affair. The fire was warm, the air was still, and the stars were bright. Our meat was tender and well cooked, and our billy provided plenty of hot tea.

However, of course, much weighed upon our minds that night. First and foremost, was our grief at the murder of Michael and Valeria, and our anxiety over the fate of young Gerald. Then there was our anger and our fatigue. Of course, we also had our doubts about Old Uncle, and whether or not this old aboriginal witch doctor truly had Gerald and would actually come to this spot.

Finally, in my own case, there were also my doubts about my companion by the fire, Cameron MacAllister.

Now that we were in isolation, with no other distractions, I found myself searching his features and reconsidering everything that I saw there. I had always regarded Cameron as a cheerful, hearty rogue – but ultimately honest and trust-worthy enough. However, the infidelities towards his wife Allison, and the unseemly passion that he evinced in trying to persuade Dougal to conspire with him that morning, disturbed me deeply.

Our conversation was polite and strained at first, before finally giving way to mutual silence. Cameron stared into the fire, and I stared into him. His eyes, normally so bright and blue, had darkened considerably, and I suspected a plotting mind behind them.

A few lonely hours passed, with nothing to break the silence but the crackling flames, and the warble of frogs from the swamp.

At some unknown hour, both Cameron and I awoke with a start.

"Good evening, gentleman. I am sorry to startle you." A sophisticated voice lilted from the shadows.

Cameron was on his feet in an instant with his rifle.

"Who goes there?" He asked in a low and authoritarian voice.

Who indeed!? Thought I.

"Steady, Cameron." I said, as my senses assembled themselves. "It may be a policeman."

"I am no policeman, Sir." Answered the voice. It was decidedly cultured and musical. "Indeed, from what I understand, there are very few policemen employed in this area. No, I am just a traveller, but I come in peace. I am looking for Mr. Dubrelle."

"You have found him." I rejoined, squinting into the darkness. "Please come forward into the light, so that I may see you, Sir."

The voice laughed gently. "Forgive me for keeping my distance in the dark. It is not meant as a disguise, but rather as a caution. I see that both of you are armed, and I do not want to be the victim of a tragic misunderstanding."

There was a brief silence as Cameron and I considered his words. In the shadows, I believed that I could make out his silhouette. He had a stillness of posture that was unnerving.

"You are not in danger, now." I announced, finally. "Please, Sir, step forward into the light."

I detected a slight inclination of the head, then he moved forward. His walk was most remarkable. He seemed to alternate between a stroll and a strut.

As he made his way into our circle of light, Cameron and I were astonished to discover that he was an aborigine.

A stockman's hat was upon his head, and the brim hid his eyes as he moved toward us. He wore long leather boots, into which he tucked his trousers, and he had a long shroud that appeared to be made of possum skins. When he finally reached us, he stood completely still and lifted his head. Bright orange eyes shone at us from the shadow of his hat.

Cameron exhaled sharply and remained rigidly

aiming his rifle at the old man. I was also alarmed and expectant.

Orange eyes considered us, rolling like those of an emu. His nose twitched perceptibly – then he began to sniff the air. He closed his eyes to consider the scent.

"Hmm. Yes, you are related to him." He mused finally, fixing his astonishing eyes upon me.

"Related to whom?" I answered, attempting to be calm despite the frantic beating of my heart.

The old aborigine smiled, and small, sharp white teeth gleamed in the fire light. "To the young boy, of course." He turned his attention to Cameron. "You too are related to him, aren't you? But more distantly, I think."

"What have ye done with the boy?!" Cameron cried. "Answer me now, or I will shoot!"

"I have done nothing to the boy." The old man answered indignantly. "It is forbidden to harm a child. No matter what tribe they come from."

"Do you know where he is?" I implored desperately.

"Oh yes." He answered with a smile. "He is quite nearby. He is quite safe. I did not bring him with me, of course. You may have been more bush-rangers. I did not want to expose the child to further risk. He has been quite traumatised, Sir. I pity him deeply, I really do."

"His parents were murdered." I announced, holding his gaze.

The aborigine sighed. "That is horrible. I am so sorry. That accounts for his behaviour completely."

"I don't trust him, Sir!" Cameron growled.

The old man's orange eyes seemed to darken, but then he smiled and gave a resigned shrug.

"Can you lead us to my grandson?" I asked plaintively. The sudden hope of his safe recovery brawled with my grief and uncertainty.

"Sir, he will lead us into a trap." Cameron warned.

"Be quiet!" I bellowed.

The aborigine raised a placating hand. "Gentlemen, please, there is no need for anxiety. I have something here to prove my goodwill."

Cameron and I tensed as the stranger reached into an animal skin bag under his shroud. He then threw something small at Cameron, who caught it eagerly.

The Scotsman let out a gasp of awe and surprise.

"What is it, man?" I inquired.

Cameron stared at the object in his cupped hands, then incredulously up into the stern face of the aborigine.

"It's Valeria's opal." He answered with awe.

"Gerald told me that you would recognise it."

"Who are you, Sir?" I asked.

"I am called many things. My tribe originally gave me the name of Dinewan."

"Very well, Mr. Dinewan. Where is my grandson?"

"He is nearby. Shall I take you to him?"

I should have been frantic with relief and gratitude. Yet, just then, a shudder went through me as though the night had suddenly chilled.

Then I heard a sound.

It was a small whine.

Cameron did not seem to hear it. "Mr. Dubrelle?"

"Hmm?" I answered, distracted.

"Did ye not hear what he said? He knows where Gerald is!" Cameron cried. "This opal is proof enough for me, Sir! Let us get the lad this instant and waste no more time about it."

"Mr. Dinewan..." I began, but not quite knowing what to say, my sentence died there.

The old aborigine continued to smile, but his eyes became piercing. "I understand. These last two days must have taken a heavy toll upon you. I assure you, Mr. Dubrelle, that your grief will soon be at an end."

Again, there was a muffled whine from the shadows.

"Did you hear that?" I exclaimed. I did not wait for an answer. I stood up and reached for some dried shrubbery that we had piled near the fire and threw it on. Almost immediately, the tiny dry leaves caught alight, and considerably widened the circle of light.

Suddenly we were surrounded by glowing green eyes.

"What the devil?" Cameron gasped.

The dingoes were stirred by the light and retreated. Some of them growled, others yawned, but they were not particularly aroused for an attack.

The aborigine's eyes seemed to glow like live coals in the expanded fire-light. What a frightening picture he was! His eyes glowed as viscously as those of the dingoes! Then he bowed his head so that the brim of his hat sheltered his eyes. To my astonishment, the pupils of his eyes dilated so that they seemed almost black.

"Are they friends of yours?" I asked with cold suspicion.

The old man lifted his head, so that his orange eyes glowed once more, and he scowled at me. His stare contained all the hatred and malice of the devil himself.

Suddenly an awful, high-pitched wailing pierced the night air. It was the scream of a horse in mortal terror.

It was then followed immediately by a tumultuous, bestial roar. Its volume and depth vibrated through the night, and the three of us nearly lost our wits. The dingoes cowered and yelped and ran in circles. A powerful thump was then heard, which made the ground shudder. Then there was a tremendous snapping, splintering sound, like a tree being torn in half by a storm.

Then silence.

I turned to Cameron, who raised his rifle in the air and fired. The dingoes scattered away into the darkness.

The old aborigine was gone.

Suddenly I saw a lighted torch hurrying across the dark clearing towards us.

Then I heard little Andrew yelling. "Mr. Dubrelle! Dad! Mr. Dubrelle! We've found Gerald! He's alive! Gerald's alive!"

"Gerald?!" I cried desperately.

We could just make out the silhouettes of our companions as they hurried toward us, Andrew running with the torch.

"Slow down, son!" Cameron shouted. "You're too far ahead, lad, they cannae see where they're headed!"

However, the excitement was too much, and Andrew did not seem to hear him. Seconds later, Andrew had dashed into our fire-light, breathless and exuberant.

"He's here, he's here, Mr. Dubrelle! Dad!"

Cameron caught up his son and held him high, as we heard the others approaching.

Then out of the shadows Dougal strode, with my dear young Gerald in his arms. The Scotsman had a broad smile and tears in his eyes, as did Old Uncle who was fast beside him.

Within an instant I had my grandson in my arms.

"Oh, my lad!" I cried, as my composure simply collapsed. I almost crushed the poor boy with my embrace. My tears fell relentlessly, and I laughed uncontrollably. "My boy, my boy! How did you find him!?"

Dougal answered, shaking his head with joy and bewilderment. "He just came out of the darkness — just walked straight to our campfire."

Gerald was pale and shaken, and clearly frightened nearly out of his wits. For moments he would not speak or seem to respond to our attention. I kissed his pale forehead and ran my hand through his golden curls. I could not get him to look me in the eyes.

Cameron approached and put Gerald's cap upon his head.

"Look, we found your cap, lad." Cameron beamed. "You're safe with us now."

With that gesture, it seemed to dawn on Gerald that he really was safe again. His wide hazel eyes suddenly got a life in them, as he looked desperately into my own eyes. Then he began to bawl in earnest.

"There, there, it's alright!" I soothed paternally. Yet, by Jove! How to describe my emotional turmoil? I felt all at once such powerful and contrary emotions that I could barely comprehend what was happening.

Joy, relief, mourning, anger, fatigue – all these brawled for the dominion of my soul.

In the end, it was joyful relief that won out. I sat there holding Gerald, laughing and crying, with his tear-stained face buried in my chest, until the dawn.

THE GRUESOME OMEN

WE WERE a day and half's ride from home. I determined that at first light, after a good breakfast, the whole company would be away as fast as we could.

The sun had been up for almost an hour, when I noticed that Dougal was not amongst us.

"Where is Dougal?" I asked, rubbing my bleary eyes.

It was our old Chinese Uncle who answered. He was reflective and solemn, sitting cross-legged by the fire. "He is not far away. Listen...his horse come now."

The old man's hearing was more acute than mine, for it was a whole minute before the horse's hooves were audible to me.

Dougal rode right up to our camp and dismounted. His face was pale and saturnine.

"Mr. Dubrelle, Sir, I need to show ye something. Please get upon Cameron's horse as soon as ye can. Cameron shall stay here a wee while with Old Uncle and the lads."

"We are all almost ready to ride now, Dougal." Cameron answered. "Is it nae something we can all see on the way?"

"Nae Cameron, it is not. I shall make it clear to ye and Uncle why soon enough. Mr. Dubrelle and I will not be away long. Come, Sir. I well ken ye're tired, but this is something that must be done."

"Very well." I conceded, a little bewildered. I was unsettled by Dougal's tone.

The Scotsman nodded. "Thank you. Wait here a moment, and I shall fetch Cameron's horse."

"Hold on, now, Dougal!" I barked contumeliously. "Why should I not ride Vernon instead?"

Dougal hesitated before answering calmly. "Vernon is not nearby, Sir. I know where he is, and Cameron's horse is much readier to hand." As always, Dougal's manner was respectful and yet authoritative.

Perplexed, and with a growing sense of foreboding, I agreed to ride Cameron's horse.

We cantered south across the clearing towards the edge of the bush. Once we were well and truly out of ear-shot of the camp, Dougal indicated that we should slow to a walk.

"Now that the young lads cannot hear us, I will bring ye into my full confidence, Mr. Dubrelle. I believe that we have danger to navigate yet."

"I gathered that you were concerned about something, Dougal."

"Aye, Sir. Though I dare admit that I am more than merely concerned. Yet I'll not say more, for now we are approaching what I wanted to show ye. I reckon that what ye see with ye own eyes will have greater impact upon ye than any words of mine. Please stop here, Sir. It is best to proceed on foot from here."

We dismounted about thirty yards from the edge of the wood. As we approached the gnarled, and dry looking gum trees, I noticed an unnatural stillness. Not one leaf was animated by a breeze.

I wanted to ask Dougal again what we were looking for, but I was compelled to remain silent. Besides, I knew with every fibre in my being that what I was about to see would be horrific.

Then I saw him. My beloved steed Vernon.

The fact that he had been killed would have been terrible enough – but not beyond my comprehension. I have seen many slaughtered animals before, both on the farm and out in the woods. Yet what I saw there will haunt me for the rest of my days.

My poor horse Vernon was lodged violently half way up an old, solid gum tree. It was inconceivable – he was a full eight feet above the ground. His blood had sprayed most of the twisted trunk, and the ground about the tree. His chestnut flanks were blood-soaked and sticky. Many branches were snapped off high above him.

I almost vomited.

The horse was grotesquely twisted, and his four legs jutted out stiffly either side of the fork in the tree. He had landed there upon his back, and then had twisted in vain to right himself. The fork of the tree itself was also split and cracked. Vernon had a gaping wound, a great slash in his flesh, out of which his viscera had slowly fallen out.

The smell was repugnant. Not only did Vernon's insides foul the air, but the poor fellow had emptied his bowels as well. His faeces were smeared down the trunk, but also scattered a good distance from the tree.

In shock I walked around behind the tree to look at Vernon's head. His teeth were bared, and his eye sockets were bloody and empty. The ravens would have taken his eyes at first light.

I gazed for a long time at my poor steed in sheer disbelief and anguish. The star on his forehead shone brightly in the morning light. Until that day, I had always thought it a lucky star. There was not a mark on it, though the rest of his chestnut face was smeared with blood.

"Dougal...what the devil happened here?" I finally gasped.

"If ye will come this way, Sir, I think I can answer that." He answered respectfully.

I turned to face him, but he had begun to walk away from the tree. With peculiar detachment, I followed him.

Dougal stopped about twenty feet from the tree and pointed to the ground.

"It happened here, Mr. Dubrelle. No doubt ye heard that monstrous roar last night, just before we recovered wee Gerald?"

"Yes." I answered. "Dare we conclude that it was a bunyip?"

"I dinnae conclude otherwise, though I can scarcely believe it." Dougal rejoined. "It was a powerful roar, Sir, was it not? The very ground shook."

"It was unlike any creature I have heard." I concurred. "The sound before-hand – the awful wailing. Now we know that it was Vernon in mortal terror for his life."

"Aye." Dougal agreed, and added passionately. "And this morning, there he is eight feet above in a gum tree!"

"Obviously this bunyip put him there after he

killed him – as a leopard will stash an antelope." I suggested, trying to master the situation.

"Nonsense, Sir! Surely ye saw the great crack in the fork of that tree? T'wasnae stashed but violently thrown!" Dougal expostulated. He then ran his hand through his mane of russet hair and took out his pipe. He sighed and continued in a more measured tone. "Do pardon me, Mr. Dubrelle. I am quite agitated."

"Dougal!" I scoffed incredulously. "I can hardly blame you for that!"

"I thank you, Sir. Now, if ye look closely at the ground here, ye can deduce what happened to poor Vernon exactly." Dougal continued. "There we see Vernon's tracks, running to this very spot. Then, he reared up, Sir, as a horse will when frightened – as Vernon always did. He was a proud, strong horse, Mr. Dubrelle – be it a snake or dog, or the sudden appearance of a kangaroo – Vernon would rear up like a warrior, ready to box with his front legs."

"That is exactly what he did." I agreed with mournful pride.

"Last night, right *here*, he did the same. And here – right *here* – are the tracks of his enemy. Just look at them, Sir! They are five feet apart, about eight inches wide and perhaps...three feet long." Dougal announced, pointing to the tracks as he spoke.

"Come now, Dougal – these cannot be animal tracks." I remonstrated, but even as I had finished speaking, I knew that they were.

The ground was reasonably soft, and a clear imprint was made. The parallel indentations showed that all the animal's weight was upon the back legs, which were elongated. At the front of the print were the toe marks, and ahead of these toe marks, was a depression that could only be made by a claw. It was a mighty, frightening pair of limbs that had made those impressions.

"The animal has a huge and heavy tail." Dougal continued excitedly. "If ye look over here, Sir, ye can see that it was creeping from the trees toward the edge of the forest there. First it leant forward on its front legs – as ye can well ken from these powerful prints the size of a dinner plate. Look, it has enormous claws on its front legs as well as the back! And don't those front prints look like those of a giant man's hands? The digits are longer than those of the hind legs, and much smaller, which suggests to me that this beast dinnae normally use its front legs for walking."

"That seems like sound reckoning, Dougal." I nodded.

"I have pondered it all morning, Sir. If we look closer, we can see how it moved. First it leaned on its front legs, then the back legs came forward. Mighty long legs! And then the long heavy tail followed. I submit to you, Sir, that the animal that made these tracks is some form of giant kangaroo."

I was struck with admiration for Dougal's reasoning, and awe at his conclusion. It all fitted the evidence perfectly. Yet by Jove! How my credulity was challenged!

"What else can you deduce from these tracks?" I asked, finally.

Dougal stood thoughtfully analysing the scene. "A kangaroo does not leave tail marks when it hops – only when it... well, walks – for want of a better description. It is the same for this bunyip. I suggest that the animal was stalking towards the clearing and encountered Vernon. Vernon reared up and then the bunyip reared up – see how there is a heavy indentation here on the tail print? The bunyip put its entire weight on its tail and gave a mighty kick with its back legs. The force of the kick was enough to send the horse twenty feet across and about fourteen feet high – as we can guess from the broken branches of the tree."

"And the claws on the feet slashed open Vernon's belly as well. The blood sprays here, and there are drops scattered from here all the way to the tree. His faeces show the same pattern." I added.

"Aye. It all fits. As for where the bunyip is now – well I think that Vernon frightened it. Likely as not, this animal had never seen a horse before. Vernon made a powerful neigh and an aggressive rearing of his body, and the bunyip responded with a roar and kick, then turned and fled through the bush. This morning I attempted to follow its tracks, but I did not get very far. They disappear quickly."

"How so?" I asked surprised. "These tracks are enormous, I should hardly think they would be difficult to find."

"With submission, Sir, do ye know how far an ordinary kangaroo can leap when in full flight?" Dougal returned.

"I have seen plenty of kangaroos in flight. The greatest leap they can make would be about ten feet, I should say."

"Pshaw, Sir! Tis much more than that. I have seen a kangaroo leap a six-foot fence with ease. I have also calculated a large male kangaroo to have bounded up to forty feet at a time. Now, an average sized kangaroo is about five, maybe six feet high. How high do ye suppose this bunyip is, Mr. Dubrelle?"

I thought about it. "Could we not guess from the length of these prints?"

"Aye, we could, Sir. If indeed we are dealing with a giant kangaroo, then it makes sense to assume that the relationship between foot length and height would be the same. I know for a fact that a kangaroo's track is about a foot long, and on average a kangaroo is about five feet high. Hence, the length of foot is one fifth of height."

"So..." I added. "These tracks are about three feet in length, which would make this animal fifteen feet high, when standing on his back legs."

Dougal gave a low whistle. "That is precisely the reckoning I came to earlier this morning. So, if an ordinary kangaroo, which is about five-foot-high, can leap let's say at least thirty feet – six times its height – then this giant kangaroo can leap...ninety feet."

"That is too big a stretch, Dougal. The relationship cannot be as linear as that. This bunyip would be very heavy, and I strongly doubt that it could leap that far."

Dougal looked right into me. "Your objection is no doubt rational. And yet, I leave room for the possibility that this animal could make such a leap. After all, we have a full-grown horse propelled twenty feet across and fourteen in the air."

"You say that you found other tracks?"

"Aye, Mr. Dubrelle. The next set of tracks are about thirty-five feet from these. It took me a few minutes to find them. They are deep as ye can well imagine, considering the weight of the animal. The bracken and the low shrubs have been damaged as it passed through. The next set of tracks were harder to find, and they were sixty feet from the previous set. We would assume that this bunyip would shoot off in a linear direction – but this is not the case. The direction is erratic. It took me half an hour to find the third set of prints amongst the bracken – I did not find the fourth. Remember that each set of prints is at least sixty feet from the last, in a haphazard direction. The forest floor is littered with logs, and bracken, shrubs and other random depressions. Tracking this beast is nae easy thing."

"Dougal, if this is a giant kangaroo, perhaps it is not as dangerous as we think? Kangaroos eat only grass and other vegetation. This animal fled after attacking Vernon, and it did not come back to feast upon him."

"There is sense in that, Sir. And yet, we both heard that roar last night. It was a deep, guttural, frightening noise – like a lion's roar – designed to scare an animal out of its wits. Nae grass eating animal could ever produce such a sound. Furthermore, the blacks are fearful of the animal as well. Why should they be so, if the animal is just a big grass-eater? I believe this bunyip to be a carnivorous creature, Sir."

I did not answer him at first, but simply allowed my mind to race through the various emotions of wonder, anguish, repulsion and fear. Dougal waited patiently for me to collect my thoughts and form my next resolution.

"Well, this bunyip certainly warrants further study, but not on this venture." I announced finally. "We must saddle the other horses and get the boys safely back to the farm. And then, we must make funeral arrangements for Michael..." The sentence came to a sudden halt, as the reality of what came next pierced my heart. In a few hours, I would have to bury my only son and my beautiful daughter in law.

Dougal stepped forward and checked my grief for the second time on that terrible adventure.

"We cannae grieve yet, Sir. There is work to be done and as I said before, danger to navigate yet."

"Surely this bunyip will not follow us home – nor attack us in broad daylight?"

"Tis not the bunyip I fear, Sir. Tis the bushrangers and the witch doctor. There is skulduggery afoot, or my name isnae Dougal MacDougall."

"What are you saying?"

"This morning, I was restless, and so I took a ride along the edge of the bush. I was hoping to see tracks of the animal we heard last night – though I never dreamed that I would stumble across poor old Vernon where he is. At any rate, before I came to where we are now, I detected a presence in the scrub, and for a brief second I saw the villainous face of one of the bushrangers we saw the night before."

I was dumbfounded by this revelation. "Why do you suppose he was here? Perhaps he and his comrades heard the roar and wanted to investigate as well?"

"It is possible. However, I ken he had other reason to be here. Remember, Sir, that we left those bushrangers a good day and half's ride away. It is possible that they heard the bunyip – but how could they ride from there to here in such a short time? And why would such a bunch of cowardly loons like that ride *towards* danger? Nae, Mr. Dubrelle, they have been following us." Dougal rejoined seriously.

"Why should they do that? It is not as though we have anything of real value. Do you think they want revenge for your visit to them?"

"It is my suspicion, Sir, that these bush-rangers have heard about wee Gerald's opal."

"And how would they know about that?"

Dougal frowned deeply with consternation. "They must have been told by someone who knew about it. I suspect that they were told about it by this same witch doctor who visited your camp last night."

I considered his theory. "It might well fit. Their story that they were scared by the witch doctor when they came across him may well have been a lie. It seems unlikely that such a pack of bullies would be intimidated by one old aborigine. They may have been in league with him this whole time."

"Aye, that is my reckoning, Sir."

"Well, one thing is certain. We need to proceed very carefully."

THE AMBUSH

When Dougal and I returned to camp, we found that Cameron, Old Uncle and the boys had packed everything away and were ready to leave immediately. Despite our desperate desire to gallop home, we were now short one horse, and so our progress was to be heavily slowed. Dougal and Cameron agreed to travel on foot, with Old Uncle and Andrew on one horse, and me and my grandson Gerald on the other.

We travelled back towards home for the entire morning, without incident. Cameron and Dougal spoke quietly to each other as they walked a few yards behind our horses. Old Uncle rode listening to Andrew's childish chatter and answering his endless questions with a patient and subtle joy. As the afternoon rolled by I came to enjoy my vicarious education through Andrew of Chinese culture. I learned with interest that the Chinese did not all speak one language, but that Chinese from different regions spoke various dialects and that they kept themselves in exclusive groups even when far away from China. This fact of segregation and xenophobia by the Chinese miners, even to their fellow Chinese, made the character of our Old Uncle all the more remarkable to me. Not only did he speak English, he even spoke at least one aboriginal dialect, that of the Djapwurrong. What motive had this old man to be a total contrast to his fellow countrymen? Why did he develop relationships with aborigines? Why did he mine for opals instead of gold? Why is he alone? The more I pondered on these questions, the more delighted and intrigued I was. I did not understand why Old Uncle was still travelling with us, given that we had recovered Gerald. Clearly, any obligation he felt to Dougal and Cameron for helping him escape the bush-rangers should then have been done with. Or was he simply seeing the matter through out of respect for his friend Michael? Well, whatever his motivations were, I had no objection to his company. In fact, I had come to welcome it. I did not wish him to part company with us at all.

Though Andrew was keen to engage Gerald in conversation, my poor frightened child remained silent and miserable. He clung to me now and then, and his little hands gripped me so firmly that I thought my heart would break. What horror he must have witnessed!

We travelled on at a good pace until high noon. It was then that we were suddenly ambushed.

Two bush-rangers casually appeared from the trees and blocked the road in front of us. They raised their rifles at our company.

Instantly, Dougal and Cameron had their own rifles aimed back at the bush-rangers, however it was no use. For behind us another two had appeared with rifles pointing at us. We were surrounded.

No one spoke a word for a tense minute. Then a fifth fellow appeared from the bush to our right. I recognised the scoundrel from Dougal's description. It was Hank Hammond.

The dirty blonde man sneered with a cold and vicious authority. None of us were impressed. We each saw him as the pitiable school bully that he was. However, his men were armed, and we were surrounded and out-numbered.

"Well, well, well, McTavish." Hank crooned. "We meet again. Only this time the surprise is on our side, eh?"

"State your business." Dougal barked.

Hank leered to his companions and laughed. "Listen to him, boys. Still speaking like a man in charge. You were very impressive the other night, Mc-Tavish. Very frightening, certainly. But then you did come at us from nowhere and we were caught off guard. Now...well, things are little bit different now, aren't they? Take their rifles, boys."

"What do you want, Mr. Hammond?" I demanded, as we were disarmed.

Hank sauntered slowly over to us. "So, McTavish has told you about us, eh? Heh. Well, mister, you can get off the horses for a start."

Carefully, we obeyed and a red-haired bushranger from behind us took the horses.

"Mind your step, Sir." The red-haired bushranger mumbled to me in a thick Irish accent as I dismounted.

"Such courtesy is hardly expected from an outlaw." I announced superciliously, looking this man square in the eye. He faltered under my gaze, then roughly led the horses away.

The six of us stood in a circle like penned sheep.

"What now, man?" I asked steadily.

Hank spat. He was clearly relishing his power over us. "You are in deep trouble now, Sir. I would be inclined to shut up and do what I was told if I were you."

"We will obey you. What do you want? We do not have much of value about our person now, but I can certainly offer a handsome sum of money in return for our freedom." I offered.

Hank seemed bemused. He fingered a whip curled at his side. "Yeah, that might do nicely. First though, we are going to teach that arrogant old chink a lesson. Then McTavish and his mate. Step forward chink."

"Now wait a minute!" I bellowed with fierce indignation. "I will not surrender a single penny to you unless you can guarantee the safety of all of us, this Chinaman included!"

Hank pointed his rifle at my throat. His cold grey eyes sparkled with lupine malice. "You are not in a position to demand anything." He growled quietly. "Step forward, chink."

Old Uncle nodded gently to me and then stepped calmly forward.

Suddenly, little Gerald pushed away from me and ran to stand in front of the old Chinaman.

"Leave him alone!" He wailed, and then stood his ground, trembling from head to foot. His blonde curls shone in the sunlight under his cap, and his cheeks were blushing. He did not look at Hank but stood staring at the ground with his little fists clenched.

All of us stood astonished at this sudden defiance. Those words were the first that we had heard young Gerald utter since we had recovered him.

Shame slithered through the gang of bushrangers and it told upon their faces. Hank sighed. "Get out of the way, boy, or you will be punished."

"I will not get out of the way!" Gerald bellowed.

Hank laughed cruelly. "You are very brave little boy, aren't you? But bravery has got nothing to do with it. You want proof? I will slit your little mate's throat right in front of you."

"Now that is enough!" Thundered Dougal, and he strode forward to meet the bushranger.

Hank pointed his knife at our brave Scotsman. "Don't you move!"

Dougal stood beside Gerald and laid a gentle hand on his shoulder. "You are a very brave lad." He soothed. "But I will handle this from here. Go to your grandfather."

"Oh, you will handle this, will you?" Hank shouted at Dougal, as Gerald came to me and I held him tight.

"Aye." Dougal answered. A controlled contempt rumbled through his deep, melodious voice. "The young lad has shown more courage and character than the likes of all five of ye cowardly loons put together. Yet, I will do ye the courtesy of allowing ye to deal with a man from now on."

"I am going to shoot you right in your arrogant face, McTavish." Hank growled through gritted teeth.

"My name is not McTavish. It is Dougal MacDougall. And you will not shoot me right in my arrogant face. You will listen to my proposition." Dougal returned. His hazel eyes held the villain.

"Heh. You got a proposition? You are seconds from hell..." Hank smirked.

"I thought it unlikely that even a group of outlaws as inept as yourselves could really be frightened away by a single old black. Ye let him go, not because ye were afraid, but because ye made an agreement with him. Is that not so?"

"Maybe we did, maybe we didn't. What of it?"

"Come man, we need not beat about the bush. Ye know of the opal, and ye could only have known about it from the old black. So what agreement has been made between ye?"

"Why should I tell you anything?"

"There is more to this old black and the opal than you know, Mr. Hammond. Agreements made with a witch doctor must be treated very, very carefully." Dougal rejoined.

Hank considered the Scotsman. "Alright. I s'pose it doesn't matter now if I tell you. Yes. We had an accord with that old nigger. He was going to sacrifice the boy to appease some spirit, so he could take the opal. Now before you judge me on that score, rest assured that we had no intention of lettin' a nigger kill a white child. We intended to do away with him as soon he delivered on his end of a bargain."

"What bargain?" I asked.

"The old nigger said that there were men chasing him and that if we took care of those men, he would reward us with gold...gold that we could obtain from an old Chinese man wandering alone through the bush. Now, not an hour later, we came across that old chink there. He was wandering all alone in the bush, just like the nigger said. We were just about to question him about the gold when you men rudely interrupted us."

Dougal turned to Old Uncle. "Pardon me, Uncle, do ye know anything about the gold these men are after? If so, please tell me now, Sir."

Old Uncle inclined his head to acknowledge the respect in Dougal's voice and manner. He then said. "Yes. There is much gold."

If Dougal was surprised by what Old Uncle had said, he did not show it.

"There ye are, then." Dougal announced with a hint of triumph. "There is gold to be had, but if ye are to get anywhere near it, ye already know the conditions. Not one of us is to be harmed – this Chinaman included."

"How much gold? How much gold are we talking about?" Hank asked with blatant greed.

Old Uncle answered. "One gold nugget."

An incredulous scoff circled through the bushrangers.

Hank raised an eye-brow laconically. "One gold nugget?"

Old Uncle nodded. "Yes. One gold nugget."

Hank looked to the sky with a mocking sigh as his cronies laughed. "Right then. How big is this one gold nugget?"

Old Uncle took a moment to calculate it. "Nearly two thousand troy ounce."

I felt my heart sink. Two thousand troy ounces

would make the gold nugget the biggest nugget ever discovered. They would never believe it.

Hank gave a low whistle. "Two thousand troy ounces, eh? Sounds very impressive, chink. In fact, I don't know whether any of us have ever heard of such a big nugget."

Old Uncle nodded seriously. "I think, biggest nugget ever found."

"Hank, I reckon he's bluffing." Answered an auburn haired, freckled ruffian with a squinting aspect.

"I don't know, Ben." Another responded. This bushranger was dark haired, pale, weak-chinned and had watery blue eyes. "If the nugget really is that big it is worth lookin' into. What do you reckon, Roy?"

"Maybe you're right, Ted, but the black didn't mention that the gold would be in nugget as big as that, did he?" A gaunt, sneering red-head answered.

"Well, why would he?" Ted returned.

"Good point." Roy conceded. "Look, I don't know. I don't trust chinks or coons. Red? What do you reckon?"

Red was also red-haired, but a shade darker than Roy. His aspect was also far less cold and violent. Red shrugged and then answered with his thick Irish accent. "I originally came to this district lookin' for gold. Maybe they are tellin' the truth, maybe they aren't. But how much will it really cost us to find out which? I have wasted weeks diggin' for gold and not getting much. I'd happily ride a day or two for the chance of a two thousand troy ounce nugget."

Hank nodded, and the other bushrangers seem to find agreement.

"Well then," the Dingo crooned. "Looks like we are going to believe you, Chink. For now. So...where to?"

Where to indeed!? Thought I.

"We have to go back to where buyip died." Old Uncle answered plainly.

Hank considered Old Uncle, and then the rest of us in turn.

"Right." He decided finally. "Back to the swamp we go then. We should be able to get there before dark if we leave right now."

Dougal interrupted him. "If ye have other horses nearby, our progress will be quicker."

Hank grunted. "That's not a bad idea. Ben and Roy, go get the other horses. And bring the mining equipment – the picks and the shovels."

Ben and Roy dutifully wandered away into the bush. Shortly they returned with seven horses, and so with our two our company now had nine.

I wondered that these men had more than one horse each nearby, but I soon learned that two were used as pack horses.

"What's your name, boy?" Hank asked Gerald.

"Gerald."

"Well, Gerald, just so there is no trouble I want

you to ride with me. Any one tries anything – and I will cut you with my knife."

"There is no need to threaten the boy." I protested. "He has been traumatised enough, surely even you can understand that? Have you no sense of human compassion and decency?"

"I will not harm you, Gerald." Hank continued, ignoring me. He addressed the child in a more conciliatory manner. "As long as you ride with me, your grandfather and these other men won't try anything. You just have sit here and keep quiet until we get to the swamp. Agreed?"

Gerald looked up into my face with a weary sadness. "It's alright, Granddad. I can ride with him."

How my heart melted at his courage, and how my blood boiled at these scoundrels!

Yet, within a few moments, we were upon our horses and on our way. Hank rode with Gerald, all the men had their own horse – including Old Uncle, and little Andrew rode with his father.

As we rode I wearily and bitterly ruminated on how much longer we were to suffer through this horrible adventure. I had thought the fate of my poor horse Vernon was the last of our calamities, and that providence might spare us further tribulation on our journey home. However, there we were being escorted back into dangerous land by dangerous men.

On the way back to the swamp, we passed an enormous old, burnt out tree stump. Upon this sat a very large iguana, with rough dark scales and bright orange eyes. It would have been about six feet from head to tail, and its claws were sharp. Some call these animals 'goanna', which to my mind sounds very similar to 'iguana'. A keen naturalist, I was struck by the uncommon nerve of the creature. Usually, these giant lizards rapidly ascend the nearest gum tree and then hide behind the trunk. This one sat still and cocky, its forked tongue languidly sliding in and out. It watched us all ride by, and its orange eyes seemed to be fixed upon each of our faces in turn. I voiced my surprise at the animal's eye colour – iguanas usually have dark eyes. Nobody seemed interested in the matter, and the rest of our journey was silent.

THE FINAL BATTLE

OUR ADVENTURE WAS CONCLUDED FAR FASTER than any of us dared hope. Even as our dismay was still fresh in our minds at having been sent back to the swamp where one monster died, and another still lived, our salvation was suddenly effected. However, there was a grave cost.

We had arrived back at our campsite near the swamp with the afternoon sun still bright and warm, though dusk was but an hour away. The tension of the bushrangers had relaxed a little in response to our cooperative behaviour over the hours of the ride. We had all just dismounted except for Cameron and Andrew, who both seemed about to dismount. However, suddenly Cameron and Andrew shouted, kicked their horse into a gallop and took off across the clearing to the trees south of the swamp.

Immediately two bushrangers fired their rifles, but neither hit the fleeing pair.

Gerald broke away from Hank and ran towards the bush from whence we had just emerged.

Hank shouted to his men to be upon their horses and after Cameron and Andrew, who were just reaching the trees. Hank then bellowed at Gerald and ran after him.

Dougal reacted instantly. He grabbed the handle of his sword packed safely on his horse, wrenched the blade free in one smooth, swift movement. The bushrangers Ben and Red had turned to fire upon him, but in three steps Dougal had slashed Red's rifle in two, spun with the arc of the swing, and continued with a second strike at Ben. Whilst Red was merely disarmed, Ben was cleaved from his neck to his breast-bone. His blood sprang from his wound in a horrible, bright red splash as he fell to the ground.

Dougal did not stop for a second to process the results of his assault. After the second sword stroke, he was already running swiftly in pursuit of Roy who was unaware of the Scotsman's attack. Roy was only just upon his horse, his attention riveted on Cameron and Andrew. He had just kicked his steed into a gallop, when he turned his head just in time to see Dougal rushing towards him. Dougal roared and charged at the horse's side, using his hip and shoulder as a battering ram. The force of his attack was enough to throw the beast off balance, and it tripped, breaking its front leg and throwing Roy off over its head. Roy hit the ground headfirst with a sickening crack. He did not move.

Red, whilst disarmed, still ran at us. He reached Old Uncle and threw a punch at the old man. I moved to assist but before I had made one step towards them, Red had been vanquished. The old Chinaman had smoothly captured the bushranger's arm during the punch and guided it with an open hand so that the momentum of the attack carried Red over Old Uncle's hips. Old Uncle had moved in such a way, that Red was literally flipped onto to his back. The Chinaman had held the bushranger's arm at the end of the throw and cut downwards as he was flipped, so that Red was forcibly slammed to the earth. Old Uncle then held his hand like a clever and chopped down upon the criminal's solar plexus. Red remained still.

Meanwhile, Dougal had turned to engage the remaining criminals, and saw that only Ted remained as Hank was running after Gerald. Ted was no threat – he was standing in utter terror at our Scotsman, his watery blue eyes bulging out of his head and his mouth open in horror. He fell to his knees and began to wail as Dougal strode towards him in a terrible, white rage.

"I give up!" Ted shrieked. "Please don't kill me! Please, Sir, don't kill me!"

"Dougal!" I shouted. "Hank is after Gerald! We'll take care of this one!"

Dougal did not seem to hear me. He raised his sword as if he were going to lop Ted's head clear off his neck. However, he merely stuck him with the handle off his sword so as to render him unconscious. He then roared after Hank.

"HANK HAMMOND!" Dougal bellowed like thunder. "COME AND FACE ME, YOU COWARD!"

Dougal then picked up a rifle and followed in hot pursuit.

I took a cue from Dougal and also picked up a rifle, cursing my slow wits as I did so. Then Old Uncle and I ran after him.

It was a frantic and desperate chase, for Gerald and Hank had disappeared from sight. Just as we entered the trees and began to trample clumsily through the bracken, we heard Gerald scream in terror.

I swore and hurled a typhoon of obscenities at the limit of my vocal chords. By Jove I was furious! I am a peaceful, gentle natured soul that abhors physical violence, yet on this occasion I was fully determined that I would brutally murder Hank Hammond. On we ran. Dougal was now out of sight, but Old Uncle and I ran towards the sound of Gerald's screams.

Finally, we found Hank holding Gerald beside a large gum tree, with a hunting knife held across my grandson's throat. He was sweating and red faced.

Gerald was bleeding copiously from his nose and tears were coursing down his little face.

"What have you done to him?!" I cried out, my voice cracked with distress. I was panting and sweating, my heart thumping me to death. I felt that I was about to collapse. Old Uncle must have sensed my plight, for he moved to me and helped me stand.

"One step closer and I will slit his throat!" Hank screeched. It was not a cold, composed threat. This man was panicking, and almost at his wit's end. "Where's that McTavish!? MacDougall! MacDougall! Show yourself or I will hurt the boy! I will kill him, Dougal! I SWEAR IT! SHOW YOURSELF!! MACDOUGALL, SHOW YOURSELF!!"

Yet Dougal was nowhere to be seen.

We moved closer. It was a mistake. Hank immediately threw Gerald to the ground, kicked him viciously, turned him on his back and then punched him savagely in the face. He then lifted the dazed child to his feet and held him as before, with the knife under his chin.

I began to sob and shriek at this horrible, merciless violence done towards my traumatised grandson.

I pleaded for Hank to stop. I fell to my knees and begged him.

I don't remember exactly what Hank said. He was hoarsely roaring threats and demands. He continued to shout for Dougal to show himself.

Soon, I too began to roar for Dougal and exhort

him from the core of my being to show himself at once.

Just as I was at my most helpless a shot rang through the scrub. A red dot appeared between Hank's eyes and he slumped forward over Gerald. Gerald crawled out from under him and ran to me.

We hugged and we both wept openly.

Dougal strode out from the trees from whence he had fired his rifle. He had obviously waited with a cold, warrior's calm for the right opportunity to fire. Dougal was renowned as a skilled marksman.

"How is the lad, Mr. Dubrelle? Is he badly hurt?" Dougal asked with a gentle kindness, his hot blood cooling as his human compassion seeped back into his veins.

To my surprise, Gerald wiped his eyes and answered for himself. "I can take it, Mr. MacDougall. Thank you for saving me."

"Brave..." Dougal smiled as tears formed in his eyes. "Brave lad."

He helped me to my feet, and we slowly made our way back to the horses.

THE CONFRONTATION WITH
DINEWAN

WHEN WE RETURNED to the clearing, we surveyed
the battle field. The horses had bolted to the southern
end of the grassy plain and then grouped together at
the forest's edge. One horse lay in agony with a
broken front leg. The bush-ranger Roy lay close by,
dead with a broken neck. Even in death, his face held
a sneer. Ben too was lying dead, the grass blood-
soaked about him.

Ted and Red were unconscious but breathing.
Within a few minutes, Dougal had shot the injured
horse, and helped Old Uncle to drag Red over to Ted
so that they lay side by side.

We each had some water, and then waited for the
two bush-rangers to regain consciousness.

Red was the first to stir. He eventually opened his
eyes, and he seemed oddly resigned. His expression

showed that he was aware of us, but he did not speak. He simply lay there, miserable and quiet.

"What is your name?" Dougal asked him civilly.

"My name is John Kelly. Also known as Red." Red answered. It was clear that this man was ready to cooperate fully with us.

"Ye have not been in the country all ye life. You're an Irishman?"

"Aye."

"And ye are a convict?"

"Aye. I was deported here in 1841. I came aboard the Prince Regent."

"What was your crime?"

Red sighed and gave a gentle, bitter laugh. He answered with a peculiar detachment. "I stole a couple of pigs. Worth maybe six pound. They belonged to a man called James Cooney...of Ballysheehan."

"Ye are a free man now?"

"Aye."

"And ye turn to bush-ranging?" Dougal suddenly barked with incredulous disgust.

Red nodded miserably. "Aye, Sir. There's no denying it. I came here lookin' for gold, and I met Hank and the lads. They seemed to offer a better life. So, I joined them."

Dougal considered the man seriously. "What will ye do now, if we let you go?"

Red swallowed and blinked. "I swear that I will

never again be a thief. I have a mind to try cattle. In a different part of the country."

The man seemed genuinely repentant. I myself had no idea what we should have done with the two men. Even though we had just put to death three men, we could not find it in ourselves to kill these men in cold blood. Should we have bound them and then taken them to the authorities? How many days would it have been before we found a policeman willing to take them into custody? As to letting them go – how could we have trusted them?

However, Dougal MacDougall was a decisive and sagacious soul, and he soon formed a resolution.

"De ye remember the old black stump we passed about five miles back? Where we saw the big goanna, on the way back here?" He asked Red.

"Aye." Red answered subserviently.

"We are going to tether two horses there, one for you and one for ye friend here, when he wakes up. In the meantime, we are going to leave you with water and provisions, including the shovels and the picks from your mining equipment. Ye are to bury the three dead men and say a prayer for each, then ye may wander towards the black stump. I suggest that ye make camp for the night here, after ye have buried the dead, and make for the horses in the morning. Are these instructions clear?"

"Aye. Aye, Mr. MacDougall they are clear. It is decent of ye. I am grateful." Red rejoined humbly.

"And I have ye word that there'll be no skulduggery? That ye will depart the district and make an honest living elsewhere?" Dougal's hazel eyes speared into the man.

Red nodded vigorously. "Aye, Sir. Ye have my word."

Dougal considered him, then nodded. "Very well. May ye live a better life from now on, man."

It wasn't long before Ted had been revived and the instructions made clear to him also. He was more insipid and obedient than Red. Barely a second had passed after Dougal had repeated his directives before Ted had picked up a shovel and was digging the first grave in earnest.

As the two men dug, Gerald, Old Uncle, Dougal and me set about gathering the horses. It was getting very near dusk. No sooner had we secured the horses than Dougal formed the next resolution.

"Mr. Dubrelle, I believe that at a brisk pace yourself, Old Uncle and Gerald can make the black stump before night truly falls." He began.

"Yes, Dougal, I dare say that we can. I don't think we want to make camp with those fellows. However, you are not coming with us?"

"No, Sir."

"You are going to pursue Cameron and Andrew? You don't think they can find their way back to the farm by themselves?"

I was not about to argue with Dougal, as his mind

was clearly set, yet I was uncomfortable with him leaving us.

"Mr. Dubrelle, I believe it prudent to track down Cameron and Andrew and make sure that they have not befallen any grief. There is a dangerous beast about and of course there is the witch doctor, as ye well ken." Dougal answered seriously.

"I see. You seemed resolved, so I shall not hinder you. You may be right about the bunyip. As for the witch doctor, I dare say he will not try anything." I opined without much conviction.

"The witch doctor may be a more cunning adversary than the bunyip, Mr. Dubrelle. However, I am confident that he will not pursue you or our Gerald anymore. He wants the opal, and he knows that Cameron has it." Dougal returned.

"Well, I don't know that I agree, Dougal. Certainly, he threw the opal to Cameron, but he cannot be certain who has it now." I rejoined.

Dougal's expression showed that he conceded the point.

Suddenly Gerald interjected. "Granddad, the Dinewan knows where the opal is. I think he knows. I don't know how. Maybe his magic."

I ruffled his hair paternally. I personally would not give credence to magic. I could well accept the existence of the bunyip – after all it is was just an animal. A terrifying, fascinating creature certainly, but a beast of flesh and blood none-the-less. Yet magic? I could not indulge such speculations.

"I think we have an even chance of encountering this witch doctor, Dougal." Said I. "If he comes after the opal, he will take his best guess as to which party has it. He will either hunt Cameron or he will hunt us. His dogs will not worry us – the horses are too big a prey for them, and we have rifles and plenty of shot. I also have no doubt that you can meet him man to man, Dougal, if you find him – but what if he is not alone?"

Old Uncle interjected solemnly. "The old black man has no ally here. The Djapwurrong fear him. He will be alone. But he is a powerful enemy."

Dougal exhaled as he thought the matter through, before he finally decided on his best course of action.

"I will find Cameron and Andrew, and then bring them back to meet you at the old black stump." Said he. "We will make camp there, and then make for home at first light. You are well armed, Mr. Dubrelle, and I am also armed. Hence, we are both able to defend ourselves should this old black approach either of us. Are we agreed?"

"Agreed, Dougal. Please take care. We shall expect you at the black stump before morning." I answered.

With that, Dougal was upon his horse and away in the direction of Cameron and Andrew. As he disappeared into the trees, I began to contemplate the day's events. It suddenly dawned on me that I did not know why Cameron had suddenly decided to bolt when he did. At first, we had all simply reacted to his impulsive move. Then, I suppose we assumed that Cameron spotted an opportunity to remove his son from danger. But if so, where was he now? Why did he not double back after a while and see the outcome of his actions? Perhaps, thought I, he would, and that Dougal, Andrew and himself would soon rejoin us and we could finally go home. Yet, another dark musing crept into my heart. Cameron had the opal. His lust for it was made apparent only two days ago. He had the opal, and he had his son. Had he simply taken his fortune in his hands and abandoned us to the mercy of the bushrangers?

I quickly banished these thoughts and upbraided my conscience. Cameron was a man of honour and had already risked his life in this venture. I was wrong to doubt his intentions.

Wearily, Old Uncle, Gerald and I were upon our horses and away towards the black stump with the spare horses in tow.

At a brisk pace, we arrived at the old black stump with the sun setting behind us. Just as we reached it, we heard a dreadful high-pitched squeal. It was a small animal wailing in panic for its life. It was a sickening shriek that vibrated through the forest about us and made our horses whinny nervously. Finally, we saw the source of the distress.

The old iguana we had seen earlier suddenly sauntered out from behind the stump, with a small animal about the size of a rabbit in its jaws. Its orange eyes glowed with gleeful hunger. The small, wallaby-like creature continued its horrified din.

The iguana seemed to delight in the plight of its prey, and it seemed to eye us haughtily as we stood watching with pity and disgust. Finally, it gave a sudden aggressive shake that broke the animal's neck and the noise ended abruptly. It greedily swallowed the creature, until only its tail hung from its mouth. It then hissed at us, and quickly ran into a burrow underneath the old black stump.

Before we could sigh with relief that the horrible lizard had gone, we heard a man coughing heavily from behind the stump.

I grabbed my rifle, ensured that it was loaded, and then held it at the ready.

"Who goes there?!" I demanded. "Show yourself at once or I will open fire!"

The coughing continued, yet no man appeared.

"If you do not appear by the count of three, I will fire." I boomed. "One...two..."

Suddenly the coughing changed to that of laughter, and then from behind the stump stepped Dinewan. He was wearing the same cloak of possum skins, and his face was hidden under the brim of his hat. He continued to laugh haughtily.

Both Gerald and Old Uncle went pale at his presence, but I aimed my rifle square at his chest and prepared myself to shoot if necessary. I was angry enough to kill the old aborigine. I reminded myself coolly that not only had this vile fellow kidnapped and terrified my grandson, he had killed my only son and beloved daughter in law.

"Dinewan...kindly desist from that revolting laughter or by Jove I will kill you where you stand." I was composed and deadly as I spoke.

The witch doctor raised his head, and his orange eyes glowed viscously in the dying light. The tail of the iguana's prey hung loosely out of the side of his mouth. He made exaggerated chewing motions on the tail and leered at us mockingly. Finally, he spat the tail to the ground and spoke.

"Keep your temper, Mr. Dubrelle. You are rightfully angry. As am I." Dinewan's voice rolled smoothly, with a sophisticated malice.

"You murdered my only son and my daughter in law. You kidnapped and abused my grandson. You placed myself and my friends in mortal danger. What possible justification can you offer for these outrages?"

Dinewan gave a long sigh. "Your pain and anger are now in sympathy with mine...Mr. Dubrelle."

I was about to object fiercely, but Dinewan held up a placating hand.

"Nay..." Said he. "Hold your scorn, now. When I was the boy's age, I watched my mother and aunties raped and murdered by white men. My father I never knew, but the other men of my tribe were hunted, shot and tortured. The children were enslaved – well, some of them. My sister was held by her ankles, and swung hard against an old gum tree, so that her brains were dashed out of her head. These are not biblically inspired exaggerations, or stories borrowed from legends of Spanish barbarity, Mr Dubrelle. These are my personal experiences."

I perceived no guile or insincerity in the witch doctor's words. He spoke with a mix of bitter rage and scornful pride. He stood defiantly waiting for my answer.

"What has happened to you Dinewan is truly horrendous. Yet I fail to see how that justifies your crimes against my family, whom have always maintained peaceful and just relations with aborigines."

Dinewan glowered. "White men serve the one queen, is that not so?"

"Yes, we all subjects of Her Majesty Queen Victoria."

"Then all white men are of one tribe, and so crimes perpetrated by that tribe will be revenged upon that tribe. That is the way of things."

"That is not how our justice system works,

Dinewan. The guilty are tried and punished. The men who committed those atrocities to your family should face trial and hang."

"Am I to comfort myself with the justice of invaders?"

As I recall the speech of Dinewan, I am astonished at how lucid and articulate he was. His knowledge of our language and his indignation were formidable. I had not before nor have ever since heard a person of aboriginal descent speak with such fluid and forceful clarity.

"I am sorry for your...tragic experiences, but I cannot allow you to remain at liberty after what you have done to my family." I answered finally. "You shall be bound and taken to the authorities to face trial. Or you shall die."

Dinewan chuckled quietly. "Given my so-called crimes and the colour of my skin, I rather suspect that I am to die in either case."

"Your *so-called* crimes? How dare you speak to me this way? DAMN YOU, HOW DARE YOU SPEAK TO ME THIS WAY?"

I was roaring hoarsely and on the brink of tears. Dinewan was taken aback by my shouting, yet he said nothing. He waited for me to speak again.

After some silence, I some-what more calmly spoke. "You feel no remorse, do you?"

"No, Mr. Dubrelle, I feel no remorse. But I do

feel...regret." Dinewan answered quietly. "I regret what must be done at times."

Another silence passed between us, as I was undecided about what to do. My thoughts were scattered, my nerves were spent, and my emotions were rampant. I could not think clearly nor act decisively anymore. The silence grew uncomfortable and so I continued with the conversation rather than tackle the practical problem of how to take the witch doctor prisoner.

"Where were you educated?" I asked, trying to be authoritative once again.

Dinewan glared contemptuously. "Are you surprised at how this ignorant savage is so able to express himself in your tongue? You are not the first."

"You do speak with an impressive command of our language. Your reference to Spanish barbarity and the bible is also telling of your education." I returned plainly. "Such education is rare among the *white* folk in this country, let alone aborigines – I mean no disrespect to your race."

"Your very presence here is disrespectful to my race." Hissed Dinewan. "However, if you must know, yes – my education has been *augmented* by the culture of white invaders. A woman called Mrs. Campbell secretly educated me. She taught me to read and she taught me history. I was her favourite person in all the world." A transient care softened Dinewan's face.

"Mrs. Campbell would be ashamed of what you have become."

"Mrs. Campbell was raped and murdered by the same man who dashed my sister's brains against a tree." Dinewan replied abruptly. "So much for Mrs. Campbell, and the God to whom she prayed for protection."

"Dinewan..." I began, but he interrupted me.

"Mr. Dubrelle, I did not come here to exchange personal histories with you, nor did I come to be your prisoner. Let us speak plainly. Your child has something that is rightfully mine. It was given to his father by the very Chinese man who rides with you now. It was not his to give. It is mine. It is medicine to me and I must have it."

I turned in the saddle to face Old Uncle. He was staring coolly into Dinewan. There was something regal about his expression.

"I have heard quite enough." I resumed abruptly. "Uncle, you did the work. You mined for the opal and so you were its rightful owner. I do not fully understand why you gave it to my son, but you did so of your own free will. Therefore, Mr. Dinewan, I do not recognise your claim to the opal and so we shall not surrender it to you."

"Then I shall be forced to resort to other means." Dinewan replied venomously. "I know where you live, Mr. Dubrelle. It is only a matter of time before I..."

Suddenly Gerald shouted, cutting Dinewan short. "We do not have the opal anymore! So, leave us alone!"

"Gerald! Be silent!" I commanded, astonished at his outburst.

"So..." Dinewan growled, his orange eyes narrowing fiercely. "You have been wasting my time."

With that, the witch doctor span on the spot and then ran through the trees. In the growing darkness his silhouette seemed to leap stochastically so that he was out of our sight very quickly.

I fired after him, but it was no use.

We set up camp and sat by the fire, waiting wearily for the sound of our companions to break the silence of the bush. Gerald finally fell asleep beside me, and I gently stroked his head.

Hours later, we heard a horse. Just one horse.

"Who goes there?" I shouted, waking Gerald.

"It is Dougal MacDougall." The Scotsman answered. His voice was tired and forlorn.

As he came closer, I saw that he had a small figure sharing his steed. I soon realised that it was Andrew. The boy was unnaturally quiet.

"Where is Cameron?" I asked, a grave premonition already freezing my heart.

Andrew stumbled to the fire and then fell to the ground, crawling up into a foetal position.

Dougal sighed heavily, and I could see that his face was wet with tears. "Cameron is no longer with us, Sir."

WHAT BECAME OF CAMERON MACALLISTER

DOUGAL RELATED to us what became of Cameron MacAllister. I shall tell it now in my own words.

As the sun had begun to set, Dougal had cantered off in the direction of Cameron and Andrew. The Scotsman had a keen eye, and he followed the trampled bracken and other traces left by the pair as they had made their escape. Soon, it became very easy to track them, as they had followed a natural track through the bush that ran alongside a shallow gully. Animals naturally make narrow dirt tracks along their regular routes, be they sheep, goats, cattle or, as was the case in this instance, wallabies, wombats and kangaroos. Dougal followed the trails as one naturally interconnected with another. It was clear that Cameron was not especially concerned with concealing his route, as he seemed to have followed which ever track through the bush was most easy to travel.

Eventually, Dougal discerned that Cameron and Andrew had travelled south away from the swamp at first, then approached it again in a roundabout way by travelling west through the bush, then north-east, so that they had arrived at the exact opposite side of the swamp to where we had camped the night before.

It was early twilight when Dougal dismounted a good fifty feet from the edge of the swamp. On this side of the swamp, the water seemed quite deep and clear. It was much more like a billabong. The surface was completely still. The stars were mirrored in the water, and the moon glowed coolly just above the trees. Frogs and other insects croaked their nocturnal symphony.

Dougal had been confused by the tracks that he had found in the soft earth. He had found where the pair had dismounted, and there were footprints made by walking. However, the horse had suddenly bolted, leaving the pair stranded. What had happened?

Andrew had run towards the bush and his tracks stopped at the base of a large eucalypt. Dougal was going to examine them further, when he decided to trace Cameron's tracks first, as they were deeper and easier to analyse. Dougal's eyes were keen even in the dark of night, yet he lit a kerosene lamp.

Cameron's tracks showed that he had strode to-wards the billabong's edge, then knelt down to take a drink. However, there were no other tracks or signs that Cameron had then left the water's edge when he had slaked his thirst. Dougal had frowned in furious thought as he tried to understand what he was seeing. It was as if Cameron had simply disappeared after he had knelt down.

Dougall saw that some mud still swirled in the water right near the edge which showed that it had recently experienced a very large disturbance. He then noticed that there was a wet region all about Cameron's imprints, showing that a large, sudden surge of water had washed up the gently sloping bank.

A shudder ran through him as he realised what had happened.

The bunyip had been lurking in the billabong, and as a crocodile suddenly lunges to take a wildebeest by the head, so it had taken Cameron into the water. There were no indications of a struggle – the animal had literally grabbed Cameron and lifted him clearly from the spot and then taken him into the depths.

Instinctively, Dougal had then backed even more quickly away from the water. For a few minutes, he was in shock and unable to do anything other than stand in a terrible awe, staring with disbelief at the peaceful billabong before him.

Gradually, Dougal's intellect reasserted itself over the fearful pounding of his heart. The horse had obviously bolted when Cameron had been taken. What had become of little Andrew?

Dougal soon remembered that Andrew's tracks had ended at the base of a large gum tree. He sighed as he suddenly deduced the reason for this.

Of course, Andrew climbed the tree. Was he still there?

Dougal approached the tree, and sure enough, Andrew was curled up in the fork of it, looking down at Dougal with a peculiar detachment.

"It is alright, lad. It is me, Dougal. Mr. Mac-Dougall. Come down from there, Andrew. Come on. I will not let any harm come to ye." Dougal had coaxed.

Andrew did not come down from the tree. Dougal had patiently exhorted him many times, but the boy did not respond. It was not clear to our Scotsman that Andrew even heard or understood him. Clearly, the poor little fellow must have been in a supremely traumatised state, as my dear Gerald was when we recovered him.

Eventually, Dougal placed the lantern on the ground and climbed into the tree, to sit opposite the boy. He did not speak further, but just sat in silence with Andrew.

After a few minutes, Andrew began to cry. He allowed Dougal to reach towards him, pick him up and hold him in his arms. Dougal admitted to me, that he too had cried with the lad as he held him tight.

Finally, they climbed down from the tree, and moved toward Dougal's horse. However, something caught Dougal's eye. Something shone brightly in the moonlight, very near where Cameron had been taken. Carefully, Dougal left Andrew by the horse and made his way towards the glowing object.

It was Gerald's opal.

Dougal carefully picked it up and then he and Andrew mounted the horse and rode carefully through the forest. The moonlight and the kerosene lamp lighted their way. They were but a few minutes ride away from the black stump, when a sudden chill lay upon them. A dreadful, suspenseful silence hung about the forest.

A ghastly voice seemed to echo from all around them.

"Beware of thieves! Beware of thieves!"

Dougal brought the horse to a halt and called out. "Who goes there?"

The ghastly voice continued, speaking a few feet away, then close beside them, then far away again.

"Beware of thieves! Beware of thieves!"

"Enough!" Dougal commanded. "Show yourself, ye pitiful coward!"

Suddenly the shadow of a man flitted here and there amongst the trees.

"Who goes there?" Dougal called again.

A chillingly familiar voice answered.

"It is Hank Hammond."

Dougal's hair stood on end. "Impossible. He is dead."

"None the less, it is I, Hank Hammond." The voice returned. Dougal described it as a passionless voice. There was absolutely no emotion it, and yet it was clearly the voice of the late bushranger.

"What do ye want, Mr. Hammond?" Dougal asked, trying to master a rising panic in his chest.

The horse began to snort and whinny nervously.

"I want you, Dougal MacDougall." The voice rejoined simply.

"If that is so, come into the light. Face me like a man." Dougal returned, his head turning this way and that, trying to place the location of the voice.

"Do you really want me to appear before you? I am a dreadful sight, Mr. MacDougall."

"Yes. I will face you, Mr. Hammond. Come forward."

A shadow of a man seemed to step out from behind a tree, about fifteen feet in front of them. It was standing absolutely still, a few steps away from the circle of light thrown by the kerosene lamp.

There was an intense suspense.

Hank Hammond spoke again, but his voice seemed to be talking right beside Dougal's ear. "Are you quite sure that your mortal heart won't seize and cease to beat for ever more, Mr. MacDougall?"

Andrew was breathing rapidly, and his arms were wrapped tightly around Dougal's waist.

"Enough of the theatrics, Mr. Hammond. I have said that I will face ye. Now, step forward at once and be recognised."

The shadow figure bowed slightly, then began to slowly stagger towards them.

One step.

Two steps.

Three...

Dougal stood his ground.

Before the figure reached the circle of light, it stopped.

"Come now, think of the boy, MacDougall." Hank implored. "He will die of fright at the sight of a ghost."

Andrew buried his head into Dougal's back and began to sob in mortal terror.

"Easy, lad." Dougal soothed quietly. "If it is ghost it cannae harm ye, and if it is a man... I will soon make him sorry for frightening ye."

"Well, Dougal?" Hank called.

"Have it ye own way, man." Dougal replied. "Stay where ye are and tell me what I am to do for you."

"I told you. I want you, Dougal MacDougall. Get off your horse and surrender yourself to me, that I may have my revenge." Hank commanded.

"Is there nothing I can do to save my life, Sir?"

Dougal asked levelly.

"There is one thing, and one thing only, that I will accept in lieu of my revenge..." Hank drawled.

"Name it."

"An opal."

A suspicion accosted Dougal's mind. He decided to test it.

"Would you accept a two thousand troy ounce gold nugget?"

"No. I want only the opal."

Dougal smirked. "You do a remarkable impression of Hank Hammond, Mr. Dinewan."

A cold silence passed.

"Come now, man." Dougal continued coolly. "The voice is an impressive likeness to that dead scoundrel – but the choice of words is entirely unlike the man."

"Very well, you have found me out." The shadow conceded. In a few stilted steps, the witch doctor moved into the circle of light, and his orange eyes gleamed balefully at the Scotsman.

"Be on your way before I run ye through with my dirk, ye disgraceful old criminal." Dougal growled. "I've killed three bushrangers already today, man. Do ye really think one more old misfit will make any difference to me?"

"I am not just a mere old misfit and you know it, Mr. MacDougall." Dinewan returned threateningly. "Pray, don't unwisely provoke me."

The old witch doctor then reached into the shadow of his possum-skin cloak and pulled out a long bone, from the leg of an emu.

"That bone is no match for cold steel, I assure ye." Dougal drawled, holding Dinewan's eyes with contempt.

"When I point this bone at a man, Dougal, his fate is sealed. He becomes weak and feverish. Within two days, his will breaks, and his heart fails. He dies." Dinewan explained coldly.

Dougal merely scoffed.

Dinewan smiled cruelly, and then imitated Dougal's voice exactly. "Ye doubt me, lad, that I can well ken."

Dougal sighed patronisingly, and then stared right into the old witch doctor, summoning all his dominance of character. "I dinnae doubt that men have died at the pointing of ye bone, Mr. Dinewan. Many a man has allowed his reason to fail at superstitions and give in to the power of imaginary devils. Often, a man causes such a strong anxiety within himself, that his nerves or his heart or his lungs fail him. It is not black magic, Mr. Dinewan. It is the practical fact behind the fragile character of some men. Now, listen closely to me. I am a man of strong will and stable mind. I cannot be bluffed by some wretched bush conjuror into causing my own destruction. I am from the mighty MacDougall clan, and we dinnae quake in fear before any foe!"

"You are a fool, Mr. MacDougall." Dinewan hissed.

"You are the fool if ye mean to frighten me with a bird's leg and gruesome folklore." Dougal barked over him. "Know this: I am your enemy and I will conquer ye. It is not I, but yeself that stands in mortal danger. I will be watching for ye ever vigilantly. Ye will not ever get close enough to strike, before I will have ye. So, heed me, witch doctor, and never cross me again!"

Dinewan suddenly snarled and hurled a dreadful sounding curse in his own guttural language, pointing the emu leg bone savagely at our Scotsman.

Dougal laughed heartily at the witch doctor.

"Two can play at war cries!" Dougal bellowed. He then drew his sword, kicked his horse into action and charged down upon the old man.

Dougal then roared his clan motto. "*Buaidh no bas!*"

Dinewan ducked just in time to avoid the swing of Dougal's sword. He then ran into the trees and disappeared quickly.

With grim triumph, Dougal then rode on to meet us at the black stump.

My tale is now quickly concluded. At first light, we made eagerly for the farm and arrived there without any further misadventure. We made the journey wearily and in silence. Though our troubles seemed to be at end, we felt no joy. The sun shone, and the light gleamed in the oily eucalyptus leaves. Magpies warbled, and Currawongs called. Butterflies danced in the grassy bushes on either side of the road. It should have been a pleasant home-coming.

All of us were thirsty. All of us had a pounding headache, and sported bruises. We travelled in a melancholy daze.

I slept fitfully in my own familiar bed. I suffered nightmares, and I cried and wailed and moaned in the early hours of the morning. The next day, we buried Michael and Valeria, and also made a memorial mound for Cameron. We sent word to the authorities, and when they arrived a few days later, Dougal and I answered their questions.

Old Uncle stayed with us for three days, and then with our thanks and exchanges of good will, he departed for his own home. He still regularly visits me, and I am glad to write that in the years after our adventure, we had many delightful dinners and chats by the fire-side. Old Uncle became my very best friend and has always been a source of joy and comfort to me.

After many, many days, with the remarkable facility of recovery that resides in children, both Andrew and Gerald found life and laughter again. Allison, Cameron's wife, was a good and loving mother to both of the boys. Dougal later married and had children of his own – however he had a very strong fatherly influence on both Gerald and Andrew.

Dougal told me only recently, that unbeknownst to me or anybody else on the farm, he rode back to the billabong with his rifle in search of the bunyip. He never found any trace of the animal. He confided in me that he thought that the beast was no more.

"Do ye remember, Mr. Dubrelle, that one of the supplies Cameron always carried with him was a tin of strychnine – in case he spied the opportunity to poison a sheep carcass and so rid the farm of a wild dingo or two?"

"Yes, I do, Dougal. It was supplied to us in bulk at one time in order to poison rats. However, I would not use the toxin – the death is far too cruel."

"I believe that he had a tin of strychnine on his person when he was taken, Sir." Dougal opined.

I stared in disbelief, as Dougal thoughtfully smoked his pipe and waited for me to draw the obvious conclusion.

"The bunyip devoured Cameron and the strychnine, and so most probably died a painful death a few hours later. Its body is probably deep under-water in the middle of the billabong." Ruminated I.

"Aye, Sir. That is my reckoning."

"I suppose if we were able to retrieve that specimen, we might become world famous." I mused with a conspiratory grin.

Dougal chuckled. "Aye, Mr. Dubrelle, I dare say

we might. However, how would we dredge that billabong? It would be an expensive exercise. Furthermore, we cannae be sure if the beast really is in there – after all these years, the bones may have been rotted away and eaten by fish and other creatures. It is an expensive gamble, Sir."

"I see you have already given the matter some serious thought." Said I, eyeing him with playful suspicion.

"Aye, I have thought about it very often, Sir." Dougal shrugged with a disarming smile. "After all, who could resist?"

We never did try to find remains of the bunyip, nor did we hear any more of it from those that had travelled the area.

Finally, this account could not be satisfactorily concluded without some discussion and speculation about the old witch doctor Dinewan. Verily, I believe that he took our Scotsman most seriously. Certainly, he may have been seen by farm-hands skulking about the edge of the property, but when Dougal and myself rode out and patrolled for him, we never saw him. For years, our nights were nervous with the possibility if his wicked mischief, and so we were vigilant. We kept lights burning brightly on all the verandas and we had four or five loyal and competent watchdogs.

Eventually, Gerald grew to be a strong and sanguine young man, and his fear of Dinewan was replaced with a defiance and contempt of him, an attitude more in keeping with that of our brave Scotsman. Gerald also safe-guarded the opal and seemed to draw much comfort from it.

I am sad to report that a rivalry over the opal eventually marred the friendship between Gerald and Andrew. Andrew grew to be a strikingly handsome young man very much like Cameron, and his sapphire eyes glowed at times with a charm and desire that I remember seeing in his father. Gerald confided in me that Andrew felt some entitlement to the jewel, a notion that his father had planted in him on their fateful ride to the billabong away from the bushrangers. Neither Gerald, Dougal, nor I recognised Andrew's claim to the opal, and whilst Andrew accepted that, he grew distant from us from that time on.

I shall never really understand how the opal bred such passion in Cameron, Andrew and also Dinewan. I am still astonished that Dinewan did not simply kill Gerald and take it from him – and I am also still puzzled at the game he played that backfired, when he tossed the jewel to Cameron on that night we first met him. I suppose he thought he would soon have it from us after his dingoes had torn us apart – but why could he not simply take it? What dark superstitions governed his thinking? I fear that I shall never know the answers to those questions.

Dear reader,

We hope you enjoyed reading *The Witch Doctor's Opal*. Please take a moment to leave a review, even if it's a short one. Your opinion is important to us.

Discover more books by Tristan A. Smith at https://www.nextchapter.pub/authors/tristan-smith

Want to know when one of our books is free or discounted? Join the newsletter at http://eepurl.com/bqqB3H

Best regards,
Tristan A. Smith and the Next Chapter Team

The story continues in:
A Web of Stories

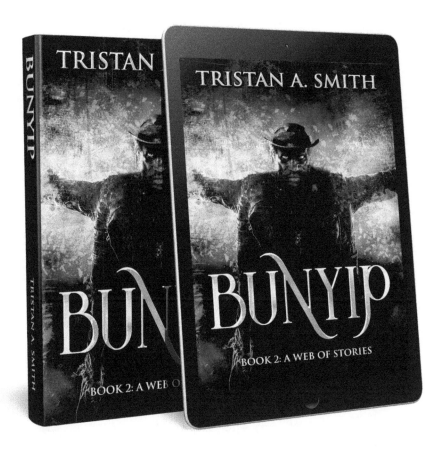

To read the first chapter for free, please head to:
https://www.nextchapter.pub/books/a-web-of-stories

AUTHOR BIOGRAPHY

Tristan A. Smith is a mis-employed zoologist who has finally committed to be being an artist. He completed a Bachelor of Science with Honours in zoology at the University of Melbourne, but now works as a Workforce Manager in a call centre. As it turns out, there is not much call in the market for someone who can do heart surgery on cane toads. Tristan's original plan in life was to be a scientist. The problem was that whilst he enjoyed learning about science, he hated doing it. He marvels at those that persist in science and is awed by their collective accomplishments, but that path is not for him. Tristan has long left the lab and prefers to go into the wild, the Australian bush, where his imagination is fired by stories old and new. *Bunyip* is his debut novel. It will not be his last.

The Witch Doctor's Opal
ISBN: 978-4-86745-951-5

Published by
Next Chapter
1-60-20 Minami-Otsuka
170-0005 Toshima-Ku, Tokyo
+818035793528

20th April 2021